LOOKING BACK

Edited by SYLVIE NICKELS

an anthology of short
stories and experiences on the
theme of hindsight and lessons learned

A team of writers has contributed to this collection of short stories and
essays based on the gift of hindsight and drawn from a wide variety of
experiences in different parts of the world at different times and
different ages. My own long life has produced a few from early
travels to the trauma of bereavement. That of my late husband,
George Spenceley, took him to far ranging adventures, from a prison
camp in World War Two to an avalanche in the Himalayas. Good
friends such as the late Ian Mathie had a truly 'inside' experience of
Africa. A fellow resident in a neighbouring retirement flat had an
unusual encounter with the local canal. Another old friend, the late
Norman Stone was a great observer of character.

And then there is a cross-section of life experiences learned through
the Cold War, and imagined incidents from a technological sci fi
future. Some are observations on a changed or changing world, others
on the comparative values of different cultures, yet others major
lessons taken from small events. On the whole the emphasis is on the
positive. It is, of course, difficult to be positive about bereavement but
there are ways of finding gratitude for the years of companionship
which created the eventual shattering loss.

Published in 2019 by FeedARead.com publishing for Oriole Press
Copyright © the editor as named on the book cover and individual
authors as named within the book.

A CIP catalogue record for this title is available from the British
Library.

By the same author

The Young Traveller in Finland, Phoenix House, 1962
The Young Traveller in Yugoslavia, Phoenix House, 1967
Travellers' Guide to Yugoslavia Cape, 1969
Travellers' Guide to Finland Cape, revised 1977
Welcome to Yugoslavia Collins, 1984
Welcome to Scandinavia Collins, revised 1987
The Big Muddy – *a canoe journey down the Mississippi,* Oriole Press,
    reprinted 2006
So, what next? - a look, with hindsight at the modern world, *a memoir,*
    Oriole Press, 2017

Fiction

Another Kind of Loving, Antony Rowe, 2005
Beyond the Broken Gate, Oriole Press, 2007
Long Shadows, Oriole Press, 2010
Village 21, *an anthology of short stories,* 2011
The Other Side of Silence, Oriole Press, 2012
Courage to Change, Oriole Press, 2013
It'll be Better Tomorrow, *anthology of short stories,* Oriole Press,
2014
Distant Echoes, *a trilogy containing 'Another Kind of Loving', 'Beyond the
  Broken Bridge' and 'Long Shadows',* Oriole Press, 2019

Educational aids

Assassination at Sarajevo, Jackdaw Publications, 1966
Caxton & the Early Printers, Jackdaw Publications, 1968
Scott and the Antarctic Jackdaw Publications, 1971
The Vikings, Jackdaw Publications, 1976

Contents

**To all our contributors,
especially those no longer with us**

Foreword

The theme of this anthology is hindsight which we all know is a great teacher - some lessons being grasped more easily than others. The first story concerns one of my best achievements in the learning stakes following the loss of my husband and best mate. Bereavement is probably one of life's hardest punishments and it took a while for me to work it out. This story relates to how I did it.

Most stories or essays in this collection are concerned with hindsight but of course this works for all of us in different ways, perhaps the main point being that it gives us a choice. Indeed, most of the stories have been chosen for the choices they gave and the results of taking them. Because they are written by different writers met over my long life, they are also set in different parts of the world - indeed most parts of the world, and reflecting most ages.

Enjoy, and perhaps share some of your own insights with other generations....

Two by two

Sylvie Nickels

It isn't something you really think about, until it's relevant to you: the fact that the world exists in couples. The coach had stopped at the Elizabeth Gate of Kew Gardens in London and James, who'd organised the day, told us the driver would be back to collect us at 4.30 that afternoon. Little groups of three or four were setting off to explore, but I didn't feel I could muscle in on them. *Anyway you'll see much more on your own,* Dan observed. Quite early on he'd started commenting on my life.

We had met, he and I, because of a common interest in Iceland, not the most obvious of holiday destinations. Dan climbed mountains, I liked rugged places. As a result, we spent a lot of time crawling in and out of tents in other non-obvious places. Dan didn't believe a tent was a tent unless you had to crawl into it. We also did serious travel in order to develop our respective careers. He taught geography, gave talks, and I wrote. He'd belonged to a climbing club, had even helped map an Antarctic island and had a glacier named after him. We didn't make much money but then our travel expenses (walking, canoeing, camping) were modest. In due course we had Rob and Beth; we and they gradually upsized. They developed their careers, moved to Australia, married, had their kids. So, we down-sized, moved to the country, bought a campervan and started roaming again.

With the advent of digitalisation, the demand for talks decreased. After retiring Dan started falling about a bit, then a lot. Short-term memory loss turned out to be early signs of dementia. Other health issues followed and finally he died quickly and peacefully. We'd just agreed to move to a flat in the middle of our attractive village, so I went ahead with that plan because what would I do with a four-bedroom house? The kids (Rob 50, Beth 45) came over from Australia to help me move.

Bereavement and moving don't combine well.

"Your mobile is rubbish, " Rob announced early on.

Apparently a lot of my stuff was 'rubbish'. Rob and Beth helped me to choose new things, but they were all so complicated. It seems it's hard to find a mobile phone that just makes telephone calls. They all have menus so that you can write emails, take photographs, read books, send texts. A telephone with menus - for heaven's sake!

My task was to take a carload of discards to the recycling depot. I watched much of my life go on landfill, the tears streaming down my face. It was hard.

No good staring back, Dan repeated in my head until I told him to back off.

Dan went on prodding me for a while before he gave up. Then, after some weeks ... no months, I was sick and tired of feeling forlorn and joined U3A in the nearest town. It's aimed at older people who want to stay physically or mentally active. Or both. I joined some discussion groups. They also organised outings - hence Kew Gardens, London's top botanical garden.

With my ticket, I acquired a map of Kew and headed for the nearest refreshment place. The map was peppered with enticing place names: Waterlily House, Rhododendron Dell, Kew Palace, Queen Charlotte's Cottage... But I was here to see trees. My grandfather had been a forester and I, as it were, had trees in the blood. In recent years I'd taken to hugging trees. Rob got quite embarrassed; Bee gave her short sharp laugh and said second childhood was clearly on its way.

Working out a route proved to be quite complicated because there were not always signposts where paths crossed. So I lost myself and found myself again by asking foreign visitors approaching me from the opposite direction where they had come from. With their help I found the Rhododendron Dell and the Woodland Glade, and I stumbled upon the Bamboo Garden by chance. But the lake, largest of the features, escaped me. I hoped Dan might prove helpful, but he stayed silent.

I asked a smiley Malaysian, a thoughtful Sikh, a young man who was watering bushes, and finally an utterly charming Norwegian who escorted me to it. *You always were a flirt,* Dan murmured.

"So you're still there?"

I'm always there, but as I said, I can't interfere.

Of course he couldn't. At the time of the move, even with all the discards, it took a long time to empty the boxes and make my new flat look like home, and a great deal longer before it felt like mine. When Dan died I'd been working on an anthology of short stories aimed at pensioners, so I decided to complete it and call it *It'll be Better Tomorrow,* which was his favourite response whenever I expressed concern about the future. Once that was done, there didn't seem a lot of point in getting up in the morning.

What about Rob and Beth and the grandchildren?

"They're in Australia," I pointed out.

What about that book you were going to write - the mystery one? You were going to make me the hero."

"It doesn't seem such a good idea now."

You're not usually so negative.

"Well, it's not been a very good time."

I can think of a great book you could write.

"On what?"

I'm not supposed to interfere.

"Oh, go away."

Thanks to the charming Norwegian I found my way to the lake, which was pleasant enough and the way back was now obvious, so there was plenty of time to go in search of more trees.

A few minutes later, I completely forgot the lake and the young Norwegian. I was sitting on one of the seats, partly because I was tired, partly because I wanted to exchange route-finding for the sheer enjoyment of my surroundings.

Does that remind you of anything? Dan's voice was very quiet.

"What? Where?"

Behind you.

I turned. Immediately behind my seat was a huge tree trunk, which I recognised as a giant sequoia straight away. A photograph of one of its relatives stared at me each time I switched on my computer. I'd taken the photograph when we visited California and somehow had managed to persuade Dan to stand beside it in a tree-hugging position. He was gazing upwards as though he were checking footholds for the best way to climb up it.

I smiled at the tree.

It had been our last major trip abroad, self-driving round the western third of the United States. We had seen wonderful things, but the giant red woods and sequoias were among the best. I'd bought some seeds but they didn't take.

"Which is just as well," a friendly forester told me. "A giant sequoia growing near an English village would probably have caused your entire community to subside."

Suddenly I was aware of a crick in my neck, and a lump in my throat. I got up and walked briskly back towards the Elizabeth Gate.

As I approached it, three women from our group greeted me. "Hello," one of them said. We exchanged our experiences without, of course, referring to head conversations or giant sequoias. Poring over the map on another bench I wondered how I'd got lost, but didn't really care as Dan and I had had a great time. Then I noticed that marked on the map was the Redwood Grove, which I had come upon by mistake. The charming Norwegian came passed. "You like lake?" I assured him I did.

Because I didn't want to get involved in a lot of chat, I wandered out through the Elizabeth Gate. *There's an ice cream van over there,* Dan commented, and suddenly there was nothing I wanted more. Wherever he was, he was still intuitive. I strolled over, bought a single cone, and stood in the shade licking it. A thought flashed through my mind. It had been such a good day, why didn't I take a break from the short stories I regularly wrote both for a publishing firm and several Websites.

To do what? Dan asked.

"Write a memoir. About us. With modern technology it need cost very little. And it'd make a nice souvenir for the grandchildren. And great grandchildren, and so on." Not to mention it would give me a chance to re-live the best parts of my life; the worst as well, of course, but no point in dwelling on that.

I'm glad you thought of that, Dan said, and I realised that's what he'd had in mind. *I could correct your mistakes,* I thought he added.

"You aren't supposed to interfere," I reminded him.

You won't even know I'm doing it.

A voice called out "Hello, lake lady!" It was the young Norwegian, waving from a distance. Yes, he was rather dishy. I heard Dan grunt. Soon after, the coach arrived.

If you get on early you won't need to be so far back, Dan suggested. *"And by the way I've thought of how to start your book."*

He was right about getting on early, but I said, "I'll start it my way if you don't mind." And the couple ahead looked back at me strangely.

Then we all got on. Two by two.

THE MARCH

George Spenceley

The rumours that a march was imminent became more positive and we were advised to make preparations for what, in our present state of physical weakness, could only be a very demanding trial. In preparation for it, George Ritchie and I somehow acquired a kit bag each, or perhaps we already had them; I can't say, and we converted these into some apology for rucksacks. We were issued with an extra allowance of black bread and margarine and early on the morning of 6th April to the usual command of *rouse, rouse, aufseigen schnell*, we stirred ourselves.

A unit of extra guards had arrived, including dog handlers with snarling Alsatians. We received the usual warning that all who attempted to escape would be shot, but many of our guards were old Wehrmacht army, some almost as ill equipped to march as were we: we developed with some a degree of friendship born of fellow suffering. And so we left Fallingbostel forever, still prisoners, but never again to be confined behind barbed wire. No one knew our destination but someone heard the word Lubeck. It seemed we might be bound for the rumoured Northern Redoubt where the Nazis would make their last stand.

We sought to make it the slowest march possible, and indeed in our half starved weak state it could be nothing other than slow. It was more a shuffle than a march. We were a tattered and teetering column, staggering along with no military discipline, a bit like a herd of cattle. But although weak and weary and our future uncertain, there was a heady excitement in the air. We were outside the barbed wire, seeing the real world of houses, trees and fields. There were people too, civilians who stared at us, some with hate, a few with pity. There were other marching columns, German infantry moving up, some mere boys with frightened faces. There were refugees and foreign workers and all day overhead a stream of Allied planes heading in formation for their targets, silver dots in the sky. How many of us were evacuated out of Fallingbostel I cannot say except that we left in several columns, each of perhaps 400 to 500 men, all moving in the same direction but not by the same route. We were rarely on asphalt roads. It was largely a rural journey, much of it on Lüneberger Heide, across which then, as indeed today, there are few roads.

I can remember few of our overnight stops except the first and last, both in barns. Otherwise we slept in the open. It was fortunate that for most of the time the weather was gentle and there was little rain. We were more fortunate than those who had been marched earlier before the Russian advance. They had suffered much from the cold and there was loss of life. In contrast we, with the aid of spruce branches which served as bed and blanket, enjoyed nights far more comfortable than those of the last winter in camp. It was only the constant hunger and accompanying weakness with which we were tormented.

After some days we were given a quarter of a loaf of bread and at one of our halts a sheep was slaughtered from which each received a minute portion of raw meat; otherwise we lived off the country raiding the fields for turnips and mangolds. Water we got from cattle troughs or even from ditches. It is impossible to say how far we marched each day but some have calculated it was between twelve and eighteen miles. Underweight, undernourished, with wasted muscles, I now wonder how it was possible. Some found it too gruelling and just dropped out: what happened to them I never knew. Others made a run for it and if they were lucky found refuge with French or Russian prisoners. A few less fortunate were picked up by the S.S. on the prowl for German deserters. It is difficult to understand the total fanaticism of the young dedicated Nazi even in their hour of defeat.

After many miles of travelling through sparsely populated country and partly forested, we approached the city of Luneburg, a city that had escaped the bombing so we were viewed with more curiosity than hate. It was early in the morning so we must have slept somewhere on the outside, still on the Heath. My only memory of our march through the streets was of a lady coming out of a baker's shop with the week's ration of bread and, while briefly left unattended on a bicycle bag, my great temptation to snatch it. Others felt likewise no doubt, but dared not do so for fear of the punishment.

Ahead lay the town of Lauenburg overlooking the Elbe, another 20 km to the east; once across they would blow the bridge. This we feared was where the Germans would make a last stand and we would be on the wrong side of the river. I have very recently motored on this road, now a busy highway of ribbon development, and have wondered how we in our weak state could cover so much distance at our pathetic pace. It was on this day, or was it another and in another place, that we were delighted to see at some landing strip a line of JU88s in flames. Were they destroyed by the R.A.F. or fired by the Germans through lack of pilots or petrol?

The old town of Lauenburg by the Elbe is now a charming tourist spot with narrow cobbled streets, 18th century houses, bars, restaurants and a few hotels. Pleasure boats and barges line the waterfront: all this we have recently seen and appreciated. It must have looked much the same to us as, on leaving the bridge, we skirted the southern end of the town, but then we were quite oblivious to its charms. How much longer have we to trudge was our only thought. For a little while we were on the main road towards the town of Boizenburg, following the river until a minor road led north. Here close to the village of Lance we were led into an open pasture for our night's halt.

If I can write of this with some precision it is because I have recently returned and before me now is a detailed map on which I can trace much of our route. A camp site is now marked but this is incorrect: it is still an open pasture. Why I write of this particular overnight halt, one of only two or three that I can now recall, it is because for the only time on the march we lay down to sleep exhausted but bloated, uncomfortably so, with an over-full stomach. This unforeseen reward was the gift of a solitary Spitfire. We had seen it earlier flying low, patrolling the Elbe in search of a suitable target. Lacking anything more military, he aimed his fire at a solitary barge slowly making its way up river. Its cargo was not arms and ammunition for the thin line of defenders, but herring roe, much of which somehow made its way to our overnight camp. Many of us suffered severe stomach problems the next morning.

It must have been the next day that the appalling slaughter occurred, a tragedy that we should have anticipated but one for which we could offer paltry protection. Our future destiny was of greater concern. Why the hurry to cross the Elbe before the bridge was blown and the urge towards Lubeck? What purpose had the march anyway when clearly the end of the war was imminent? The threat of being held as hostages in some fanatical Nazi redoubt was beginning to assume some reality. For this we showed some apprehension; the

14

threat of friendly fire we unwisely ignored. With clear skies the Allied air forces were active throughout the day, but neither the high flying bomber formations or the low flying fighters gave us concern, only joy at our mastery of the sky. Some ground attack machines flew low to check us out at which we waved but, satisfied that we were just one of the many marching column of refugees or prisoners, they turned away. It seemed impossible that our widely spread out ragged column of totally unmilitary, ill dressed men could ever be seen as a worthy target. Tragically, we were wrong.

Two such columns of our men marching parallel to each other were approaching the village of Gresse. A flight of six British Typhoons came over to look and then seemingly satisfied flew south again, but then at a lower level returned now ominously in line astern. Their aim was directed towards the other column. We watched horrified as we saw puffs of smoke appearing from under the wing of the first Typhoon. Five attacked first with rockets, then cannon, the sixth aircraft turned off, perhaps aware of the error. The ultimate tragedy had occurred: our own air force in which we had all served, killing and maiming their own men.

Our immediate thought was to rush over to the devastated column but any such movement was barred by our guards. We were ordered to continue, our escort no doubt anxious to seek some concealment in the forest ahead. At least we were spared the trauma of viewing the mutilated remains of our fellow airmen. Amongst them were men who had been prisoners for four years, killed within two weeks of release.

There have been several accounts written of this 'incident' of the 19th April as it is described by the authorities and there is some dispute as to the number of Typhoons and of those killed. Dixie Dean has said sixty were killed, some of whom died of their injuries in the hospital at Boizenburg. One account says the bodies were buried in a mass grave in the churchyard at Gresse after a service given by the local Pastor. What is certain is that all have now been reinterred by the British and Commonwealth War Graves Commission. Fifty nine years later I returned to the scene of the tragedy along with my wife Sylvie. We drove along the road where the tragedy occurred, through a hamlet of new houses now called Heidekrug (a familiar name) to the village of Gresse. In the churchyard there is a line of military graves where lie the bodies of five of our guards. We spoke to one elderly man who knew of the 'incident'.

Of the remaining weeks of the march only a few memories stand out clearly. We must have cast anxious eyes on the sky above, but now in an ever weakened state, we had become a long straggling line of men stretching into the distance, much less of an obvious target. The guards were strung out as we were and also, in their own way suffering, they were all much older men, non combatants, and perhaps equally ill fed. Starvation was ravaging the column and very soon another plague: dysentery. With dysentery a man loses all self respect. We came to drop our trousers whenever the necessity arose, often in places most public with total loss of any embarrassment. I remember performing with several others in what in England we would call a village green, regardless of the passing of the women of the village.

While much has been lost, a few incidents of those last weeks of marching starkly stand out beyond those of general weariness and hunger. There was the day we found a dead horse beside the road. Decomposed as it decidedly was, there was a rush to cut off pieces of meat with knives or bayonets borrowed from our guards. Some chewed the raw meat there and then. Personal survival was the major thought in every mind and there were tales of physical fighting for food, but of this I have no knowledge. Quite the contrary, I can recall acts of kindness with the less weak helping their companions of greater weakness. One unexpected act of self sacrifice I clearly recall. Our column became more widely scattered as the days passed, we ourselves to some extent dictating pace and time and length of the breaks. Had we been Russian prisoners, laggards would have been shot. One break of our group was at the gates of a substantial farm where Russian or Polish women slave labourers worked. Our starving state was evident and it must have been their midday break for they came to us with plates – yes, plates, if only tin ones – laden with hot potatoes and vegetables, their own meal for the day. This was the first genuinely kind act from the outside world.

Many of our German escort of Luftwaffe guards had for the most part been with us since Heyderkrug and gave us little trouble: they were elderly, unfit and disillusioned. They shared something of our sufferings and a certain sympathy developed between us. Faced with the imminent defeat of their country they were surely aware that our roles would shortly be reversed. At our night camps any order they had earlier sought to impose was now substantially relaxed so that we could freely forage for food or wood. Any earlier arrogance was replaced by a degree of servility. But there were exceptions when on slim excuse a prisoner could feel the full fury of a disillusioned, demented German: and so I was once to suffer.

Returning with an armful of wood with which to boil up some stolen swedes I was halted by a loud gutteral command. Some distance away stood two Luftwaffe N.C.O.s, a *feldwebel* and an *unteroffizier* and between them one of the fearsome guard dogs, an Alsatian trained in the pursuit of escapees. With another command the senior of the two released the dog which with a few bounds came rushing towards me. I dared not move. I stood absolutely still. Now, I had been brought up with dogs and if I ever considered myself to have with them a special relationship then this was going to be the big test. The dog reached my feet, looked up in a friendly way and wagged its tail. Less friendly was the *unteroffizier,* both at the dog for its neglect of duty and, of course, me for having found a four-footed friend. He drew his Mauser, thrusting it into my face, his hand shaking with emotion. It was then that I recognised him, a hated figure, the recipient of many taunts. We called him the Victory Parader. With Hitler's march through France, he had left his home among the Bronx of New York to join the Victorious German forces. With his command of English he was to become a *dolmetscher* serving in a P.O.W. camp. Some days later there was to be a sequel to this event when the life of the man lay literally in my hands.

Looking now at a map east of the Elbe it is possible for me roughly to trace the route that we must have taken, following the tragedy near Gresse. It is marked *Lauenburgische reservat Schael-See* an attractive, sparsely populated area of lake and forest now given over to recreation. Sylvie and I recently enjoyed our drive through this land, following as far as we could the line of our march fifty nine years earlier. Then, for us, the beauty and peace that now attract the tourist were entirely lost; survival was more on our minds. And for our German escort, the uncertainty of their future must have been much on their mind too, a fate more uncertain then ours. Weakened by hunger and dysentery it was we, the prisoners, who now dictated the pace and demanded too the frequency and length of our halts. Our guards were compelled to take a secondary role. While for a few fanatical S.S. remnants the struggle might continue, for our guards, almost as weary as ourselves, the end could only be welcome.

And for me particularly a speedy end to the march had become more vital, that is unless I was to suffer serious injury even, if prolonged, possible amputation. Apart from the German issue of wooden clogs my only footwear was a pair of ill-fitting French army boots worn with disintegrating socks. Not surprisingly I developed a seriously septic foot, each day becoming increasingly painful and swollen. So swollen in the end that no longer could I wear the boot at all. I could but hobble, the foot wrapped in sacking, unable to keep pace with the column. Somehow I managed to shuffle forward, not merely at the back but many yards to the rear, my only companion George Ritchie who refused to be separated from me, and a solitary guard, nervous and unhappy at being parted from his fellows. We too were nervous at being away from the column and felt highly vulnerable. There were tales of nasty fanatical Nazis, the S.S. and their like, roaming the country ready to shoot or string up those they considered deserters or escapees. Later we were to see much evidence of this last minute obsession. How long could I continue in this state of hunger and pain, I wondered, but happily this was to be the last day of the march.

For some there was good reason for fear. The Russians were near, some said their guns could be heard, and the greatest dread in every German's heart was Russian captivity. Few had any illusions as to the treatment to be expected. It must have been for this reason we noticed the direction of the march had been changed, no longer north but west back towards the Elbe. If the roles were to be reversed, our guards to be prisoners, then let it be the Western allies who would decide their future. Such thoughts were in more minds than those of our guards. Small groups of German soldiers, remnants of some fighting unit, were also hurrying west along the same road, their spirit broken, all now eager to escape the Russian clutches. Some stopped to talk; one even helped me with my load until weary of my slow pace.

At the small village of Salem we caught up with the main body of the marchers, who were preparing to settle in for the night. It seemed we were now closer to the advancing British than the feared Russians in the east. There would be no further marching; here we would await events, liberation for us, captivity for our guards.

Relief for us perhaps, but for the civilians of the village, many of whom were women evacuees from much bombed Hamburg, there was deep apprehension. Few Germans could be unaware of the horrors their forces had inflicted upon Russia and now their conquering army was almost at their gate, bent upon revenge. Their fears were very real. Indeed as we were later to learn the threat of

Russian rape was fully justified. To the women of the village it seemed that the arrival of a bunch of weak and starving *terror fliegers* was the lesser of the two evils. More than that our presence in the village was positively welcomed for could we not guard the womenfolk from Russian rape and pillage? After all, although military enemies, were we not fellow members of the Aryan race, not the unspeakable *untermenchen* from the east? It is for this reason rather than for charity that doors were flung open to offer us the comfort of their homes. It should be added that all German control over us had now been lost; our former guards, at least those that were still around, were meek and amenable, anxious only to seek favour. Unhindered by them, George and I could have sought the comfort of a bed, but so hardened to discomfort were we that we settled down to sleep on the hard ground of the nearest barn, too weak to stretch up for a bale of hay above.

These were historic days, vital to those involved on whatever side. I would dearly love to relive them, two days of very varied emotions and expectations. There was fear and uncertainty, as we have seen, in the minds of the women in the village, a mixture of relief and uncertainty among our guards and all the other uniformed flotsam who were hurrying west. They were no doubt grateful for the war's end and their survival but still full of apprehension for their future as prisoners. For us, of course, who would shortly be released from that state there could only be unalloyed joy and relief. There were others who shared our joy, a handful of Russian prisoners from some nearby work camp. Gaunt and ragged, a few of them seemed bent on mischief. Somehow they had found guns and were on the rampage seeking loot and drink, perhaps even revenge against their former slave masters.. This need not have been a matter of any concern to us but even while understanding their motives after pitiless privation, years of German imprisonment had not destroyed our civilised values. Among us were a few who could speak Russian who were able to impose upon them some restraint.

On our second day in Salem the unarmed defeated German soldiery continued to stream west. We had heard no Russian gunfire but there was much real apprehension in the minds of the villagers and perhaps they welcomed, as we did, the sound of our own military activity in the west: occasional small arms fire and the trundle of tanks or other tracked vehicles. Our expectations were high but they did not come until the afternoon.

RELEASE

It was an outburst of many shouts of joy that first advised us of the long awaited moment of liberation. A line of British armoured vehicles trundled slowly into the village from the west; it was May 2nd. There was much laughter and shouting and vehicles were surrounded by deliriously happy men; there was weeping too and one man I saw knelt in prayer. I, now in much pain, could only hobble but the Major in the leading vehicle told me to go to the tail of the column where a medical sergeant could dress my septic foot. It was then that I became abruptly aware of the contrasting attitudes towards the enemy between these battle hardened soldiers and our more gentlemanly selves. It came as something of a shock. These men in many months of combat had seen death and destruction at close quarters and, in Holland, many German atrocities. From these horrors we the airmen had been protected. Truly, we in Bomber Command over the years had inflicted death and destruction on a massive scale, as death had been inflicted upon us also, but it was all so remote: flashes on the ground, flames in the sky. We might have been appalled if able to witness individual suffering below but for us in the sky we were in a place apart, our sensitivity never coarsened or brutalised.

The wide gulf in attitude towards the enemy between us, the recently released prisoners and the still actively serving sergeant, was quickly illustrated. To cover my swollen foot something more substantial than sacking was required. He rushed across to the nearest house and, where we might have knocked at the door, without ceremony he kicked it open. He returned with an assortment of right footed slippers. By cutting the longest half open, it served me better than the sacking. While this was going on the remnants of our former guards were being rounded up as if for inspection or retaliation. 'How did they treat you?' we were asked and it seemed difficult for our liberators to understand that we had few complaints. My memory is vague but at some point our *dolmetscher*, the Victory Parader, was pointed out as the man who had set the dog on me. I was surprised to see him still around but he must have felt more secure remaining with his unit of guards. My sergeant reacted immediately, picking up a Sten gun with the intention of taking him round the corner. We dissuaded him but it was good to see stark fear on the man's face, and better to illustrate that we had not lost our humanity.

Events now happened in a haze of relief and joy. For the first time in years I could relax and let things happen with no effort on my part, only knowing it was for my good. George and I must at some time have returned to the barn to pick up what little there was worth retaining. More than half a century later with my wife Sylvie I returned to the village of Salem. We approached it along the same road from the east as I had done so long ago with my right foot clothed in sacking. As we entered the village I said there would be a barn on the left, and there it was; now surrounded by modern houses it remains, along with the church, almost the only old building. No longer in use, it's retained as a monument of earlier days.

The armoured column soon left. They were anxious to push on to Lubeck, but a small unit was left behind to organise our evacuation which was done in captured German vehicles driven by ourselves. I suppose we must have retained some military escort. I can remember little of the drive except more unarmed Germany soldiery trundling west and, while few civilians were about, white sheets were draped from many windows. At the bridgehead at Lauenburg I parted from my old companion George Ritchie and the others and I was taken to a field casualty station. I was deloused by what looked like a bicycle tyre pump and placed on a stretcher beside a wounded German soldier, and then taken across the Elbe on some amphibious vehicle. This long, eventful memorable day ended for me lying in a hospital bed in Luneburg attended by an attractive nurse. I wept when I heard her Yorkshire accent "Ee, thou dust look thin lad". A miracle had occurred. I had been washed, I was wearing pyjamas and lying between clean sheets. Beside me on a table were English magazines and newspapers, a source of enormous fascination.

The next day I was taken to the theatre for attention to my foot, now vastly swollen and painful. Under a local anasthetic a drain was inserted and I received my first course of penicillin, but for some days I was unable to walk except on crutches. In one respect I was more fortunate than most of my fellow prisoners, all anxious for a flight home. Some had to wait a long time, but those with injuries or who had suffered unusual privations were given priority. The next day I was taken to an airfield on *Luneburger Heide* where I received further medical attention, this time from a doctor from Harrogate, formerly a pupil from my old school. When I flew out in a Dakota to Brussels I had a bottle of champagne beside me.

In Brussels I was taken to the Edith Cavell Hospital where I was visited by a kind English-speaking Belgian lady. The war for me was over. I was going home. I really didn't need cheering up. My final flight was in a converted Lancaster, along with army wounded and a further bottle of champagne under my blanket to, I think, Boscombe Down. We were taken to a hangar where a group of enormously well meaning ladies of the W.V.S. had prepared a meal which to me, or any other ex-prisoner, was over rich and lavish. My much depleted stomach rebelled and it was some days before it would accept anything but a very basic diet. My memories of my first night in England in the station sick quarters is of hugs and kisses from drunken nurses, for was this not 8th May, V.E. Day?

Finally an ambulance drive to some R.A.F. hospital unit in the Midlands to join other recovering ex-kriegies to be gently led back under professional care to acceptable health and strength. It was here I was issued with a new uniform and fully kitted out for return to Harrogate and loving parents. I was 24 years old.

A sequel to my stay in the Catholic hospital in Rheinber, June 1942 :

In the late summer of 2004, my wife Sylvie and I were planning to motor through Germany passing close to the town of Rheinberg. It occurred to me that it would be of interest to visit the hospital where sixty-two years earlier I had been cared for after being shot down. Through the internet we were able to get into contact with the Archive Department of Rheinberg. We learnt that the hospital no longer existed but Sabine Sweetsir of that department showed interest in my story for a future publication concerned with Rheinberg during the Nazi period.

Further email correspondence followed finally containing this extract from the diary of one of the nuns, Sister Bernhild…"*One night two planes were shot down near the hospital. All personnel of the planes died except one English pilot. He had a gaping wound on his forehead. This one was fed 5 weeks long by our sisters and then removed to Frankfurt.*"

It was undoubtedly me; I have the scars to prove it!

IMMIGRATION CONTROL

Ian Mathie

Meeting the baggage weight limits when flying can be problematical if you have to take everything with you. When you have to unpack the suitcase in the booking hall and change your apparel specifically to meet the limit, it can be inconvenient to say the least. But the problems are not solely about weight and they don't necessarily end there. Sometimes they follow you all the way to your destination, raising their heads anew when you arrive at an immigration officer's desk. After this they may continue to haunt you for years afterwards, as I found out when I first went to Togo.

After five weeks leave in Britain, I went to Accra for a week, to attend the African Population Conference. I was to go on from there to Lomé in Togo, which is all of sixty five miles along the coast. There was no coach service in those days, and if one did not have a private car, road travel depended on bush taxis or mammy wagons. The only other alternative was to fly on the twice weekly service provided by Air Afrique with an antiquated Dakota. I would have been happy to go by bush taxi, crammed into an overcrowded car with at least eight other adults and a huge pile of luggage strapped to the roof, but my masters insisted that I went by air.

Inevitably the flight was delayed by a technical problem and the sun was high and the air already baking hot by the time we walked across the apron to the waiting aircraft at Accra airport. There had already been some good entertainment in the terminal for the Air Afrique staff insisted on weighing every item of baggage very carefully and would not let a single pound of overweight luggage go on board, regardless of whether one was willing to pay. The flight was full, they said, and the weight factor was critical. One very large American lady, who was predisposed to whine about everything, made a tremendous fuss about having to discard thirty pounds from her matching luggage. The rest of us simply opened our cases and removed dispensable items, like toiletries, that could be replaced easily and repacked our bags. Having done this I found my bag was still about four pounds overweight. There was only one thing for it, I took my bag to the gents and repacked it. In went the lightweight tropical suit I had been wearing and I emerged a few minutes later wearing my heavy kilt with all the accoutrements and my bag weighing less than the required limit. The people waiting for flights that day were a colourful lot and nobody took any notice or saw anything out of place about my attire.

The bags were checked and taken out to be loaded into the plane's hold. Eventually the passengers were summoned to board and a long crocodile of droopy people straggled across the roasting apron towards a line of waiting planes. As it became clear which plane we were to board, the whining American started again.

"Ah dun payed fer a prapper airplane ride, not a trip in some anti deeloovian death trap like that tin can! I wanna proper plane!" she wailed as her husband tried to look as though she was nothing to do with him.

The pilot, a phlegmatic Frenchman with a world weary face, was waiting at the foot of the boarding ladder. As the woman hung back and repeated her protest he turned and shrugged.

"Madame, in two minutes I shall close the door," he announced "Then I will start les moteurs and we shall depart. If you are not on board, I shall leave you be'ind." With this he skipped up the rickety ladder and disappeared inside the aircraft. The American woman, whose husband had already boarded, hurried after him and the door slammed closed behind her.

It was not worth climbing to any altitude for a twenty five minute flight, so the pilot stayed low and we were treated to a grandstand view of the coastal plain from just over two thousand feet. We had the coast on one side and lush palm groves and fields of corn and cassava stretching away northwards to the forest on the other. In the hot tropical air turbulence was already building up and so the pilot left the 'fasten seat belts' sign illuminated. The only other member of the crew, a pretty African stewardess, handed out sweets and cool moist face cloths for our comfort. The only unpleasant part of the flight was the incessant whining of the fat American woman. We had not been airborne more than ten minutes before the pilot engaged his autopilot, left his seat and came back into the cabin to ask her to be quiet.

Hijackings were unheard of in those days and there was no door between the cabin and the flight deck. We could all see that there was no co-pilot, so when the pilot came back and spoke to the American woman there was nobody up front. When he had said his piece and calm was momentarily restored, the woman unfortunately made this same observation.

"Hey! Who's flying this darn crate with you standin' here?" she demanded.

"Nobody madame," the pilot replied. "There was too much distraction from you and I could not even 'ear my radio. If you do not shut up I will not go back. Then we will crash in the sea and the sharks can get fat eating you!" He turned to the other passengers and shrugged a Gallic shrug.

The woman immediately started another wailing protest which stopped abruptly a moment later as her husband's fist landed heavily on the point of her jaw. As she sagged unconscious in her seat he looked up and said "Sorry about that, Captain. She'll be quiet now."

The pilot gave another shrug and returned to his seat. Soon afterwards we flew over the city of Lomé and landed at the new airport. The terminal building was airy and cool after the confined cabin of the plane. Lines of whirring fans hung above our heads and blew a gentle breeze over us as we queued to have our passports checked. When my turn came the Immigration Officer's eyes flicked briefly over me before he examined my passport. He looked at the photograph which had been taken at a time when my beard was much shorter and checked it against my face. Then he looked down at my feet and his eyes travelled slowly upwards until he again reached my face. Holding up my passport and waving it he spoke to one of his colleagues, who also came over to inspect me. After a look at the passport photo his eyes too inspected me from shoes to face.

"Mais c'est fantastique!" he declared. "C'est Monsieur ou Mademoiselle?"

Needless to say everyone, except the Americans, who spoke no French, thought this was outrageously funny and the whole terminal joined in the laughter. When I presented my bag at the customs bench the joke was repeated and we all laughed some more as the officers scribbled their chalk marks on every bag that was presented without so much as a question about the contents. Goodness knows what contraband came through undetected that morning, but nobody's baggage got opened, even the Americans'.

I don't know how many times my hand was shaken that morning, but I believe I must have been greeted by every official in the place and I was very tempted to get my bagpipes out and play them. Eventually I made it to the exit door and found someone waiting to meet me. I tossed my baggage into the back of the dusty Landrover and we headed into the city in the direction of a cold beer and lunch.

Six weeks later I had cause to fly from Lomé up to Niamey, in Niger. The local travel agent provided a ticket and advised me to be at the check-in desk at least half an hour before the departure time. The security checks we are so familiar with today were not even thought of at that time and check-in was certain to be brief since I would be returning within two days and was only taking a small bag. I arrived at the check-in with a little time to spare and presented my ticket. A boarding pass was issued and I headed towards passport control and the departure lounge.

As I presented my passport I recognised the Immigration Officer. He was the same man I had met when I arrived. He looked at my passport, inspected me from head to toe and shook his head, apparently with disapproval.

"Ça ne va pas," he announced. "Vous êtes arrivé en Mademoiselle, vous ne pouvez pas partir en Monsieur."

"What do you mean?" I asked

"The kilt," he said, grinning. "You must wear it to pass control."

"But it is at my house. I will miss the flight."

"The plane will wait," he said. "You must wear it."

"Really? Is it necessary? I'll have to go all the way home to change," I protested.

"Oui. C'est néccésaire."

There was nothing for it but to go home and change. I arrived back in a taxi with the wheels squealing round the corners, but needn't have worried about rushing. True to his word, the flight had been held up for almost an hour. The passengers had been served iced drinks and word had obviously gone round among them to explain the delay. They gave me a rousing cheer when I finally climbed the steps and took my seat.

I made eleven more flights in or out of Lomé airport over the next eighteen months and every time it was the same. I was required to wear my kilt. After the first couple of flights, when I turned up 'properly dressed', I didn't even need to show my passport. I soon got to know all the airport officials and in those eighteen months found I had made some very good friends.

THE HISTORY CLASS

Sammy Birch

"I've joined a history class," Jess announced at Sunday lunch. "Wednesday evenings. Before my brain totally atrophies." She didn't need to add *since I moved in next door.*

Jess, Jessica Grey, Greg's arty widowed Mum, an amazing 90 years old. We'd moved to Donnington soon after Greg's retirement to be near her. Greg had taken to "just popping over to see if she needs anything" and Thursday had become his Jess-day, part of life's routine like the weekly supermarket shop. Except for the occasional outing I managed to exclude myself from these encounters.

"I just don't see the problem Shona love," Greg said (it's always *Shona love* when he professes I baffle him). "Jess is forever on about how marvellous it is the way you cope with home, and kids, and me, and part-time job" (in the local health centre) "and all those charity involvements" (two actually).

He never had understood it was the *way* she went on about it that made it quite clear I scored zero as a daughter-in-law when it came to creative talent which, of course, was what Really Counted. Because I knew he adored Jess I let it go. And with the length of a largeish village between us it hadn't been important.

And then she had started falling about and Greg had said "That's the third fall this week. That house is much too big, and anyway she shouldn't be on her own."

. There had followed a silence in which I knew I was supposed to say "She could come and live with us." But I didn't, knowing in that far-back bit of my mind where unacknowledged things lie, this was something I had always dreaded.

Greg put his arms round me. "The obvious thing would be to move her into the residential home next door. She already has a couple of acquaintances there, the rooms are pleasant, the food good and the staff angelic."

Which was all very well, but she'd be there with her disapproval, permanently just the other side of a wall.

"The twins will be glad," I said, and knew I'd given in.

Ben and Becky, aged ten, were the progeny of our daughter who had moved to Australia, married, moved back to the UK and settled within ten miles of us following a divorce. The children went to Donnington school, had supper with us, and probably spent as much time with us as their high-flying mother who had carved a rather good career for herself in television. They adored Jess who insisted we all called her that because "it keeps me young."

Decision finally taken, Jess set about disposing of her huge furniture and her too-big house without, it must be said, a trace of self-pity. One of her architect friends turned a derelict outhouse in our garden into a studio with a tiny conservatory "where I can unfold in the morning sun." Somehow she reached an arrangement with Freshfields that she came and went as she pleased as long as we took full responsibility for her medication and hospital visits.

It was OK at first. Apart from joining us for Sunday lunch and materialising in her studio most days, Jess didn't really intrude on our daily lives. Rather it was the other way round.

"Why can't Jess eat with us every day?" Ben demanded very soon.

Greg avoided my eye. "She likes to be by herself. And you're *not* to pester her."

They did, of course, bursting in on her as soon as they got home from school. And Greg wasn't much better with his "just nipping over to see if she needs anything," most evenings after supper.

"What's achoffies?" Ben wanted to know now.

"Atrophies. Sort of shrivels up. Like your brain will if you don't do your homework," Greg said. "Trouble is, Jess, Wednesday's the one evening I'm late home."

Jess said briskly "I'm perfectly capable of walking a few hundred yards to the village hall."

The tutor, James, was a retired academic who'd moved to the area from nearby Brum. Jess was delighted with him and his class. Then on the third Wednesday she tripped as she was leaving the village hall.

James brought her home by car, cross and bruised but otherwise undamaged. "She really shouldn't be walking on her own," he said sounding sharp.

"Stop fussing James," Jess said "I'll use that infernal stick the doctor keeps wittering on about."

I heard myself say "I'll take you."

"That's that then." James stopped sounding sharp and beamed at me. "There are a couple of vacancies on the course if you want to join us. No obligation of course."

I had absolutely no intention of doing so, but when I delivered Jess the following Wednesday and James said "Why not stay, see what you think?" I couldn't quickly produce a convincing reason why not.

History was not a subject I'd given much thought to before. The complexities and demands of here-and-now seemed quite enough to be getting on with. But James certainly had a way with him. Quite unexpectedly and absorbingly in the next two hours, I got the first glimmerings of how the past was as relevant to the present as the present was to the future: that we were all miniscule cogs in the wheel of time; that today was tomorrow's history.

Somehow it was taken for granted that I'd stay on for the course. Jess had found a soulmate called Anne from a neighbouring village and made it clear she would continue sitting with her at the front of the class. That left me to skulk unnoticed at the back, which was fine by me.

James was concentrating on a general history of our area. He wanted us, he explained, to look at our surroundings with new eyes: observe old field boundaries, tell-tale humps marking deserted farms; ferret out the original lay-out of the village. The twins had recently got interested in the Vikings - I suspect the horned helmets were the main attraction - so I took special note on learning that Donnington actually straddled the old frontier between the Viking-settled areas and the Anglo Saxons. When I imparted this nugget of knowledge to the twins Ben said airily "Jess has already told us all about that."

Becky added "Have you noticed how her brain has stopped shrivelling?"

I tried to discuss the odd historical point with Jess, as one student to another as it were; but she was not encouraging

About two-thirds of the way through the course James produced the idea of celebrating Donnington's millennium in 2020. "A sort of DNA of Donnington," he elaborated. "Old diaries, parish records, maps, photographs, prints - everything that combines to make Donnington uniquely what it is."

It would need a lot of research, he went on, and should keep us occupied right up to 2020 when the aim was to display our findings in a special exhibition for all to see.

"But I need a co-ordinator," James concluded. "And I'd like to suggest Jessica whose artistic flair will be invaluable."

There was a general rumble of agreement. Jess was obviously chuffed to pieces.

"And Shona." Suddenly all eyes swivelled in my direction as James addressed me across the class. "If you could be available for a bit of chauffeuring ....?"

"Anne's already offered," Jess said firmly, belying Anne's startled look, "And she's a wizard with a computer, which means we can start out with a proper data base."

Why was it that, instead of feeling let off the hook, I actually felt rather miffed?

The effect of the project on Jess was remarkable. "As if she's been given a completely new lease of life," Greg said.

The twins complained her brain had become so big and busy perhaps it would be better if it shrivelled again meaning that she no longer lavished so much time on them. Indeed she was out and about all over the place, usually with Anne in tow, checking this museum or that library. And when she wasn't, there was a steady flow of telephone calls or visits from other members of the class delegated to fulfill various tasks.

By the end of the course James had superficially covered Donnington's life story. "We'll be looking at its more important chapters in detail during the next terms," he said. In the meantime the last class before the holidays would become our own personal update: Donnington within our times, seen through our eyes and according to our experience.

I wondered if he'd really thought that idea through. A lot of the class were relatively new to the village - that is within the last twenty years which is extremely new by Donnington standards. Indeed, Jess - fourth generation born and bred - was the only Donningtonian in the fullest sense.

Not surprisingly the reminiscences got off to a slow start. There were predictable contributions about how attractive the village and its setting were, and the general joys of the countryside. Then a peevish note was struck as one or two started homing in on the lack of facilities for the youngsters, the ever-decreasing shops, the limited public transport. I could see James was beginning to regret the idea.

Then into a quiet lull came Jess's voice. She had a good voice and spoke thoughtfully, almost as if reminiscing to herself which, in the end I realised was exactly what she was doing. And before long any fidgetting or shifting of papers ceased.

"In 1944 there was just a dusty lane," she said. "The main road was five miles further than it is now. It took the fire brigade and ambulance an hour to get here that night the V1 fell. Doodlebugs we called them because you couldn't be afraid of something with such a silly name. But it was a direct hit so Father was killed outright. Mother and I were out in the fields. Just a few scratches, but I remember the terrible noise and everything crashing down and the dust. I was eight."

A couple of years younger than the twins.

"It's true public transport was better after the war than now; there weren't all those cars. But we did a lot of walking. Three miles each way when I graduated to the Seniors. And of course you don't miss what you don't have so instead of TV we had darts, and pingpong - in this very room come to think of it; and local hops - our version of the disco; or went bluebelling or blackberrying or mushrooming. There was the village fair twice a year until no one had time to organise it any more. so they reduced it to once, then did away with it altogether."

She must have gone on for a full quarter of an hour, and I could actually visualise a Donnington I'd never known. And began to visualise a Jess I'd never stopped to think about. A young Jess who'd worked her way through art school without a Dad and, in due course, brought up a son without a husband. Greg's father had died in an accident when Greg was eleven.

A year older than the twins.

I'd chanced upon a file of cheap greeting cards and calendars that Jess must have produced when she needed every penny she could earn. It hadn't occurred to me at the time but, knowing her bold (and for me difficult) abstract style, I guessed now she must have hated doing them. Of course she would never have let on to Greg.

And what else wouldn't she have let on? That she didn't want other people completely taking over her life, popping in every other minute, giving her lifts, requiring her to be grateful?

"It wasn't easy for someone as dreamy as I was," she was saying now. "Young women nowadays are so well organised, so sure of themselves. Still we knew what we needed to do, and did it, and we survived." She stopped quite suddenly; there was a small silence, and then a ripple of sound grew into applause. Jess looked up puzzled, then dismayed, and hurriedly left the hall. I went after her.

I found her struggling into her coat, cursing her stick and muttering "What on earth possessed you woman..."

She glared at me as I took the stick. I said "I thought *I* was the inadequate one."

She went on fighting her coat for a moment, then stopped. The glare gave way to astonishment. *"You?"*

We stood looking at each other. It seemed like a long time. I began to think of just some of the ways phrases or gestures can be misinterpreted, multiplying over the years.

Tentatively I held out an arm. "Start again?" I said.

For a brief moment Jess looked cautious. Then, uncharacteristically, she gave me a hug. "Start again" she said.

THE HALL OF FUTURES

Nicholas Wood

As usual, the lights were low in the Hall of Futures, but it was not gloomy. Rather the silent busyness triggered an impression of forward movement that brought its own clarity, a knowledge there would be light at the end of a tunnel however long, and in whichever parallel universe.

The rows of desks stretched into infinite distance, each occupied by an assiduous occupant completely focussed on his or her task. There was little feeling of stress, but a great deal of small movement: perhaps a jerk of impatience, a head lifted as communication with a colleague was established, a brief nod of satisfaction as a job was completed.

The occupants of the desks were small gnome-like people. Those in the front ranks had been there for eons beyond counting and were the most senior and experienced. They communicated by specifically directed thought and could not be interrupted. One of them, Noah, spoke across the ranks to Moab. "So Jade is in trouble again." It was more a statement than a question.

"Yes, she's in her flat in that place Grimsbury," Moab responded.

"That place on Earth? Perhaps it's the name that troubles her. Has her sickness returned?" Noah was aware that Jade's condition affected him more than was usual or sensible.

Throughout his immeasurable time in the Hall of Futures, Noah had learned to detach from his experiences in those other worlds in which he had lived and from which he had acquired his ability to contribute to the future of those still inhabiting them. But occasionally one of them would trigger a sensation that lay so deep he would not be able to trace its origins. Jade was a case in point. Noah knew he had lived through her despair and that it had had profound effects on him.

The causes were different - indeed he had long since forgotten them; but the effects were similar though he could not remember exactly what they were. Certainly he had no memory of starving himself because he was the wrong shape, nor of cutting himself until he bled. But there had been something: some intake of substance that changed and troubled his psyche.

He now gathered that Moab had intercepted a message from Sam, far back in the ranks where the gnomes were much less experienced and quite often made errors so that they were obliged to return to their worlds to improve their knowledge. Sometimes they were returned to other worlds. Lacking the skills for directed thought, their forms of communication were various and often noisy, though mostly by means of computerised machines similar to those available in a number of worlds. These were innumerable and offering ever-improving programmes which could also have the effect of modifying the errors, not always for the better. As for Jade...

Before responding to Noah Moab sent an urgent message back through the ranks to Sam. *She must not call her mother. Her friend Ruby is just passing Jade's door and has decided to visit.*

So, hunched up on the sofa in her flat in Grimsbury, Jade contemplated the cut she had just made on her forearm and wondered what on earth was the point in being alive. She was just reaching for her mobile to ring her mother when the doorbell rang.

"Hi Jade," her best friend Ruby said, coming in without being invited. "You look dreadful."

"Everything *is* dreadful," Jade said in a flat monotone, and burst into tears.

Tracey gave her a big quick hug and went into the kitchen to put the kettle on.

It intrigued those in the Hall of Futures who had time to think about it why putting the kettle on was the first thing many - especially some Earth People - did in the face of a crisis. Mostly they decided that this acted as a form of distraction. But then there were many things that puzzled them, however senior they were, about the behaviour of those in lower worlds.

Noah was pleased to note that Moab had managed to divert Jade's phone call to her mother, who was a nervous woman completely uncomprehending of the way the modern younger Earth People reacted to each other. Noah would have shared her bewilderment if he had not long ago acquired, through experience, the ability to act for rather than react to those put in his charge.

Ruby brought two mugs of steaming dark brown liquid into Jade's small living room and said, "You've been cutting yourself again. That's really stupid."

Noah thought it was really stupid too, but he had learned that doing this strange act apparently released tension in some Earth People and telling them it was stupid did not stop them from doing it.

Ruby went on, "Is it that Rose?"

Jade nodded. "She's been putting stuff on Facebook again."

Facebook particularly intrigued Noah because it was an important part of the Earth People's world. Those who 'put stuff' on Facebook often gave great details of what they had had for their last meal. Or they put photographs of themselves looking so extraordinary that it was incomprehensible that they should wish to so demean themselves. Another major purpose for which they used it was to be unkind to each other and this clearly was what had upset Jade and caused the cutting.

The messages, Noah knew, were about Jade's appearance (skeletal), brain power (moronic) and lack of popularity (rejected) according to Rose who was very popular herself at the school to which they both went, but seemed upset by Jade's academic achievements.

Ruby said, "But Jade, cutting yourself won't hurt Rose - or stop her. Rose will only understand when she has to face the result of her actions."

Noah found himself nodding. He noted that Ruby had diplomatically not mentioned that Rose had once had a similar eating problem. Jade's friend had good comprehension and he could even visualise her one day in the Hall of Futures. It was interesting that the Earth People gave themselves such names as flowers and precious stones, though they bore no relation to them either in appearance or character: unyielding jade, delicate rose. Noah had had his own name so long he no longer thought about it, though he knew it came from a religious book. Most of the names in the Hall of Futures originated in religious books from one world or another, though the less senior ones liked to reduce them to one syllable like Josh or Sam or Jude. When it came to Rose, she was a monster. Undoubtedly a pretty one in Earth's terms, but a monster all the same.

"And how is that going to happen?" Jade asked, sulkily. "She's even started nicking my Smartphone and putting horrible messages before leaving it somewhere I can't miss it."

"That's interesting," Ruby said. And Noah realised she was reflecting his thoughts.

Smartphones were instruments that Earth People held to their ears so they could hear other Earth People who were in quite different places. Or they put pictures on a screen and spent a lot of time staring at these screens instead of looking where they were going. Doing this they often ignored the person who was walking by their side, even their own child.

Ruby started talking to Jade in a very low voice, almost as though she were afraid someone might overhear them. But Noah did not need volume of sound to hear Earth People. And as he listened, he nodded in approval.

Jade's expression was showing approval too as she understood Ruby's plan. "Except," she said, "I'm not sure how to do it."

"I'll show you. It's a doddle."

Frustratingly, it was a while before they could put it into practice, as Rose was away. On her return Ruby took Jade's Smartphone and pressed some buttons. Then she handed it back to Jade and said, "Three-thirty."

Noah smiled, understanding what she was doing. Moab, who had spent less time with Earth People, was very puzzled, so Noah explained it to him. It was important to share knowledge.

That afternoon the class was writing essays on 20th Century English Literature. They were to discuss authors between the two World Wars. Jade found it difficult to concentrate and kept looking at her watch, noting time crawl by. At nearly three thirty, she held up her hand, "Excuse me, Mrs. Johnson. I just wanted to ask if anyone had seen my Smartphone. It keeps disappearing and sometimes when I find it there are messages on it as though someone has been using it. Some of them are a bit weird, quite nasty. And then ...." She was interrupted by the shrill sound of a mobile from the second row of the class. "That's it!" she exclaimed, "That's my Smartphone!"

Mrs Johnson stood up, head forward like a ferret scenting a prey "Isn't that coming from your desk, Rose dear" she enquired.

In fact, it was coming from the pocket of Rose's shocking pink jacket. Reluctantly she pulled it out, and pressed a button. Silence fell.

"And how did it get there, Rose dear?" Mrs. Johnson enquired. "Well, the class will be over soon, so we'll discuss it after that. We can check the messages and see if they give us a clue. I'm sure you'll want to help Jade with such a nasty experience."

Ruby grinned at Jade. Jade looked uncomfortable, but not nearly as uncomfortable as Rose. Noah briefly had the sense of a job well done, even though he was not sure exactly what he had done.

Nor would he have had time. For, as the end-of-class bell rang and the pupils streamed out, all except Rose, a new urgent message was already coming through.

"I'm right here," Noah said to someone called Nigel who sounded very agitated. "Take deep breaths and just calm down." Already he was engaged with the next problem, with just a very small feeling of regret that he would have to wait before he heard the very end of Jade's story. Though he could make a fair guess at what it would be.

MAN OVERBOARD!!

Peter Cottrell

Anyway, it seems that this old guy had been to the Spiceball Gym on his scooter to attend a series of talks on how to improve his breathing!! On the way back to Foxhall Court residential flats where he lived, he took a wrong turning and found himself in Spiceball Children's playground. Nothing daunted, he took a canal path (barely wide enough for the scooter). All went well – he enquired of a rare passer-by as to where the path went, and was told that it led to the old Alcan Works – that seemed to be in the right general direction, and as there was not enough room to either reverse or turn around anyway, he pressed on.

Suddenly, to his dismay, the width of the path got so narrow that the scooter decided that it was no longer wide enough, and so it took a leap into the canal, taking its passenger with it. Now this was more serious than it first appeared because the old fellah was strapped in to the machine, and was totally under water. Surprisingly, perhaps, he neither felt cold nor frightened. Quickly releasing himself from the straps, he now found himself standing in about nine inches of sludge on the canal bed; walking was impossible, so casting off his raincoat , hat and scarf, he struck out a couple of strokes to the bank. If he thought, then, that he could now just scramble out of the canal, he was wrong. He found that whatever he grabbed to assist his landing gave way in his hand. Finding a strip of gravel at the edge of the canal bed, he settled down to await rescue. The water was just up to his chest sitting down. He saw that he was not far from civilisation because of the sight and sound of the busy road (he presumed Southam Road) behind the trees on the other side of the canal, and a bridge about two hundred yards away. He caught sight of his scooter, lying, forlornly, on its side with one wheel only showing above the surface, and managed to rescue his raincoat.

Relief came in about ten minutes (surprisingly his watch was still ticking), when a welcome voice from above called "hello, mate, are you alright there". Our friend gasped words to the effect that he was not alright, and would be grateful for a pull out. With that the rescuer grabbed hold of the scruff of his shirt and pulled him out on to the bank, half throttling him in the process, not to mention pulling off his shirt buttons, one by one.

Luckily, the rescuer had his mobile with him, and he asked whom he should ring. The Ambulance or maybe the Police. 999 anyway, the soaking wet body suggested. He heard the man on the phone saying "I don't know – about seventy I suppose" - which was gratifying being nearly twenty years short. There then followed a discussion as to where an Ambulance or Police Van could park. The rescuer then advised that he had better get to his feet as he could easily roll off back into the canal .

This proved virtually impossible as the victim was, by this time, frozen stiff!! Just then a canal boat passed by and the rescuer cried out a request for an old blanket – a horse blanket perhaps that he could spare. A Police Constable then came along the tow-path from the bridge over the canal. He lifted the casualty to his feet holding him in a bear hug to help him get warm. He then asked the crewman on the canal boat if he could possibly give a lift into Banbury. The latter agreed and after a fair amount of manoeuvring, managed to get his craft close enough for the Constable to get the old boy aboard. The Ambulance was waiting in the park from where his adventure started.

From then on, it was all routine except for the stripping naked in the ambulance and being warmed up with a corrugated sheet into which a tube of hot air was infused at the bottom – no, not up his bottom!! His body temperature was, apparently, very low and hypothermia was feared. He was then kept in hospital overnight for this and to check that he had not "injested" too much of the canal!! At A&E he was greeted by no less than six lovely nurses who had heard of the incident, but needed to see for themselves to make sure it was true !! One even enquired if he had enjoyed the "dive". Apart from the jesting, he was spoilt rotten for the next 24 hours and began to think that it had all been worthwhile.

PS At the time of going to press, the scooter has been recovered from the canal (how is not yet known), and will be returned to normal "soon".

PPS   Six months later: how long is "soon"?

BUNTY AND THE PERHAPS-ANGEL

Sylvie Nickels

"I'm off," Emmie said to the head cook at Freshfields Care Home, slipping out of her apron. On her way she paused at the open conservatory door peer across the garden to a figure bent over the flower beds. "Hi, just off. Don't forget Bunty's bringing the sprog over this evening."

The figure waved an arm in acknowledgement and Emmie headed out of Freshfields, round the corner to one of the cottages overlooking the market place and switched on the kettle. It was part of an almost daily routine: that and the cup of tea that she would take out on to the patio among the tubs of geraniums where she would, as likely as not, indulge in her favourite memories. It was a daydream that would take her back twenty-five years.

"Look Mummy, an angel!" Bunty had shrieked that long-ago December, her long fair hair swinging.

All too familiar with the excesses of her daughter's fertile imagination, Emmie Gregson began "Don't be ...." but hadn't got as far as "... silly sweetie" when she stopped. Across the market place with the December sunshine highlighting his white sweater and creating a curious halo effect about his head, the man did look disconcertingly angel-like. Not least because he was playing a very large harp.

As they approached, the sound rippled like dappled sunshine on a woodland stream. Emmie found herself smiling at the sheer pleasure of it. As a piano teacher music was an essential part of her life. By the time they reached him the halo had dissolved and the

42

harpist had paused to attend to an older man who was saying "…. they *will* be pleased Stefan." It was then Emmie saw he was collecting for the local hospice.

"Are you really an angel?" Bunty was hopping from one foot to another.

The older man laughed but Stefan looked at Bunty quite seriously and said "Perhaps one day if I am good enough." Emmie noted the slight foreign accent; then he smiled and she thought *that is a very attractive man.*

She turned away. She was through with attractive men, or indeed any other kind. Four years of living with Gerry had seen to that.

But Bunty was tugging at her arm. "*Wait* Mummy, I want to give the Perhaps-Angel some of my pocket money." Emmie paused resignedly while her daughter made a great performance of extracting 50p from the patchwork purse that hung round her neck.

Stefan said "Thank you. You are a golden girl with a good heart."

As they moved out of hearing Emmie said "I don't like it when you show off."

"I *wasn't*," Bunty protested. "The Perhaps-Angel was pleased." She glanced sideways at Emmie and added "And I expect Daddy would have been too."

She had discovered quite recently that mention of her father usually cut short any scolding. It worked. Emmie sighed and fell silent as they headed for the car and home. Gerry had actively encouraged Bunty's precociousness; it was one of the many things they had come to disagree on.

It was four years now since he had left for New South Wales with a sleek Ozzie redhead over in the UK on a short training course. Though Emmie had fallen out of love with him long before, this sudden and crude rejection had turned her life upside down, blown apart her self-confidence. Only three at the time Bunty remembered him hazily as a Mr Nice-Guy who gave her presents and made her laugh. After days of agonising over what to tell her, Emmie settled for "Daddy's gone to work a long way away in Australia for a while" and hoped that time would do the rest. And, thankfully, for a long while it had.

That evening as Emmie came to the end of her nightly story, Bunty said drowsily "Can we go and see the Perhaps-Angel again?"

"He's just a nice man, not an angel sweetie, not even a 'perhaps' one," Emmie said, but her daughter was already asleep, golden hair splayed out on the pillow looking heart-meltingly like an angel herself.

Emmie went on sitting there quietly, watching her. The fact that she loved her to bits didn't blind her to the precociousness that also showed up in Bunty's writing and drawing skills; and likewise had sometimes tested her teachers' patience to the limit. Getting the balance right between stick and carrot could be really hard when you were responsible for wielding both. Then the difficult questions had begun three months ago.

"Has Daddy died?" Bunty had suddenly asked soon after learning of the death of one of her friends' grannies.

"Of course not," Emmie said firmly. Though how could she be sure? It was well over a year since the last contact.

Soon after came the question she had always dreaded because of the deep-down sense of failure, however unjustified, associated with it. "Mummy, are you and Daddy vorsed?" Bunty asked as she scooped up fluffy mounds of bubblebath one evening. She frowned over the unfamiliar word, and hurried on "Because Jennie Peters said her auntie vorsed her uncle and he went away too."

Emmie reached across for a towel and said quietly. "It's called divorced sweetie, when Mummys and Daddys decided to live apart. And yes, that's what we decided to do." To her relief that seemed to suffice.

Thankfully Bunty didn't seem to remember the rows, increasing in number and vehemence, until they seemed to disagree about everything. How could it have happened? Oh quite easily, Emmie acknowledged when, long ago, she had accepted her own part in it. Infatuation, the dizzy joy that someone as gorgeous and streetwise as Gerry had actually fallen for her had stifled completely the small voice of doubt somewhere deep down.

They had been both so young: still at college, Emmie with her music, Gerry with his sights set on high finance. Far too young to take on board that the attraction of opposites was not always the best basis for a stable long-term partnership. Though she had tried, she really had.

There was no sign of Stefan or his harp in the market place a few days later.

"I expect he's working," Emmie said, quite sorry not to hear that mellow flow of sound.

"Making all those sick people better," said Bunty clearly fostering vivid images of a harp-toting ministering angel. But her attention was soon distracted by the many signs that now presaged not only Christmas but her own birthday. The big Christmas tree from their twin-town in Austria now sparkled in a corner of the market place; stalls were wreathed in tinsel and fairy lights; and wall-to-wall Christmas carols filled the air. In a week's time Bunty would be eight, in two weeks it would be their fifth Christmas without Gerry. Tucked away in Emmie's wardrobe was the Barbie outfit she had made secretly in the evenings after Bunty was in bed; and a small easel to encourage those early daubs which were showing such promise. She had also booked matinée seats at the local Arts Theatre for a revival of *The Sound of Music*.

On the eve of the great day they were indulging in pre-birthday tea and chocolate cake in their favourite teashop, when a voice from the next table exclaimed "It is the golden girl with a good heart!"

"Mummy, it's the Perhaps-Angel," Bunty was bouncing with excitement.

Emmie smiled. In jeans and bomber-jacket, he looked a good deal more of an earthling than on their previous encounter. He said "It's nice to be a Perhaps-Angel. But otherwise my name is Stefan."

"And I'm Bunty," Bunty said. "And I shall be eight years old tomorrow. And this is Mummy. She plays the piano."

"Happy birthday tomorrow, Bunty." Stefan glanced at Emmie questioningly.

"Emmie Gregson." She gave a rueful smile. "I'm afraid my daughter can be impossibly precocious at times."

"I have a niece in Poland - my sister's daughter. She is very much like Bunty, with long beautiful hair, and likes to pretend she is bold."

"Where is Poland?" Bunty wanted to know. "Is it far? Like Australia?"

Stefan laughed. "Not *so* far, but far enough."

"It must be lonely away from your home," Emmie said.

He shrugged. "I came to stay with my aunt and English uncle here at the time of some political troubles problems many years ago. I'd just qualified as an engineer and I was lucky enough to be able to stay. So now *this* is home." He paused. "So you play the piano?"

45

"I give lessons, and sometimes play for friends."

"You could play together!" Bunty said, clearly pleased with such a clever thought.

Stefan looked at Emmie. "I would like that." Then after a pause that went on too long, he said "But in any case you will find me on the market place most mornings before Christmas."

Emmie shrugged into her coat as she said "We'll probably see you there then. Come on young lady." She turned and gave Stefan a small apologetic smile.

Bunty was lost in a television programme on monkeys that evening when the telephone rang. "Good morning England," drawled a voice Emmie had never thought to hear again.

"Good evening Gerry," she said coolly.

"Yeah. Evening, of course.. And here we are basking in early morning sunshine on the terrace, sipping our breakfast orange juice..." Emmie glanced at raindrops glinting on the window pane and found she was hugely glad not to be sipping orange juice in far away early morning sunshine. Gerry was saying "So my little Bunty's birthday hasn't yet begun - I was just telling Jaz here about her and she said why not call...?" Jaz? That was a new one. "I guess she must be all of seven by now."

"Eight," Emmie said shortly.

"Is that right? Yeah I guess it's a while since I've been in touch."

Quite suddenly Emmie didn't want to be talking to him any more. She said "I expect Bunty would like to speak to you. But I really don't have anything more to say."

A few moments later she closed the door on the excited "Daddy? Daddy .... it's my birthday tomorrow and ...."

Hearing the unbroken flow of chatter, Emmie marvelled at her daughter's ability to pick up the threads of a relationship she surely could barely remember. But perhaps had continued to practise privately within the confines of that fertile imagination? At last there was quite a long silence, the click of the phone and Bunty came in looking thoughtful.

"All right sweetie?"

She nodded. "I don't think Daddy's coming back."

Emmie knelt down and hugged the small figure tightly. She said "No he isn't," and waited for the questions to follow.

"He sounded ... funny."

46

"They speak a bit differently in Australia."

"Not that sort of funny," Bunty said. She wriggled away. "Oh, bother, I've missed the end of the monkeys." She put on a theatrically wistful expression. "Oh I do *wish* we could have a monkey."

Thank God for a child's resilience.

It was a relief next morning to find her still seemingly unphased by the contact with her father. Indeed she was far too preoccupied with opening presents and cards, and making ever wilder guesses at the nature of that afternoon's promised treat. Her expression when they finally entered the theatre was a joy to see, and she settled into her seat near the front of the stalls, hugging herself with anticipation. Emmie found almost as much pleasure in watching her as in the show, though it was a colourful performance with an excellent cast.

Then, after the second interval, the musicians returned to the orchestra pit and "Look!" shrieked Bunty. "The Perhaps-Angel."

And so it really was, Emmie saw with equal if quieter amazement, observing for the first time the very large harp and the familiar figure beside it. She also observed that Bunty's clear voice had caused an amused murmur through the auditorium and an infinitesmal flicker across Stefan's face.

Thankfully, once the curtain had risen Bunty was so absorbed in the show once more that her further outbursts merged with the rest of the audience's reactions. Emmie felt strangely still.

Afterwards they waited for him at the stage door.

"Bunty and I have come to apologise," Emmie said as Stefan emerged, thankfully alone.

"I knew it could only have been you, Golden Girl" he said, squatting down in front of Bunty. He took her hands. "Happy Birthday again. But I think now I must tell you the truth: I am not an angel, not even a 'perhaps' one."

"That's what Daddy said when he rang me yesterday. But then I thought perhaps they don't have angels in Australia?" Bunty looked at him hopefully.

"Her father lives in Australia now," Emmie explained.

"Ah," Stefan said. There was a small pause before he went on "Not in Australia. Not anywhere where you can *see* them. They're like a lot of things - happy feelings and liking feelings. You can't *see* them, but it doesn't mean they're not there."

47

Emmie thought *Gerry wouldn't have left her with that chink of hope. Anyway who really, really knows?* "It means." she said, "that sometimes you have to take things on trust."

And how long since you've put that into practice my girl, she wondered fleetingly.

Time to examine that thought later. In the meanwhile "Would you like to join us for a birthday supper Stefan?" she said.

They had never looked back. They had married a few months later, Bunty had in due course done media studies and worked her way up to being editor of an arts magazine. Emmie and Stefan had a son who eventually decided to travel the world and finally ended up in the Polish community in Canada.

They had done a lot of travelling themselves, too. Stefan proved to be a natural with computers and jetted from one continent to the other sorting out big business IT problems. When retirement began to poke its nose above the horizon, they settled in Donnington in the Midlands where Stefan got a job as handyman at the care home, and Emmie worked part time in the kitchen.

Bunty came to visit quite often, now with two-year-old Trixy who was fast heading towards being the next Perhaps-Angel in Emmie's life.

A Man of Passage

Ian Mathie

In 1973 the monsoon failed a second time and drought struck Ethiopia. While vast relief efforts were poured into the mountains of Wollo and Tigre provinces, nobody gave a thought to the people down in the Danakil Desert.

Lying between the high escarpment of the Ethiopian massif and the Red Sea to the east, the Danakil is one of the hottest places on earth. Temperatures soar daily to over 140°F, there is no water and life is like being in a slow oven. The Afar tribes who live there are pastoralists, scratching an existence as their goats and sheep browse the sparse vegetation whilst never seeing rain from one generation to the next. Most of their livestock and many of the people died before any help arrived. Those who had lost everything just wandered alone from one encampment to the next, hoping for a little sustenance until they too died.

We had been surveying down beyond the Chelaka for five days when the man came. The job was going well and we were almost finished. Two more days would see the whole thing completed.

We sat in the shade of an enormous acacia tree and discussed the results of the morning's activities. It was the only tree on this side of the river where the land was covered with dense thorn scrub and sparse patches of dry grass. The survey had been made more difficult because it was almost impossible to see more than about forty yards through the scrub. Frequent moves of the theodolite had been necessary and these wasted a considerable amount of time.

We had pitched our tent close to the edge of the river bank, beneath the sweeping boughs of the huge tree. It was in shade for most of the day and, being more or less in the open, had not so far become a target for the troop of olive baboons that had taken up residence below the bend on the other side of the river. Calling it a river was a generous description. There was almost no flow in this unnamed stream and the level was low enough for the baboons to cross with ease and without getting unduly wet. So far they had left us alone, although we often heard them barking, particularly at dawn.

The heat haze was always bad during the midday hours so we normally stopped work from noon until around three and sat in our patch of shade after lunch to do the paperwork. The others calculated out their theodolite readings and transferred the levels and angles to the plan. I sorted through the morning's collection of samples, made some preliminary tests and recorded the results in my book, cross-referencing with the plan to identify locations from which the samples had been taken. The series of tests was complete and I was just packing up the box of reagents, since they would not be needed again, when the man appeared as if from nowhere, and emerged from the surrounding scrub.

He walked slowly round our camp and finally stopped in front of the open tent flap. Very slowly he squatted down on his heels, just outside the dense shade of the tree, next to a leafless thorn bush. He was an old man, the oldest any of us had yet seen in this forsaken land where everything was shrivelled by drought and burned up by the sun.

The normal life expectancy here was little more than thirty five. This desiccated creature must have been nearer sixty five. Almost bald with a sparse grey friar's fringe at the back of his head, he had a thin white beard which had been carefully clipped. He was terribly thin and the skin hung in loose wrinkles over his spindly limbs.

In silence he squatted. With eyes screwed up against the glare of the sun he watched and examined us minutely. His bony left hand rested on his knee with the gnarled forefinger hooked loosely through the handle of a battered, soot encrusted, aluminium kettle. His right hand held firmly onto a short forked stick which he had been carrying over his shoulders and which now served to steady him in his pose.

"Hello," we said.

The man remained immobile, staring at the three of us in turn as if trying to decide whether or not we were fit to be spoken to. When he eventually made up his mind and spoke it was with a voice that was as old as time and as desiccated as the desert surrounding us.

"You have come here," he said.

"Yes," Mohamed replied. "We came five days before."

The old man said nothing but continued his scrutiny.

We had just brewed some tea. Without asking Mohamed ladled sugar into a glassful and held it out towards the visitor. He looked at it for a moment then set down his kettle, transferred the stick to his left hand and, with a slight nod, accepted the glass.

I thought it was curious the way this solitary wanderer had been so silent. I was intrigued, but dared not ask. We often received visits from the nomads who lived in this region and had learned their ritual of greeting. That garrulous process could last for anything up to twenty minutes and enquired in microscopic detail into the wellbeing of one's father, brothers, mother, grandfather, children, livestock and the world and his wife in general before moving on to enquiries about news and grazing. Only when all this was done should one approach business or any other topic. It was a wordy process, common enough across Africa, designed to enable each to weigh up the other. This old man had been squatting there for at least a quarter of an hour and had only uttered four words.

He wore the usual rough cotton *gaabi* draped over his scrawny shoulders, with a piece of similar cloth round his waist. On his feet he had a pair of crude sandals made from untanned goat skin. Apart from the kettle and his hand-worn stick, these appeared to be his only possessions.

The old man continued to watch us for a long time as he slurped noisily at the scalding tea.

"Do you want to buy a camel?" he asked after some time.

I shook my head and looked at the other two.

"Want a camel, Mo?" I asked. Mohamed shook his head. "Yusuf?" I enquired. He too shook his head.

"No thanks," Mohamed said to the old man, "We have no need of a camel."

The old man seemed unmoved and unsurprised, and said nothing. We looked around for the subject of the proposed bargain, but there was no sign of any camel.

Mohamed gave the man some more tea. He accepted it in silence, with only the same slight nod of thanks as before, and sucked noisily at the sticky sweet brew. He continued to watch us with his rheumy old eyes and said nothing more.

A baboon barked on the far side of the river. The yellow weaver birds chattered raucously in the canopy above us, where they fluttered about adding to their globular nests hanging precariously from the tips of the thorny branches. These were the only sounds as the world

51

around us dozed through the midday heat.

The old man finished his tea and placed the empty glass on its side in the dust beside him. Transferring the stick to his right hand, he hooked a finger through the handle of his kettle, resumed his former position, and continued to watch us in silence.

After a while he stood up, turned, and at the same unhurried pace at which he had arrived, walked off into the scrub with no word either of thanks or farewell.

"Do you want some tea?" I called after him and picked up a large handful of teabags. He stopped and turned slowly back towards me as I walked over and placed the teabags in his thin hand. For a long moment he stared at them with expressionless eyes, then turned his hand over and let them fall to the ground. He turned to go again.

"What's the matter?" I asked him, "Don't you want tea?"

He stared at me with a look of total bewilderment but said nothing. I had spoken in the local language, but suddenly wondered if he had understood what I had said.

"Open them," Mohamed called from behind me. "He has probably never seen a teabag before."

I picked up the fallen white squares, tore one open, and poured the contents into the palm of my hand. Mohamed brought an empty tin can and I tipped the tea into it. As more bags were torn open and decanted comprehension dawned and the old man's eyes lit up. He watched closely as all the fallen bags were retrieved and their contents added to the tin. When I held the tin out to him he took it hesitantly and peered inside. Then, with a wrinkled black finger, he slowly stirred the dry leaves. He looked up and the eyes that met mine twinkled with delight.

Yusuf brought another tin with some sugar in it and gave it to the man, receiving a nod of thanks but no words. Mohamed brought one of our goatskin water bags and refilled the old man's battered kettle. When the lid had been replaced the man looked at each of us in turn, nodded once, then turned without a word and once more walked off and disappeared in the scrub.

We stood for a long time, staring after him in silence.

Our reverie was broken by another series of harsh barks from the baboons across the river. I looked enquiringly at Mohamed. These were his people. Surely there must be an explanation. The best part of an hour had passed since the old man had appeared and he had spoken less than a dozen words.

A hundred questions filled my mind. Mohamed must have sensed my confusion.

"He is a man of passage," he said, as if this explained everything.

"A what?" Yusuf and I asked together.

"His family are all dead. His animals are all taken by raiders. He has no more than you see," Mohamed explained.

"Then how does he live? Where does he get food?" I asked.

"He will be fed wherever he goes. He is a Man of Passage."

Miss Finlayson comes to tea

Norman Stone

When the doorbell rang, Emily and Jim Dix were preparing their usual old-fashioned Sunday tea - paper-thin cucumber sandwiches, thick Victoria sponge.

On the quarry-tiled doorstep stood a little old lady. Barely five feet tall, fluffy white hair, eyes of faded blue, cheeks like the skin of a Worcester Pearmain, she was shabby but tidy. She wore a neat little brown felt hat and clutched a large, well-worn shopping bag.

"Good afternoon." Her soft speech was pure Morningside. "My name is Miss Finlayson. I do hope you won't think me impertinent, but over sixty-five years ago I lived in this very house - your house now - and if I may, I would like, for the last time" - her voice wobbled - "to see the rooms where I lived and worked, for so many years, so long ago,"

There was a silence. Miss Finlayson hurried on. "They're at the very top of the house, but it would only take a few minutes. Please?"

Emily's heart-shaped face lit up. "Yes, oh yes. Do come in."

Nodding approvingly at the highly polished front door knob and letter box, the old lady stepped into the hall. She kept up a constant flow of murmured half sentences.

"So kind. No wish to disturb. Teatime. Apologies. Not good manners."

The mention of manners prompted Emily to remember her own. "Please. You're very welcome to see your old rooms, though I doubt you'll recognise them."

"Oh, why not?" Miss Finlayson was almost sharp. "Unless

they've changed very much, I think I'd recognise all the rooms."

"Then you must look over the house," Emily soothed. "And afterwards, you'll stay to tea, won't you?"

Jim seemed about to say something but the look she gave him made him think better of it. He pushed his unruly hair back from his forehead. "Yes, of course," he said. "Please stay", and his smile showed that he meant it.

Miss Finlaysoon coloured a little and protested that it would be an imposition. Even so, it was not too difficult to persuade her that tea would be unthinkable without her.

They climbed the stairs to the first floor, then the half landing and so to the upper flight. Miss Finlayson was short of breath. but managed to wheeze that it was thirty-three treads and thirty-three risers, and she would never forget a single one of them. On the very top landing, the old lady got her breath back and explained that the room on her left had been the bedroom she shared with the maid of all work. Opposite was the sitting room that had been hers and hers alone. It was there that she had mended and darned and done all the sewing jobs that a so-called dressmaker actually carried out.

She was fascinated to discover that each of these rooms was now a modern office. "His and Hers", said Jim. "I run my business from this one - I'm an accountant - and Emily writesin hers. One day that will be her business."

"Not for a long time yet!" laughed Emily. "I've still to sell anything."

Miss Finlayson was sure it would be only a matter of time for her talent to be recognised - "perhaps even a best seller, who knows?"

They went downstairs, taking in each room as they passed, while Miss Finlayson's refined Anglo-Scottish tones gave a running commentary. "These brass stair rods are almost exactly the same as the ones the family had when I was here. The gouges in that newel post - have they always been there? - that would be where young Master William tested his pocket knife. He did rather too often."

In the dining room, Jim found himself explaining that though the three-storey , turn of the century villa cost a bit more than they had wanted to pay, it was a lot of house for the money. And, of course, added Emily, it would be a lovely place to bring up a family in, when the time came. So much space. And all that history.

The old lady seemed to take that as some sort of cue. She stood by - indeed under - the mantel and described everything that used to be on it. Jim and Emily could practically see the Tunbridgeware spill jar, the leather framed photographs, the art-deco tobacco box and the big mirror, with its arched head and black and gold frame.

Carton-pierre, she called it, and Jim had to admit that he had no idea what that was. Miss Finlayson diffidently spoken about a mixture of paper pulp and whiting and glue that could be moulded before it set rock hard, ready for painting or gilding. Emily discreetly made a note to look for a *carton-pierre* mantel mirror inthe sale rooms and antiques fairs.

Then it was time for tea. Politeness itself, Miss Finlayson sat straight backed on the edge of her chair and allowed herself to be cajoled into eating. Smiling and chatting the whole time though she was, somehow she never once spoke with her mouth full. Even so, she managed to put away far more than was ladylike and Emily suddenly realised that it could have been the first meal she'd had all day.

One more cup of tea, one last slice of Victoria sponge- "Oh, I shouldn't. Well, perhaps just the one, then. Thank you",- and she wanted to leave, in time to catch the half-past-five bus. Emily asked if she had far to go. "Oh no, just a few stops on the bus and then a wee walk." When pressed on just how wee the walk would be, she answered briskly, almost bravely, "Not far. With luck I'll be home by half-ast six - or quarter to seven at the latest, maybe."

Jim was outraged - "My dear Miss Finlayson...."

The old lady, quietly firm, said "If you're going to offer to drive me home, please don't."

Since Jim had not intended to do so, he had no difficulty in agreeing "But what I will do, Miss Finlayson, is call for a taxi."

"Oh no!" She was obviously distressed. "Please. The expense. I couldn't possibly afford..."

"And you'll surely allow me..."

"Jim," Emily spoke a shade anxiously. "Miss Finlayson may be offended."

"No, I wouldn't." The frail voice was quite brisk. "I mean, of course if that is what you wish to do, then it would be churlish of me to refuse. I accept your kind offer in the spirit in which it is intended."

With Jim's twenty-pound note tucked into her shopper, alongside the huge bag of cakes and sandwiches she had been given to take away with her, the old lady was ready to go home.

"Thank you so much for a most enjoyable afternoon, and for all your kindness. You really have done wonders with the old house."

The taxi arrived, there was a flurry of thank yous on all sides and she had gone.

Later that evening, over micro-waved pizzas and supermarket red, the couple talked about the events of the afternoon.

"Amazing memory," enthused Jim. "Picked out all the significant details. Really made the past live."

"Yes, and when she stood by the dining room fireplace, and told us all the things that used to be on the mantelpiece -"

"The way she reeled them off, she could almost have learned them by heart."

"As a matter of fact," said Emily in a very small voice. "She probably did."

"Eh?"

"Oh Jim, I should have told you. Soon after we moved in I had a friendly call from the Residents Association."

"What about?"

"They told me about this sweet little old lady who calls on newcomers, tells them she used to work in their house, and stays to tea."

"Well, she might have worked here."

"Maybe Jim, but she couldn't possibly have worked in so many, surely?"

"Probably not. And you knew all this, and kept it from me? That's not like you Emily."

"I know, and I am sorry - I just didn't expect her so soon. Once she was actually here, she was so obviously enjoying herself that I hadn't the heart to challenge her. I suppose I thought that as long as one of us knew, she wasn't really deceiving us, it would be all right."

Jim said Emily was silly, and a soft touch, a real pussy cat, but he loved her anyway. Besides which he had something he wanted to own up to himself. Maybe she could guess?

"You don't mean...?" Emily was wide-eyed.

"'Fraid so. I got a tip off when I went to sign on at the Business Club. Apparently they, too, warn newcomers to the area about Miss Finlayson."

"And you didn't think to tell me?"

"Well, I thought about it, and decided that as long as one of us knew it would be all right."

Emily pointed out that one person already knew anyway, and

that was Miss Finlayson.

A wee walk from her bus stop, Miss Finlayon let herself in to what the estate agent had callled a 'bijou garden flat', but which she acknowledged to herself was just a tiny basement. She made a cup of Early Grey and thought about Emily and Jim Dix. Such a charming couple, and generous too. She had really enjoyed her tea and, with care, the takeaway bag of goodies would last her a good few days.

The £20 note had been a complete surprise and rather embarrassing. She had not been looking for charity. But Mr Dix had been quite firm, and she hadn't wanted to offend him. Besides, there was no denying that the money would be very useful and, after all, it had been freely given, hadn't it?

She began to think about tomorrow and going to the Library. She knew exactly what books she wanted.

A fortnight later, Anne Murchison was in the new kitchen of her late-Regency townhouse in Hamilton Crescent, admiring the carefully-casual unfitted look, while her husband Joe was at the Business Club, when the front doorbell rang.

"Good afternoon," said the little old lady on the doorstep. "I do hope you won't think me impertinent, but over sixty-five years ago I lived in this very house...."

Was it something I said...?

By M. E. Fearon

I throw nothing away yet know where nothing is. I have kept so many scraps of myself that tell me very little and a few that tell me too much. My yearly scurry to make good my debt to the nation tends to exhume evidence of memories haphazardly buried.

Passive pleadings from the taxman prod my inbox with familiar alarm and, as January progresses, alarming familiarity. Yet no matter how genial the reminders, it is only when the looming deadline can cast no darker shadow that fear provokes me into action. The action being to unearth enough evidence of expenses to turn my profits from the meagre to the pitiful.

Filing a tax return as February beckons proves to me that time is relative. While the salaried look forward full of those twin fallacies, hope and self-deception, I live in a past that can never catch up with the present. All I have to navigate this foreign terrain is the sketchy evidence of the incomings and outgoings of a time best forgotten, that must now be relived in minutiae.

I do this sitting in an armchair that belonged to my former father-in-law. Whatever the time of day, although I usually try to start in daylight, I undertake the task in the company of a cut crystal tumbler, also once my former father-in-law's. Strictly speaking, it still is. I once found myself an inebriated but not uninterested bystander in a game of Russian roulette. I couldn't tell you where, but I have dreamt of the wood-panelled walls that formed the backdrop. I watched without flinching, expectant. I recall it now to describe the emotional pitch I reach while sitting in that armchair.

I use a letter opener that belonged to my former father-in-law's former lover. She gifted me the blade as a mark of allegiance; I think she felt we were allied in a kinship only understood by outsiders. The slice of each envelope resounds with trigger-click echoes. I acknowledge every blank chamber with a refill.

I read once, in a newspaper that is still around here somewhere, that by two years ago we will have become a paperless society. I have stood in defiance of very little in my life but paper I will defend to the death. I have an email account, the password is long forgotten and the verifying phone long lost, but I do remember that I set up an automatic response: *I will be honest with you: I will never read your email. If your missive is important, please send it to my home address. If you do not know my home address or have no other way of contacting me, it is safe to assume that I have no particular wish to hear from you.*

Despite my best efforts, my home address is known to more people than seems democratic. Each letter that comes in, no matter its apparent import, is subject to the same process: first, a period within the holding pen of my post-box; then, as space necessitates, graduation to a place in my in-tray (pinched from the stationery cupboard of a publication that once employed me); at which point they remain in quarantine until I have a guest.

As a general rule, the next stage of the process depends on whether the guest is unexpected or not. Another general rule is that, over the course of a tax year, I forget to expect roughly half of all expected guests. It's also worth noting that since adding a sign to my front door - 'unsolicited visitors and mail encouraged' - I have received twice as much of both.

Before this begins to sound too much like a problem that leaves Fred with two green apples and a resentment, I will set out the next stage of the process as implemented if the guest is expected. If you have been working out the sum in your margin then, for this explanation, you will have calculated that there is little point in paying attention: most envelopes bypass this system.

Long in advance of the doorbell being rung by the expected guest, I will open as many envelopes as my heart can take and file them away in the appropriate drawers, either: 'invoices', 'receipts' or, that go-to of the absent-minded, 'miscellaneous': that overworked servant of the slovenly, close cousin of *et cetera*, proud ancestor to *Any Other Business*. Defined as *"consisting of a mixture of various things that are not usually connected with each other"*; from the Latin *miscere*, to mix. What joy to know that I chose entirely the right label for each of the four overstuffed drawers that bear the name and more so to know that those decadent Romans would approve of their designation.

I must confess though that the most I have ever processed in such a way was seven. My industry that day was arrested by the revelation of a County Court Judgement. It put me in such a bad humour for the visit of my guest that I vowed to never open another envelope unless absolutely necessary. As for the process employed when I am visited quite unexpectedly, I think most recently of the ladies from Christian Aid.

It was some time before eight o'clock in the evening but certainly after a quarter-past six. I know this because that was the time my automatic-quartz movement watch stopped moving. I had been inactive that day and I always take my watch off before falling asleep; it never does to be reminded of the time when one first wakes.

It was dark out, and in, for that matter. I recall three shin slams just to reach the desk lamp that, once switched on, shone a light on a papery mess that had an upturned in-tray as its source. It appeared I had spent the time before slumber engaged in demonstration of the leaflet drops used by Allied bombers to warn cities of impending doom. Whether I had an audience or not for such folly is hard to say. My nap left me with little chance to evacuate and now the air raid sirens were going off again in the form of a second ring of the bell. During more drawn-curtained times, I conducted careful analysis that showed that charity doorknockers with a Christian connection were the most persistent. I once endured a thirteen-bell ring by a young man from a charity called Tearfund. I still do not know the correct pronunciation of that first syllable. I should have answered, if only to ask if he was collecting for the sartorially, or the lachrymosely, challenged.

Before the fifth ring, I had shovelled, using an old beach spade that had belonged to my daughter, most of the leaflet drop debris into a cellophane storage container that fitted in the under-cavity of my sofa. That, near enough always, was the filing process employed ahead of an unexpected visit.

Experience had taught me that the container fitted near enough exactly 16 months' worth of correspondence; it is a moot point as to whether a letter must be answered for it to be considered correspondence, or even opened for that matter. Another question for that Tearfund boy, perhaps this one would have to be shouted down the street through the open window: '*Boy, if I hand over another pound will you tell me at what point a letter becomes correspondence?*'

I invited the ladies in. They were both married, that was my first observation. If I read their shared glances correctly, it was just as safe to assume that their first observation also pertained to my marital status. In an attempt to kick away the lingering detritus of paper, a red-and-white Christian Aid envelope stuck to the sole of my foot. I don't believe in an interventionist God but that did give me pause for thought. After bending over with a flexibility that betrayed my clinging vanity, I turned my back on them to prop the envelope up against the coffee mug on my desk. I hoped to create a sense of ripe expectancy.

Noticing Luke's Gospel being used to prevent the storeroom door knocking in the gusts, the younger one asked if I had God in my life. I didn't have the heart to tell her that it was one of several (12 to be precise) I had filched from various events during last year's University mission week. The free food had drawn me in but the free books kept me coming back. I kept one beside the toilet, one on each side of the bed, one in the pocket of my winter jacket (a leather and lambswool overcoat made exclusively for Saks Fifth Avenue that belonged to my former father-in-law and is now mine by right), one in the pocket of my suit and the other six were given away as need required, mine or the recipient's, sometimes both. I have always been struck by the sincerity of Luke's line, "*since I myself have carefully investigated everything from the beginning, I too decided to write an orderly account for you*". It feels a perfectly rotten thing to recall right now.

I offered them a cup of something instead of answering her question. I presumed they said yes, they usually do, the Christian ones. Once a volunteer from the Salvation Army said yes to the best part of half a bottle of Scotch. He left me the worst part. I found out from a woman I gave one of the Luke's to that he was a recovering alcoholic and that he still mentions me in AA meetings. I had thought all along that he was merely a flugelhorn player with a thirst for Christ.

The trip to the kitchen afforded me some time to compose myself, with all the shovelling of papers and the alacrity necessary to greet my unexpected guests, I was in need of a drink myself. I keep a bottle of white in the fridge for the more expected of guests and, under the kitchen sink in a well-scrubbed W5 bottle, vodka for such emergencies. Nothing takes the edge off alacrity faster than a throat-constricting wince of the cheap stuff. If the mood takes me, and it did that evening, I give it a vigorous squirt rather than unscrew the top.

They were new to this, probably stepped in at the last minute following a guilt-ridden plea by the vicar last Sunday, which makes me wonder what day it was that day. They were silent when I returned with three glasses and picking at the hems of their skirts. I had presumed they would feel too uncomfortable to refuse the wine. I placed all three glasses down on my desk, steadied myself under the pretence of picking up a pencil sharpener and then handed them their two glasses.

They weren't really picking at the hems of their skirts. I can't even remember what they were wearing that night. I only remember that they were married. They asked about the envelope. I gestured towards it with the hint of a flourish, a little movement that said, 'it has been processed: from post box to in-tray to out-tray via the relevant office for action and the head of department for sign-off and now it is ready to be collected at the appointed time.' Except it wasn't, ready.

Cue flourish number two as I produced, as if I did so frequently, a £20 note from my leather and lambswool jacket pocket. It must have been a cold evening if I was still wearing that jacket and I don't recall having been out that day. I picked up the envelope, slipped the note inside, sealed it with my third flourish and handed it over to the elder of the two; she seemed more trustworthy.

I sat down in my armchair raised my glass to salute the transaction. God the wine was good, but God knows who I was expecting to have splashed out on something so potable. It was as I strained to recall the reason behind such extravagance that I remembered that I had handed over all my cash to these two nice Christian ladies sitting on my sofa.

I was struck indignant at the exorbitant tithes finagled from my ancestors by a Church heaven-bent on raising blood-stained spires. Instead of thinking aloud, I asked them about what they knew of the doleful black girl, who caught my eye from the red-and-white envelope still held between the older one's folded hands. 'Is that so?' I heard myself respond. 'How barbaric. How much our ancestors' Scramble for Africa is to blame. Do you mind if I take the envelope again? I'll be right back. Fancy a top up?'

I presumed they said no, they usually do to the second, the Christian ones. Once out of view, I began the delicate operation of unsealing the envelope without obvious signs of a break-in. I thought of boiling water but was put off by the boredom that would set in while I waited for my charity shop kettle to boil. I opened *that* kitchen drawer, always two to the right of the hob.

Beneath the tape measure that definitely wasn't there the last time I was searching for it, was the letter opener. I teased apart the glued folds and ever-so silently slid out the £20 note. Back in the drawer, I tore out four sheets from an old spiral-bound journalist's notebook. Using the £20 note, I cut out the replicant outline from the four sheets. Before I folded them in half, slipped them back in and sealed up the envelope with a lidless gluestick, on each of them I wrote,

> "*Looking up at the stars, I know quite well*
> *That for all they care, I can go to hell.*"

I must have been longer than my sense of time assumed, or perhaps my subterfuge was not as original as I had imagined; when I got back to the front room, the ladies from Christian Aid had gone. A pity they missed my couplet, but that was their loss. All that remained were two empty wine glasses and an empty wine bottle, which surprised me until I followed the lingering vinous reek right to the soil of my potted succulents. I spent the rest of the evening working out whether their act of disposal was callous or caring, and went to sleep giving them the benefit of my doubt.

SORRY, BARNIE

Nicholas Wood

The sounds, small, inexorable, chipped away at consciousness as Jason drifted in and out of oblivion. Somewhere, bluebottles were scouring the surface of a sunlit window, desperate for release. He remembered them from that seaside holiday as a kid: in that wretched boarding house where he had a tiny cupboard of a room on the top floor. He'd watch them drone up to the top of the window, then drop down, sometimes falling stunned and silent, legs flailing. He'd bet with himself about how long it would be before they eventually struggled upright to start again. Bzzzz …pssss….mmm ….

He opened an eye.

"Welcome back," said Staff Nurse Michelle, checking his notes at the foot of the bed.

"What'sa noise?"

"What? Oh." She smiled and nodded towards the window. "I'll be along for your blood pressure in a mo."

Bzzz … mmmm … bzzzz. Jason's mind grappled with the meaning of the movement of Staff's head. He rolled his, just enough to check. It hurt. A lot. But the window was closed, so no explanation there. He noticed the bed next to his was empty, and in the one beyond – the one next to the window – an old boy was watching the TV screen that hung over his bed. Its flickering lights were reflected in the window.

Bzzz … mmm …

So that was it. The silly old fool wasn't using his earphones. Jason felt protest rise and fade. Too much effort. He drifted back into the warm welcome silence of unknowing.

Later he resurfaced reluctantly several layers closer to full awareness. He wondered what the time was, couldn't be bothered to check. It was broad daylight.

And …. bzzz … psss … mmm

"Christ, will you use your bloody earphones," he shouted; or tried to shout. It came out an angry whisper.

"It's best if you stay calm." Senior Staff Michelle said, wheeling in her blood pressure machine.

"What's he in for anyway?"

"Barnie?" He felt the band tighten round his arm. "He's a bit fed up because his operation was postponed until tomorrow."

"I've just had mine," Jason pointed out, "and need my rest." But as he drifted off again he wondered briefly whether the emergency he'd become was responsible for postponing Barnie's op.

When he opened his eyes the old boy was sitting on the big armchair by his bed.

"You shouldn't call on the name of the Lord in vain," Barnie said.

"Wouldn't have been in vain if you'd used those bloody earphones."

"You're right." Barnie grinned, displaying spectacular toothlessness. Jason tried to sit up, felt a wave of nausea and sank back again. After a while he asked "What you in for?"

"Stomach." There was a silence that was strangely companionable.

"Gave us all a right rotten night, you did," Barnie said at last. "Road accident, was it?"

"Yeah." He must have been well over the limit when his bike swerved off the road and hit a tree. Hadn't even learned yet the extent of the damage; only that the bits of him that weren't numb hurt like hell, and it was like he'd been kicked in the stomach by a wild horse.

"Don't overtire him Barnie," A blonde nurse paused a moment in passing.

Michelle was dark and curly. Jason frowned. "Where's Michelle?"

"Changed shifts. Three o'clock. That'll be Emma who's on till nine and then the night lot come on."

"I'd got used to Michelle." To his horror Jason felt tears welling, then uncontrollable nausea. Someone shoved a vomit pan at him just in time.

"It'll have been the anaesthetic," Barnie said consolingly when he returned after the nausea had passed and Emma had tidied Jason up. "Not much I don't know about anaesthetics. They say them epidurals are better but Sister said I can't have one of those. I'm major, you

66

see." Barnie sounded quite proud. "Top of the list for tomorrow."
Without rancour he added, "I reckon it was you what scuppered my
chances today. It's my fourth … op … you know. Sister keeps that
bed for me. She knows I like the window so I can look out, like.
Watch the kids in the park. We go back a long way Sister and me."

Jason slid in and out awareness. There'd been an injection:
the nausea had gone and the pain retreated far away to the rim of
consciousness. Mostly Barnie was there when he came to, yacking
away about the kids in the park, and how they reminded him of his
grandkids and what a shame they all lived so far away they couldn't
come and visit.

"You got kids?" he asked suddenly.

"No." There'd been plenty of women in his life, Jason
reflected, but not the maternal kind. Dad had always been on about
kids, grandkids, continuity, all that stuff. God, what a boring old fool
he could be, too. He and Barnie had a lot in common.

And yet. And yet it was OK, waking up and finding him there,
hearing him go on about a couple of kids he'd seen out there that
afternoon with a pretty nursemaid. Of course it wouldn't be a
nursemaid these days. An *au pair* more like. It was too much effort to
say all that so he just asked what she looked like, because it would be
nice to picture a real live woman.

"Blonde," Barnie said. "Long blonde hair that curls in at the
ends. Like Virginia Lake. But I don't s'pose you're old enough to
know about her. She'd a bright red woolly hat on the back of her
head." He paused, obviously savouring the memory. "Looked a
proper treat, with one of them white coats – you know, made of that
squashy material.

"Quilted?"

"Yeah, quilted. And the two kids were curly-haired, dark –
boy about eight and little girl of four. Bundled up like footballs, one
green, one blue. Reminded me of my Joe and Susie, only we didn't
have no nursemaid."

When Jason came to the next time, Emma had brought a tray of
herb tea and dry toast. Barnie was over by the window, but it was
getting dark now so he wouldn't be seeing much. "What's going on
out there?" Jason called and Barnie wandered back to join him.
"Want a bit of toast?"

"I'm Nil by Mouth," Barnie said.

"Don't let him overtire you," Emma shook her head at them, without specifying who might overtire whom.

To his surprise Jason was glad to see the old boy, noticed he didn't look any too bright himself. Probably worried about tomorrow's op, which he might have had by now if it hadn't been for Jason.

"So what was your line?" Jason asked to take the old man's mind off tomorrow as much as because he wanted to know.

"Ran a shop, with my missus. Ironmongers. 'Bring us any problem and we'll hit the nail on the head' – that was our motto." Barnie chuckled. " 'We'll make sure you never have a screw loose'. That was another."

Jason laughed dutifully and noted that his head didn't hurt as much any more. "My Dad had a shop. Newsagents. 'You heard it first from here' – that's what he'd tell all his new customers." Not to mentioned anyone else who'd stop long enough to listen. "Wanted me to take over from him."

"Can't imagine that would have been your cup of tea," Barnie said. He had leaned his head back in the armchair, closed his eyes. "That's the trouble ain't it? Like father like son – only it doesn't often work out that way."

"You can say that again." Jason felt suddenly sorry that they – he and dad, neither of them – had ever seen it each other's way. "Still he did pass on his flare for selling – insurance, cars, mobiles, whistles and bells and gizmos, you name it I can always sell it. Then I went dot com – you know, on the Internet." That was when he'd changed himself from Jack to Jason. He stopped. Not likely the old boy would have a clue what he was talking about. For a moment he thought he'd gone to sleep, then Barnie said "We've got one of them computer things in our local library. The librarian sent a … what d'you call it … for me to my Joe in Australia."

"Email?"

"That's it. Joe in Australia and Susie up in Edinburgh. Good thing, keeping in touch with your kids. She's coming down tomorrow to see me, my Susie. After the op." He levered himself up. "Reckon I'll rest a bit now. See you tomorrow, eh? When I get back?"

It took Jason a long time to get off and, when he eventually did, they kept waking him to check this or that. He found himself thinking about what Barnie had said about keeping in touch with the kids. Not about the kids keeping in touch with him. He was glad Barnie's Susie was coming tomorrow.

When he finally woke to broad daylight, Barnie's bed was empty. This time he got butter on his toast, and proper tea. The doc came with a couple of students and told him he'd been very lucky and could probably go next day. He was allowed up for a shower – bloody awkward lugging a catheter like a ball and chain. Barnie still hadn't returned when he got back, and he was so tired after all that effort he crashed right out again.

Michelle was back on duty, flicking through his notes, when he awoke more refreshed than he'd felt for a while. But still no Barnie. "Finally got his op then?" he said.

Michelle kept her head bent. "I'm afraid he didn't make it through."

Jason didn't immediately understand. Then he protested "But his daughter Susie's coming to see him." As though that had anything to do with anything.

He couldn't get the old boy out of his head, even when some of his mates drifted in to see him, full of alien blasts from the normal world out there. Briefly, he saw Barnie's Susie come and go, a brisk middle-aged woman who suddenly crumpled as Sister was speaking quietly to her.

That evening, still a bit wobbly, Jason wandered over to look out of Barnie's window.

And stood transfixed.

The view consisted entirely of a blank grey wall and a scrap of wasteland.

"Some imagination that Barnie had," Jason said. He felt a bit cheated as though Barnie had pulled a fast one, and it was too late to have his own back.

"I think he'd call it making the best of things. Like the TV – he said the sound helped him to make the pictures," Michelle said. "You hadn't realised he was blind?"

Had he, hell!

Jason gripped the window ledge, swallowed hard. "Christ," he said eventually, then very softly "Sorry, Barnie."

Understand Much

Sylvie Nickels

Jessica sometimes regretted that Vicar John had quite such unquestioning faith in her.

"I'd be so grateful if you could take this on for me, Jessica. I know you will have the interests of our guest at heart. And it really is a very generous offer from Larry – er …"

"Hardcastle," Jessica said. "Larry Hardcastle."

"Yes, indeed, a *most* generous offer which will undoubtedly give a great boost to the church's fundraising project for creating new wells in T'bal. And, of course, it will be quite delightful to welcome someone from a corner of the world so profoundly less blessed than our own."

Jessica suppressed a sigh. She loved Vicar John deeply - in the most spiritual sense of course - but did wish at times that his academic skills had equipped him better for the realities of life amongst his flock in this small industrial town in middle England. He had recently come to them from some seminary devoted to studying the finer and most abstruse points of Hebrew – or was it Aramaic? - texts. Her own forty-one years of marriage with associated motherhood, grandmotherhood, widowhood and involvement in two generations of teenage traumas, had brought her insights which she sensed, so far, Vicar John, had not acquired.

So," he resumed. "As I understand it, Mr. Hardcastle's newspaper – the, er, *Dursham Mercury?* - will finance the travel arrangements for whoever is chosen to represent T'bal. He and his friend Mr Bradwell, who I understand runs a chain of youth facilities, will arrange a series of fundraising events highlighting the desperate plight of that community. And you have kindly said our guest may stay with you. I gather their precise identity has yet to be decided?"

"We're making the decision tonight – over at Larry's … Mr Hardcastle's house."

Something seemed suddenly to occur to Vicar John as Jessica rose to go. "It has to be said Mr Hardcastle, er, does not come across as the most likely of ministering angels. Mysterious indeed are the ways of the Lord."

"You've absolutely got to take into account the A-a-a-h-h factor," Larry Hardcastle said a few hours later. They were in his converted barn overlooking a wildflower meadow he had donated to the community. Photographs were scattered over a table. He went on "No wrinklies, no glowering teenagers with kalashnikovs shoved up their sweatshirts, no snotty kids."

"That just about rules out the lot." Scott Bradwell shuffled through the photographs unhopefully.

"What a cynical pair you are," Jessica chided. Unlike Vicar John, she did not find the ways of the Lord so mysterious. Larry Hardcastle was desperate to get into politics. With the right publicity this T'bal business could soften his reputation as a hardnosed opportunist, and who better to ensure the right publicity than the owner of the local tabloid himself. As for Scott Bradwell, his chain of youth facilities – more commonly known as discos - round the county was patently in need of a boost; and while his paunchy profile barely suggested a second coming of Bob Geldof, Jessica had no illusions regarding his motives.

Larry looked pained. "Not cynical, merely realistic, Jess, my sweet. We all want this to be a wow, get everyone digging deep into pockets, zap the help out to those poor folk in T'bal. Don't we? And if anyone can …" He stopped in mid-sentence to lean forward and tweak a photograph out of the untidy pile of Scott's shufflings, and then said happily "There she is. There's the one with the a-a-a-h-h factor in bucketloads."

She was seventeen, eighteen. Perhaps younger. They grew up so quickly in those unforgiving environments. Her long black hair hid part of her face, and from behind it large dark eyes looked up at the camera. And the sadness in the expression had no place in one so young.

Larry turned the photo over and read from the scrawly writing on the back: *"name – Sabria. Age – 16. Eldest of eleven children, nine surviving. Mother crippled.* Hell, eleven children! *Father subsistence farmer.* Except there ain't nothing to subsist on any more." He flipped the photograph over. "God, those eyes. That expression." He could not take his eyes off the picture. "I feel a headline coming on….."

Jessica said firmly "You're not to exploit her, Larry. She's just a kid out of nowhere."

He looked at her in amazement. "Exploit? She'll be treated like a princess. And we'll appoint you her personal chaperone to make sure none of those seedy Canary Wharf types get any wrong idea."

So it was Canary Wharf now, was it? Next stop Westminster.

For several days before Sabria's arrival, Larry ran a 'Say Hello' campaign on the front page of the *Mercury*. Alongside a picture of her, a punchy paragraph outlined the plight of the mountainous drought-struck enclave of T'bal, caught between warring minor states in central Asia. Sabria would be their honoured guest, so the *Mercury* informed its readers, as she came to raise help. And the editor was banking on every one of them to 'Say Hello' and make her feel at home.

Jessica insisted that she should meet Sabria at the airport alone, hoping to help temper the cultural shock. The first surprise was the poise and calm with which this child from the back of beyond handled the mayhem of Terminal Four. The charity in T'Bal had kitted her out in a sari-type garment in flame with a high-necked blouse; her black hair was pulled back into a long tight pigtail that reached to below her waist. The second surprise was her English. "Understand much, speak little," she said her huge dark gaze fixed on Jessica's face as they headed for the car park. Settled in the car, the girl was clearly fascinated, though not always favourably. by everything she saw.

The one-hour drive was accompanied by a terse commentary "So much cars" "T'Bal much people, no cars", "You not have mountains?" Jessica had the distinct feeling that T'Bal was, comparatively, more than holding its own against first impressions of England's green and pleasant land, though she did exclaim at the fine buildings.

72

The poise began to crack a little when they reached Jessica's cottage – quintessential England in honey-coloured stone with roses round the door; and it broke down completely when Sabria was introduced to the bathroom. As Jessica showed her the workings of the shower, Sabria turned into an excited child let loose in a room full of toys. Yes, Jessica assured her, she could stand under the shower for as long as she wished. No, the water would not suddenly stop or go black, though it might turn cold if she stayed under it too long.

The girl was too excited to eat. She wandered round the small living room, touching some of the treasures Jessica had brought back from a lifetime of travels. "Beautiful house. I like very much. You so kind lady."

Jessica was feeling more responsible for her by the minute, deeply wished that she did not have to expose this charming creature to a media circus, not even one of Dursham proportions.

Larry came round to discuss the coming week's programme: a reception at the town hall, concert at Scott's main youth club, a string of minor appearances at schools and local organisations; and, of course, daily interviews with the *Mercury*. He could not take his eyes of Sabria. "She's exquisite. My God, that photo didn't do her justice."

"You'd better know she understands more than you might think."

"Understand much, speak little," Sabria said, her poise recovered.

Jessica took her to meet Vicar John in the parish church next morning. Standing in the middle of the Gothic nave, staring up at the intricate tracery and ribbed vaulting, Sabria for the first time seemed quite overwhelmed. "Like mountains," she said at last. "Like in T'bal." And Vicar John seemed to know exactly what she meant.

Larry's 'Say Hello' campaign proved hugely effective. Dursham took Sabria to its heart. 'Hello Sabria's pursued them wherever they went, usually accompanied by broad smiles and occasional wolf whistles that had to be carefully explained. The reception at the town hall was a doddle, the Great and the Good falling over themselves to pledge material support to benighted T'Bal. In the schools, even the most fidgety kids became still after exposure to a video of life for their peers in that distant place. The organisations –

from WIs to retired firemen and wildlife groups to computer geeks - all fell in love with her.

Jessica observed with growing amusement the interaction between Larry and Vicar John over the unfolding arrangements for Sabria's stay.

"Just you leave it to me, Rev," Larry said. "This girl is a natural. You just stand back and wait for the shekels to roll in."

Jessica noted Vicar John's left eyebrow lift in gentle irony at Larry's choice of expression, but all he said was "On behalf of the people of T'bal I am profoundly grateful to you Mr Hardcastle for your efforts." She hoped he wouldn't add "which will undoubtedly earn you a place in the next Kingdom," and he didn't.

He did, though, murmur more than once "We must not overtire the child. All this must be quite overwhelming for her."

"Rest assured, Rev, rest assured. Jess is watching over her like a Mother Superior." Pause. "Sorry, Rev, no offence meant."

Again that gentle lift of the left eyebrow. "None taken, Mr Hardcastle, none taken."

But the success beyond all measure was the concert at Scott's main youth centre. A local band-made-good got the concert off to a great start. Then Sabria asked if she could sing some songs from her country: simple T'bali themes that were soon taken up by all the kids in the audience, and then by the band.

"Bob Geldof, eat your heart out," Scott was heard to murmur.

It was on the last afternoon, just before the 'let's-say -goodbye-to-Sabria' junket that she dropped her bombshell. Or not so much dropped it as inadvertently let it slip out. Sabria was making tea for herself and Jessica in the way she had been taught, and Jessica was musing on the success of the week and the pleasure it had been to have her company. She could not help wondering what had been going on in that pretty head, so prompted, "I have so enjoyed your company Sabria and do hope you will come again,"

"I like, too," Sabria said, warming the teapot.

"You're quite a remarkable young lady," Jessica said. "It must have been a huge culture shock coming here. Though it is quite amazing how much you have learned of the world from your isolated home."

"Father very much like radio." Sabria paused to count three teaspoons of tea into the pot and pour in the boiling water. "He say we must try and understand all. He say to understand is to live. When I was child at time of Chernobyl…." She stopped. Her gaze met Jessica's steadily, both registering almost simultaneously that at the time of Chernobyl, Sabria was not supposed to have been born.

Jessica raised a questioning eyebrow. Sabria took a deep breath and her English underwent a startling transformation. She said "Most is true. I promise. Mother have eleven children. That is true. Now very tired and sick. That is also true. Only not-true thing is I am not sixteen, but twenty-six. I work for agency for five years. I learn much about all sad things in world, and how difficult it is to get help for my T'bal." Her mouth quirked into a knowing smile. "I learn many things, like how rich countries like pretty girls, especially young pretty girls. It can help to get money. We so much need money.... So I put in my picture – old picture when I was young. In my country, no pictures in newspapers of young girls. They stay with family, are very much – how you say?"

"Protected," suggested Jessica.

She nodded, waited, allowing the question mark to grow in the silence before asking in a small voice "You tell this to Larry, to Vicar John?"

Jessica let the silence linger a while longer before she said, then "Understand much, speak little," she said. "I reckon you can pour out the tea now, Sabria."

Through the Iron Curtain

George Spenceley

Following my return from a canoeing adventure in Canada with my climbing friend Tom Price, Sylvie had announced "next time, I'm coming with you!" This was a grand thought but clearly had to be given careful consideration. We would need to find a river which did not involve a lot of heavy portaging and that would take us through interesting countries to provide me with a new lecture and Sylvie with articles and possibly a book.

After a lot of thought I came up with the idea of the Danube. What could be more interesting than a river that traversed more or less the whole of Europe and which, at the time, provided a unique route through that part of Europe which lay beyond the (then) so-called Iron Curtain?

As Sylvie was then editing guidebooks on several East European countries for Fodor Guides, she had good contacts with the relevant national tourist offices in London. We went to see them. Most of them were somewhat surprised by our plans. There would be a plethora of paperwork involving visas, some of which could only be made valid from specific dates which, at that stage, we could not precisely forecast. In some cases we would need to apply for visas at the border or in some major city in the country preceding our arrival. Happily three capital cities – Vienna, Budapest, Belgrade – were actually on the Danube and a fourth, Bucharest, not far from it. It sounded complicated so we asked for, and were granted, a letter of introduction in the language of each country along our route. In those days we would be travelling through seven countries, five of them 'Iron Country'. The first would be Czechoslovakia and Vera of their London office, warned us that we may be welcomed by a military escort when we crossed from Austria. It sounded intriguing.

Sylvie is quite a good linguist, though her repertoire did not include any of those along our route except for a smattering of Serbo-Croat. She decided to do a crash course in German. We also contacted one or two friends along the way, notably in Budapest and Belgrade. In between our lecturing and writing commitments we made vast lists of what to take with us, revising them many times. Also, in Sylvie's case, her canoeing experience was limited to a few short stretches of the upper Thames, so we fitted in as many paddles on the Oxford Canal as we could. Finally, on Sunday, 20th May, 1979, we were as ready as we would ever be and we set off, canoe firmly fixed to the roof of our car, for the Felixstowe-Zeebrugge ferry crossing.

Two days later we were high in the Black Forest above Furtwangen, beside a small chapel and one of the typically timbered houses of the region by which a trickle of water poured into a rocky pool. Above it, a small tablet informed us that this was the source of the Danube, at 1089 metres above sea level, and 2,888 km. from its outlet into the Black Sea. The source tablet in fact marks the river Breg, and it does not bear its adult name until it is joined by the Brigach at Donaueschingen. Here in the grounds of the Fürtenburg Palace is the better known source: a 19th century decorated pool embellished with classical statuary. The river, for it soon ceases to be a mountain stream, flows east through a limestone valley by attractive towns and villages, but it was not until we reached Ulm that we abandoned road for river and cast off in our five-metre open canoe.

A swift current swept us past the medieval ramparts but we soon slowed down before the first of the twenty-one H.E.P. barrages that interrupt the flow between Ulm and Vienna. This was preceded some distance ahead by a large sign announcing *lebensgefahr* which Sylvie translated as 'danger to life' before scrabbling anxiously through the dictionary to find what the danger was. It proved to be simply a warning that the barrage lay ahead and we should approach it on the appropriate side of the river to go through the attendant locks. Those before Regensburg were (except for the first) all self-operated. Beyond Regensburg, where the river becomes a channel for larger vessels, they are controlled by some remote and unseen hand, instruction given through loudspeakers by a disembodied voice. We usually had to wait to share the lock with some massive tug or push boat with its flock of barges from any one of the eight Danube nations.

The Danube links much of industrial Europe, but it is often far from evident. There were many towns and several great cities: the industrial complexes of Linz and Budapest took us half a day to pass. There were sections when the river was flanked by roads and railways and we were compelled to camp amid the roar of traffic. Once we camped on a garbage dump, another time on a factory site; on the other hand for much of the way we were alone with nature. For long sections there were just forests of poplar and willow with no evidence of man's work beyond the regular kilometre posts marking the distance to the Black Sea.

Among the early historic landmarks were attractive towns like Dillingen and Donauworth, and the relics of Blenheim at Höchstadt. Near Eining on the right bank we visited the well preserved Roman remains of Abusina. Opposite, evidence of the Limes reminded us that this was for much of its history the Roman frontier. Beyond the Benedictine Monastery of Weltenburg is a scenic highlight of the river, Kelheim Gorge. Here in their narrows we had our first encounter with a potential hazard that was to become a familiar feature: the wash and backwash of passing vessels.

At the town of Kelheim we saw the Danube terminal of the old Ludwig Canal, completed in 1846. The rivalry of the railways condemned it to failure, but the dream of a great European waterway has been reborn and realised. In due course. a little below Kelheim the outlet of the Rhine-Main-Danube Waterway, was completed in 1992.

The medieval gems of Regensburg and Passau are the historic highlights of the German Danube. The fast flow of the Inn which joins the Danube at Passau added a fresh infusion of energy to the river which swept us swiftly into Austria, whose 350 km. share was one of the most varied and picturesque of the journey There are still plains and prosperous farms, but for much of the way the river is contained between steep forested and craggy walls. Between Melk and Krems comes the dramatic stretch of the Wachau, where the Danube has carved a course through the granite of the Waldviertel, the last modest foothills of the Bohemian mountains. There is nothing modest about Melk, however, whose massive baroque monastery dominates the town said to be the Medilick of the Nibelungen. Napoleon was an uninvited guest here in 1809. The turbulent history of these parts is reflected in the many ruins of medieval castles, like Aggstein, whose robber baron owners exacted tolls or ransome from passing travellers, and Dürnstein where Richard I of England was held prisoner after the

Third Crusade. But today, below the grim fortresses are vine clad slopes for the Wachau provides much of Vienna's wine, and charming villages with narrow streets and 'onion' shaped baroque church towers, popular destinations for the capital's visitors.

It was at this point that we had our first lesson in the Danube's unpredictable temperament. As we paddled through the Wachau we were delighted, if also a little alarmed at the speed of travel. Sometimes it was impossible to stop. The melting snows of Spring brings the highest water to the Austrian Danube in May and early June, anyway, but now heavy rain in the mountains had added to the normal swell. It reached its peak in Vienna where the river rose three metres in three days. The authorities halted all shipping, and that included us.

Life suddenly became complicated. The weather was diabolical, the river continued to rise steadily and we developed visa problems. Only a few days earlier we had noticed that our passports, tucked away in the side pocket of what we had assumed was a waterproof bag, had got pretty wet during one of our encounters with the wash of other vessels. Our Hungarian visas were slightly smudged, the Czechoslovak ones badly so, and all our efforts to dry them out had not improved their appearance. The pleasant girl at Čedok, the Czechoslovak Travel Bureau in Vienna, agreed that it would be wise to check their validity and arranged that the Visa Section of her Embassy, though officially closed by then, would see us that afternoon. Full of confidence, we dodged through a succession of heavy showers to the remoter parts of the city.

A Mr. Krameš soon deflated us. Though he spoke no English, he made it crystal clear that so far as he was concerned, not only were our visas not valid but our passports were unacceptable too. Astonished, we re-examined them – slightly buckled it is true, but with indisputable clarity and courtesy requesting that we should be granted passage without let or hindrance, etc. Mr. Krameš thought otherwise. Thumping the passports down on to the table, he departed, effectively ending the discussion.

Much chastened we invested in expensive taxis in search of the British Embassy. By the time we found it, it too was officially closed but earned our eternal gratitude by allowing us entry and listening to our sorry tale. The air of calm reassurance was majestic and the pro-Consul remained splendidly unsurprised that two of Her Majesty's citizens had dampened their passports in the Danube. They were, he affirmed, perfectly valid but regrettably he was not able to put this in writing since this would imply there might have been reasonable grounds for doubting their validity! Unfortunately the Embassy would be officially closed the next day as it was Her Majesty's birthday. However, he continued, barely giving us time to groan, if we cared to return to the Czechoslovak Embassy at 9.30 a.m., he thought we would find everything in order. We did and it was. With very little delay, we emerged with clear, new visas stamped in our same old passports by a same old unsmiling Mr. Krameš.

While we waited for the river levels to drop, we revisited old haunts in Vienna: the famous coffee shops, wine taverns, wide boulevards and famous music associations. Indeed you can hardly turn a corner in the city without coming across a statue, or a memorial plaque, or a building connected in some way with one of a dozen famous composers who made this city their home. Not least of these was Beethoven who once conducted a concert with over 1000 musicians in the 18th century hall of yet another very Viennese institution, the Spanish Riding School where we watched fine Lippizaners and their riders display their superb skills beneath glittering chandeliers to the rhythms of the great composers.

It was a week before we were again paddling and still in a current more than usually fast. We managed to stop near Petronell to see the Roman remains of Carnuntum, but totally failed to halt at the official Austrian border exit point. We were swept on, seemingly unnoticed, towards the so-called Iron Curtain into Czechoslovakia.

There can be few tourists who entered communist Europe as we did, much at the mercy of the current, mid-stream down the Danube. We were a little apprehensive. A river patrol boat came alongside and escorted us past the long line of barbed wire and watch towers to a military check point where, with some amusement, young soldiers completed the formalities

About 250 years earlier, Maria Theresa had exchanged all the glitter of Vienna for what must have been comparatively the very provincial atmosphere of Bratislava. All the same, Pressburg as it was then to the Austrians, or Pozsony as the Hungarians called it, had been since the fall of Budapest to the Turks the capital of Hungary-without-Turkey, and eleven kings and eight queens were crowned in its Cathedral between 1563-1830. Among them, in 1740, was Maria Theresa herself, inheriting the Hungarian crown among a plethora of other titles, from her father Emperor Charles VI

Bratislava Castle, sitting four-square on its hills, provides a distinctive silhouette for a considerable distance in most directions. It owes its present appearance mainly to the Habsburgs who built it in the 15th-16th centuries, and especially Maria Theresa who had it Baroquised in the late 18th. Following a fire in 1811, its reconstruction in original style was only completed in the 1960s. Maria Theresa's intermittent presence acted as a magnet to the noble and the ambitious, resulting in the fine patrician houses that line the narrow streets of old Bratislava and are among its main attractions.

Beyond Bratislava the Slovak shore of the Danube is a real paradise for the bird watcher and naturalist. Forests of willow cover the half-submerged banks behind which is a complex tracery of smaller channels and a multitude of islands. One could leave the main river and dawdle for days through this watery network, seeing nothing of man, hearing only the call of the night heron and bittern. The Danube here has a primeval quality more akin to the Amazon and we were not surprised to learn that it had been the setting for jungle films.

We crossed to the right bank and entered Hungary at Komarom after two wild and wet days of almost constant rain. Weather and spirits did not revive until we reached Esztergom, which like so many Danube settlements was originally Roman – Marcus Aurelius wrote his *Reflections* here – but it was to become under the Árpáds, the Magyars' first capital. It remained important as the seat of the Archbishop of Esztergom, Primate of the Hungarian Church.

We were now at the beginning of the Danube Bend, where the river leaves the plains of the Little Alföld to cut through a southern spur of the Carpathian foothills. Scenically this is the best section of Hungary's share of the river. Beyond Višegrad, the river is split almost all the way to Budapest by Szentendre Island. We followed the right arm and visited the little town of that name. A charming place of pastel washed baroque houses, Szentendre was settled by Serbians during the great movement of population, following the advance of the Turks. We visited its artists' colony including at that time an exhibition of work by that brilliant ceramic artist Margit Kóvács.

Budapest is a handsome city. Lady Mary Montagu who passed through it in 1717 would not recognise the place, for then its most beautiful buildings had been wholly destroyed in the sieges and battles that punctuated the Turkish occupation from 1541-1686. Of the castle she wrote, "the Prospect is very noble" but beneath it, the people's "Houses stand in rows, many 1,000s of them so close together they appear at a little distance like odd fashion'd thatch'd Tents (consisting) every one of them, of one hovel above and another under ground."

It is remarkable how almost all traces of that Turkish occupation have disappeared, other than in museums. Indeed, there is far more to be seen of the Roman presence a millennium and a half earlier, when the Danube formed the northern boundary of their Empire and Aquincum was the capital of the province of Pannonia Inferior. Aquincum is on the northern outskirts of the city with its own station on the electric suburban rail route. The Roman town, still being excavated at the time, is well worth seeing.

The Danube waters plenty of large cities, but in no other is it such an integral part as Budapest whose very heart it has penetrated ever since hilly Royal Buda on the west bank finally became one with flat administrative Pest in 1873. The British engineer Adam Clark was responsible for the first bridge (the Chain Bridge, re-built like all of them since World War II) in 1849. Most of Pest dates from the late 19th century onwards. For greater age you must cross to Castle Hill where the much-restored former royal palace is now a vast and splendid museum complex. The narrow streets that twirl up and down the Castle Hill district have many of the city's oldest houses and some of her most famous restaurants; bur Pest can claim some of the finest churches, the smartest shops and several of the best coffee houses.

Our fears that the long straight section south of Budapest would be both sluggish in current and dreary in scenery proved unfounded. The current was still adequate and while the flat plain of the Great Alföld offered no scenic grandeur, there was great beauty of detail. Also we could escape from the shipping channel behind islands or reed beds to fine secluded camp sites disturbed only by the solitary fisherman, by now representing our most frequent companions.

` Hungary's official exit point is at Mohács where we were received and sent on our way with much jocularity, but a strict injunction not to halt before Yugoslavia, in those days still undivided. It was dusk before we reached Beždam, the first Yugoslav community, but somehow news of our approach had preceded us and three uniformed officials were awaiting our arrival. In due course I signed a splendid document in which I was described as "Commandant de Yachte".

Of all the Danube countries at that time, Yugoslavia held the greatest share with some 590 km of the river, as well as offering many causes for delay, not least some of the best bird watching in central

Europe. Beyond the junction with the Drava, the Pannonian Plains are broken to the south by the forested and vine clad slopes of the Fruška Gora. At Novi Sad, we took a day off to explore them by car visiting the monasteries of Krušedol, Hopova and Vrdnik. Following the advance of the conquering Turks, many Serbs fled north seeking sanctuary in Habsburg territory and these monasteries reflect the continuity of Serbian life in exile.

On the right bank, opposite Novi Sad, is the great fortress of Petrovaradin, once the main bulwark against the Turks with a history as long and almost as turbulent as Kalemegdan which dominates the confluence of the Sava and Danube at Belgrade. It is the oldest part of the capital for few cities have been burned and sacked so many times, so that today Belgrade is largely a new city.

A day's paddling down river is Smederovo, Europe's most massive fortress. But of all the Danube's castles, the most magnificently sited must be Golubac with its nine ruined towers overlooking the rock entrance to the first of that series of gorges that terminate at Djerdap, or the Iron Gate.

The 130 km from Golubac to Kladovo, where the Danube has cut a deep cleft through the Carpathian barriers, is the dramatic highlight of the river and the Kazan Gorge is the most exciting of its several narrows. Its statistics are impressive for where the river flows between limestone walls, rising to 700 metres, the gorge is only 150 metres wide. More even than the rapids and whirlpools of the Wachau, the narrow defiles above Djerdap for centuries set a fearsome problem for Danube boatmen.

The Romans were the first to solve it; they built a tow path. All evidence of this is now lost below the recently raised water, but Trajan's Tablet, the plaque to commemorate its completion, has been re-sited at a higher level. Since the completion of the Djerdap H.E.P. Station in 1972 – a joint Yugoslav-Romanian project – the level of the water has been raised by 30 metres. The 100 km above the dam is now a lake, if a very elongated one. Dead forests with only the topmost branches breaking the water, and half-submerged villages punctuate the shore.

Below the two-tier lock of the Iron Gate we were once more thankfully in the grasp of a helpful current and in a few more days, at Kladovo, we completed the rather prolonged exit formalities for Yugoslavia. Indeed, they were especially prolonged as apparently, through ignorance and neglect of some river regulations we had omitted to report to the police at several points and incurred much displeasure. Fortunately good humour and reason prevailed.

It would be difficult to describe the Danube bank settlements of Bulgaria as attractive, although some, like the predominantly Turkish town of Nicopol, have a degree of charm. But what the towns lacked in distinction the people made up for in friendliness. Wherever we halted for a lunch time picnic or wilderness camp, peasant farmers or fishermen came to join us. Their welcome was overwhelming and we always departed laden with a mountain of melons, tomatoes, corn on the cob, fruit or freshly caught fish.

We had quite early on our journey decided that the people of the river were rather special, a breed apart; even the border officials were more friendly and relaxed than elsewhere. The river, like an ocean highway, seemed to bind together the citizens of many nations who, in their different ways, depended upon it for their livelihood.

And so, in due course, we reached Ruse, Bulgaria's greatest Danube port. We had paddled 2,100 km from Ulm. There remained a further 495 km to the Black Sea. Another country lay ahead and much of interest, not least the fascination of the Danube Delta. It would be folly to rush it, we felt, and so we decided to postpone the bulk of the Romanian Danube for another year.

So, in 1980, we set off by car with the canoe fixed to the roof to retrace our journey to Ruse, only on this occasion aiming for one its Romanian counterparts, Călăraşi, about   120 km downstream. Our first camp wasn't particularly auspicious as we suffered an invasion of beetles that kept both of us awake; but at least we got off to an early start and put into practise our plan to break camp early and canoe some distance before a breakfast stop. Those early morning sections became a magical part of each day.

There are few towns of any size along this section and many of the villages lie some distance back behind protective dikes, so there was often an illusion of travelling through a virtually uninhabited landscape. Most of our encounters were with fishing folk and farm workers, along with flocks of sheep huddled under the trees in the noonday heat while their guardians dozed or fished. Women laundered carpets and clothing at the water's edge, sometimes wading in fully dressed and waist deep to rinse tangles masses of raw wool. Once we came across charcoal burners.

Compared with their sociable counterparts in Bulgaria, the Romanian country folk showed little interest in us. For the first time we had problems with drinking water. This was especially surprising as on all our earlier land journeys through Romania, one of the attractive features had been the proliferation of wells, often housed in beautiful little structures carved and decorated with traditional designs. Once we asked a family, confidently trotting out the phrase taught us by a Romanian friend – *Ivo viz keram?* – but they merely looked puzzled and pointed to the river. We became very sparing with our own precious supplies of water, filling up when we could at some standpipe in the middle of a village.

This region of the Dobrudja, caught between the Black Sea and the angular course of the Danube, has a story quite different from much of Romania. For up to 400 years it was under the Turks. Later it became yet another pawn in the political chess of major and lesser powers, and whoever had it never did much with the unpromising material offered by large tracts of arid prairie or equally unprofitable expanses of soggy marsh. In the last few decades things have dramatically changed, but backwaters remain and we were travelling through one of them.

The gateway to the Danube Delta is the Romanian port of Tulcea. It lies more or less at the apex formed by the three main distributaries of the Delta. Of these, the greatest in terms of volume of water is the Chilia Channel which forms the border with the Soviet Union to the north. In the centre is the much canalised shipping channel of Sulina and, to the south, the meandering arm of Sfintu Gheorghe. The whole area of the Delta amounts to 5460 sq km of which less than 10% is permanently dry land. Most of it is a complex pattern of channels and lakes, and countless floating and moving islands of reed and mattresses of other vegetation, all in a constant state of change.

The uniqueness of the Delta is fortunately appreciated by the Romanian authorities as is the need for conservation. At Tulcea there has been set up a Delta Museum where visitors can gain a better understanding of the region, its history, economy, flora and fauna. We had decided to follow the southern arm of the Delta, the Sfintu Gheorghe Channel, deviating from it as time would permit. Once we had paddled past the industrial complex of Tulcea and the point where the Sulina Channel carries its cargoes to and from the sea, we were on a river little disturbed by passing vessels. The banks were of permanently dry land lined with willow and white poplar, and it was like much else of the lower Danube, except for the villages. The houses here were of white washed mud or clay with reed thatched roofs, each house enclosed by a fence of reed, neatly woven to some pattern; in the centre of each yard was the summer kitchen with a sunken clay oven for baking bread.

Some of the people tried to speak to us in a tongue we recognised as Slavic. The population of the Delta is very mixed, including many Ukrainians and others of a strange Russian religious sect called Lipovans, dissenters holding to the "old beliefs" during the time of Peter the Great. They were expelled to this fringe of the Empire where for centuries Tsar and Sultan had contended. A handful still follow all the tenets of the faith and do not shave. We saw a few of them, massively bearded Tolstoy-like figures.

If the newest occupation of the Delta is the harvesting of the reeds for pulp and paper and the manufacture of cellulose, the oldest and still the most important is fishing. There are catfish and carp, bream and barbell – more than a hundred other species have been identified; but economically the most important are sturgeon, famous for their caviar. We first saw the fishermen at Uzlina. They were returning with their day's catch, each fisherman sitting in the stern of the graceful slim boats of the Deklta, known locally as *lodka*. A long line of them, a dozen or more in number, were being towed by a motor vessel back to their co-operative fishing station. We had left the main channel and paddled into a series of lakes, lush and colourful with a floating blanket of lilies. The purpose of this deviation was birds.

Of course we had been watching birds for days now, for the Danube Delta is ornithologically one of the most rewarding areas in Europe. We had seen little egrets, glossy ibis, and all the European herons daily and in great numbers, and on every mud bank waders galore; there were countless warblers which we failed to identify, while almost every tree clump was the perch of a hobby, and twice soaring high above us we saw the white-tailed eagle. But the pride of the Delta are the pelicans; both the Dalmatian and white pelicans nest here, the latter in fairly substantial numbers. It was at Uzlina that we first saw them. Perhaps 300 or more were feeding in the lake from which they took off majestically with strong, unhurried wing beats. Rising on thermals they circled silently overhead, alternately displaying their black-edged underwing and then, as if by some command, banking to show their upper parts brilliantly white against the blue sky. It was a spectacular aerial ballet.

Another and completely contrasting aspect of the Delta we did not see until almost the last day. The banks of reed by which we had been paddling for some hours abruptly gave way to a pocket of luxuriant vegetation, tropical in density. A narrow channel of crystal clear water enticed us to explore its dark interior. On both sides of the stream tall oaks were interlaced with creepers which formed a massive canopy overhead cutting out the sun. This was more akin to some Equatorial jungle than any European forest.

Another day of paddling, surprisingly on a still perceptible current, and we reached the mouth of the Sfintu Gheorghe Channel. Here, just beyond the little fishing town of the same name, the Danube flows out into the Black Sea and we hitched a ride from a local fisherman. For him it was just another day; for us, and especially Sylvie, it was the culmination of a major adventure.

Discovering Miss Austen

Alison Day

Not for the first time, they were discussing Jane Austen. This time it was regarding a course about her being offered on line. Someone said, "You're quite a Janeite, aren't you?'

Was she a Janeite? She didn't think so, she just enjoyed reading her novels …autobiographies …the modern rewrites … watching the many and varied television adaptations and films.

Her voyage of discovery started about 50 years ago. An exchange with her mother all those years ago was still as clear in her head as if it were yesterday.

'What are you reading?'

'An Agatha Christie' was her rather abrupt reply.

'Isn't it time you started reading other things? You're really of an age when you should be reading something more literary'.

On her 15th birthday she was given a copy of *Pride and Prejudice*. She resisted reading it for some time and it remained on the shelf as she continued to read of the exploits of Miss Marple and Hercule Poirot.

Her stubbornness, however, finally gave way to curiosity and she started to read Miss Austen's novel. She couldn't put it down. Her voyage of discovery had begun. It was a page turner in exactly the same way as any of the 'whodunnits' she had read. What was going to happen next in the world of sensibilities, manners and morality? What incisive and witty comment would Elizabeth Bennett come out with next? Even to this day she could still recall Elizabeth's stinging rebuke to Mr Darcy's marriage proposal:

"From the very beginning— from the first moment, I may almost say— of my acquaintance with you, your manners, impressing me with the fullest belief of your arrogance, your conceit, and your selfish disdain of the feelings of others, were such as to form the groundwork of disapprobation on which succeeding events have built so immovable a dislike; and I had not known you a month before I felt that you were the last man in the world whom I could ever be prevailed on to marry". Oh, to be able to be able to come up with such words today and have the confidence to deliver them.

That was it; she was hooked. Over the years she discovered the rest of Jane Austen's novels: *Sense and Sensibility*, *Northanger Abbey*, *Pride and Prejudice, Mansfield Park, Emma*, and *Persuasion*. She enjoyed them so much and found them such a rewarding read that she found herself rereading them, particularly *Pride and Prejudice*. She was often asked 'why do you keep going back to Jane Austen'. She would trot out the 'standard' answers: it's her brilliant wit, subtle irony and insight into women's lives.

She also found that every time she reread one of the novels, she discovered subtleties and connections she hadn't noticed before. It was only in recent years, however, that she started to consider this more deeply and realised, that, yes it was all those things, but *Pride and Prejudice* was her comfort. It was the book she turned to when life was getting on top of her. It was an escape, a safe place. Yes, Jane Austen's subject matter was narrow, and it may seem rather trivial to be excited about balls, amateur dramatics and needlework when England was at war with France under Napoleon. But to her it was part of the attraction to be able to read about the everyday lives and concerns of a few families in a small country circle.

Back to the matter in hand, was she going to sign up for this course? She thought there was a delicious irony in that the course was to be delivered online. The web was a modern medium that could be toxic, rude and undiscerning: a strange choice to study a writer known for her strict moral code, even if, at times, her tongue was firmly in her cheek. But there again, Jane Austen was something of a mould breaker: it was not the done thing for a genteel woman to write, let alone sell her stories. Perhaps Miss Austen would have approved of and made use of the World Wide Web. Her interest in Jane Austen and her works was such that she had discovered that the novels were published anonymously during her lifetime and made very little money and that it wasn't until the late 19th century that her novels gained popularity.

If Jane Austen became popular in the 19th century this was transformed into veneration in the 21st. The Austen Project saw six contemporary authors that included Joanna Trollope and Val McDermid rework Jane Austen 's most popular novels. Of course she had read them, and it was fascinating to see how the stories translated so easily and well into a modern setting, even *Northanger Abbey*, Jane's wonderful parody of the gothic novel. Then there was the wonderful and highly entertaining television serial *Lost in Austen* a twist on *Pride and Prejudice*, when a 21st century fan, Amanda, 'swaps' her life with Elizabeth Bennett. Needless to say, Elizabeth takes to modern life like a duck to water, but Amanda finds her new life a lot more challenging. There is a magnificent moment when Amanda is invited to sing, and she hesitantly launches into Petula Clark's *Downtown* for her bemused hosts.

'What's your decision? Are you going to register for the course on Jane Austen?'

'I'm still thinking about it'.

'Well, if you're unsure they're also running a course on the Brontes'.

LESSONS LEARNED

Jenny Sakamoto

As a "War Baby" born in 1943, I still remember queuing up with my mother and three siblings for rationed food, or playing with friends in the sandpit that my father had ingeniously built on the roof of the air-raid shelter in our back garden. But the threat of air strikes and war was far from our young minds, since we lived some ten miles north of Birmingham.

At the age of six, following a severe bout of measles, I developed a squint and became a miserable, self-conscious little girl, unhappy both at home, where I was teased constantly by my siblings, and at school where I felt shunned by my peers. Fortunately, my mother had trained as a doctor, so took me promptly to the Birmingham Eye Hospital to be assessed. Once the squint was diagnosed I embarked on a series of tests and treatments that I came to dread. Squints can be of various types but in my case the right eye turned inwards, hampering my vision. I was afraid of the elderly male consultant, who leaned so close to me that I could smell the fusty material of his dark suit, and feel his wheezing breath on my face whilst he shone dazzling lights into my eyes. I could barely read the lists of letters on the display and was frustrated, in particular, by one annoying challenge. With one eye covered and the other eye pressed against a little window in what seemed a huge machine, I managed to see a lion in its cage, but with the other eye the lion was always once again outside it. Each time I failed to perform a test correctly I felt ashamed.

Worst of all was the indignity of having to wear little pink NHS spectacles and a patch over the good eye to make the lazy eye work harder. At first the patch was simply a sticking plaster and when it was changed it felt as though eyebrows and eyelashes were being ripped off. My mother thought doing this quickly would hurt less. Fortunately, someone discovered the less painful alternative of a tinted lens.

Children, especially in those days, could be cruel if someone seemed odd or different. At school, I found myself mostly left alone at break times and wept copiously in the safety of my bedroom, earning the nickname "South Staffordshire Waterworks" from my gleeful sisters. Loneliness prompted me to mutter under my breath "I'll show them, I'll show them," so I worked hard at all my lessons. There was one teacher, Miss Higgs, who helped me more than anyone else at this low point in my life. Without fuss, she managed to make me feel important in little ways, setting me classroom tasks like cleaning the blackboard or collecting up books and, best of all, choosing me to be swashbuckling, eye-patch wearing Captain Hook in the class performance of Peter Pan. How proud I felt.

Eventually, the decision was made to operate to tighten the muscles of my right eye. Unlike nowadays, when this can be performed during day surgery, I spent over a week in the Eye Hospital, most of the time with both eyes bandaged. Hearing childish voices around me, I soon realized this was a children's ward, a fact confirmed when the kindly nurses lined us up in a crocodile, each clasping the waist of the child in front, to shuffle to the toilets and back. In this way, I realized we were all "blind" so I was one of a "team". My mother bought me a musical box, which, thanks to her quirky sense of humour, played the melody of "Drink to me only with thy eyes", a popular song at the time. It became a favourite with the other children, especially when I turned the handle so as to play the tune backwards. Suddenly, I had friends, swopping names, chatting and laughing. But once home, though the lazy eye had been successfully corrected, I once more reverted to feeling lonely and friendless.

In the final class of Primary School, I noticed that one of the girls had unusually exotic snacks for break time and lunch. Living within walking distance of the school I went home at lunchtimes, but began asking to go to the toilet just before the morning break, in order to sneak a few goodies from her lunch box. Then when we were all out in the playground, I offered my classmates dried apricots, cherries or walnuts in a desperate effort to win friends. Of course, this didn't last for long. One day, I returned to school to find my whole class sitting in silence. Somebody had been stealing from Pam's lunch box. I'm not sure if I blushed, or how I was found out, but that evening my mother pulled down my knickers and swiped my bottom with the back of her hairbrush, saying afterwards: 'well, I doubt if you needed that. I'm sure it's punishment enough for all your class to know you're a thief. Maybe that will teach you never to steal again.'

It certainly did. In fact, what happened subsequently changed not only the remainder of my schooldays but my attitude to life forever.

'Why didn't you ask to share some of my lunch?' queried Pam the next day. 'Come on Jenny, I've got something special today. Do you like figs?'

This was the start of a friendship that lasted from that moment to present times. Soon, other friends were joining in with us, and at last I was just one of the girls. Pam and I, though parted by distance, keep in touch and meet at least twice annually, best friends for over sixty years throughout all the usual ups and downs of life. I learnt so many important lessons from that relatively brief period of having a squint, but perhaps most significant, how bad experiences can trigger positive and heartwarming results.

THE WILD WOOD

Olive Hill

Heather Armitage had few illusions about her popularity in Dorringham: despite all she had done for the village in the five years since she chose to retire in it. But then she had learned quite early in her business career that neither success nor altruism necessarily inspired affection. The villagers, especially ones like that appalling old Joseph Forrester, had merely confirmed this. Nevertheless it was hard to believe anyone would deliberately sabotage Whirling Wood just to spite her.

"Don't be absurd," Fiona said when she suggested it. "It must be a nutter."

Heather's lips pursed in disagreement. The fact was that the wild wood for which she had fund-raised, fought and laboured to make a reality a mile out of the village, appeared to be under siege. Now in their fourth winter, the trees were being systematically pruned. Species by species her beloved infant wild wood was being tamed. It was intolerable.

Fiona glanced at her friend's intelligent, uncompromising expression. More than a mere millennium project it had become, she judged, the child Heather had never had, the mark she intended to bestow upon posterity. Interesting how a small green dot on the Midlands map could acquire such importance to someone who appeared to have it all.

Now she suggested "You need a sleuth. What about that pallid boy with the black dog who's always down there? Lives on the new housing estate out that way. Single Mum."

"That Mrs. Armitage wants to see you," Spud's mother told him when he came home next day. She hoped it might penetrate his uncanny silence since Blackie was killed three days earlier. It was no one's fault. Blackie had nudged open the front gate that never latched properly and hurtled after a cat. The van driver stood no chance of avoiding him.

Spud found out on his return from school. His mother, unusually gentle, had already dug a grave in the garden. They had placed Blackie in it carefully, wrapped in a blanket, then filled in the hole and put two pieces of wood to make a cross.

"What's she want?" Spud asked now. Mrs Armitage had a plummy voice, ran the village magazine and alarmed him.

"One way of finding out" his mother said.

A couple of days later, Spud shifted uneasily from one foot to another in Mrs Armitage's kitchen, gulping lemonade and desperately suppressing a burp.

She said "I understand you take your little dog down to Whirling Wood... er - Spud."

Spud shook his head. "Blackie's run over," he said, adding "Dead" in case he hadn't made himself clear.

"Oh," Mrs. Armitage said. "Oh dear, I was depending on you." A pause, then "And I'm very sorry about your little dog."

Another pause, then because he couldn't think of anything else to say Spud blurted out "But, like, I can go for you anyway."

"*Could* you? Could you go every day for a while - say, for 50p a time?"

Spud stared at her in amazement. He was to be *paid* for going to his favourite place! Already he had forgotten his vow never to go there again now Blackie was dead.

Mrs Armitage said he was to look out for someone who was cutting off branches; and if he could tell her who it was, there would be £5 for him.

As he surveyed the young ash critically Joseph Forrester caught himself humming. He stopped, grunted. Hadn't hummed since Maggie died and that would be ten years tomorrow.

There wasn't a day he didn't think of her, but the thinking was never so hard when he was outside, practising what he had learned over nearly 70 years of working with nature.

"Reckon if you stood still long enough you'd grow roots," Maggie used to tease him.

They'd both wanted a kid but it wasn't to be. He guessed she really minded too, but they'd each kept it to themselves. Then much later she'd suddenly got thin. A tumour, they said. They didn't talk about it but he'd done his best for her those last five years. While she could, she'd quite often come to the gardens at Langham Grey where he worked for the Major. When the pain got too much they put her in the hospital and she'd slipped away while he was holding her hand.

He took to working from dawn to dusk, filling the dark hours of winter with repair and renovating jobs. But the time came three years ago when even he recognised it needed a younger man. The Major said "You'll always be welcome at Langham Grey, Joseph. After all these gardens are your creation."

He soon stopped going, though, unable to stomach the new-fangled short-cut ways of doing things. It was the worst time in his life, waking up to long purposeless days. At midday he went across to the Red Lion but an hour was enough and he didn't invite conversation. And the village had changed so much: the bakery and butcher's shop gone, replaced by a hairdresser and a dentist; the village store turned into a mini-market; and the old folks' club closed down. He blamed the off-comers who shopped in the big supermarkets and had gradually taken over the village with their play reading groups - whatever they were - and theatre outings.

Like that Mrs Armitage who was into everything. Once in the village shop she'd had the nerve to ask him if he could spare a couple of hours to sort out her garden.

"I don't do folks' gardens," he'd said curtly and turned his back on her.

Now he said sharply "Get on with it you old fool," and gently but firmly took his secateurs to the new branch forming from the main stem of the young ash.

It was the Major who had told him, "I hear they're planting a millennium wood on the north edge of the parish. They'll appreciate your expertise."

But no one had asked Joseph his opinion. In the Red Lion he picked up the odd snippet. "That Mrs Armitage is organising a wild flower planting day." "Someone said you can't see the trees for dock and thistles!" "Them environment people are building an otter holt by the stream."

"The mink'll find it first," Joseph couldn't resist saying.

His curiosity eventually got the better of him on a fresh early morning last spring. He had been torn between delight, approval and fury. Delight at the shimmer of young growth and the tangle of ragged robin, buttercup and oxeye daisy in a clearing by the stream; approval of the sowing of tough grasses to compete with unwanted rank vegetation; and fury at the neglect of the trees themselves. A line of willows bowed low and unattended in the path of the prevailing wind. Not a single tree had been pruned to give it shape and grace in decades to come. It was a long time since he had felt such outrage.

Too late to do anything then, but come the following winter ....

It was the first time Spud had ever gone to Whirling Wood on his own. The late February afternoon sunshine slanted low over the young trees making silvery sparks of the catkins on the willows and gleaming blood red on the dogwood stems. Spud did not notice such things but, with no Blackie to hurtle after every real and imaginary rabbit, he was aware of stillness.

A stillness broken by the crackle of twigs underfoot and a faint tuneless humming.

Spud crept on, half scared, half excited. Oh *crumbs,* it was that horrible old Mr Forrester who used to shout at Blackie for digging holes. His heart plummeted and, without warning, he gave an explosive sneeze.

Old he might be but Joseph Forrester's grip on the scruff of Spud's neck felt like a steel clamp. "Leggo," he yelled, as he was unceremoniously dumped on his feet.

"And what d'you think you're up to?" the old man demanded. He looked at Spud more closely. "Oh it's you, is it?"

Spud thought if he legged it home the old man would never catch him. Then all he had to do was report to Mrs Armitage, collect his fiver and go. But he felt oddly cheated: all those 50ps - and he'd gone and solved the mystery in one go. He was also curious.

He mumbled "Wondered, like, why you're cutting all them branches off."

It was a long time since anyone had shown any interest in what Joseph Forrester did. He also remembered hearing in the Red Lion about the dog, and said gruffly "Not any old branches; just particular ones so the tree will grow straight and strong and a good shape."

Spud was puzzled. Mr Forrester didn't look a bit guilty as though he'd been caught doing something he shouldn't. "So that's a good thing, isn't it?"

"Of course it's a good thing," the old man said impatiently. "Been doing it all my life, helping things grow strong, making everything look better."

Spud's puzzlement grew. So what was Mrs Armitage on about? It must be great to help things grow strong, make everything look better. He said "Could'ya teach me?"

Something was unexpectedly constricting Joseph's throat and he cleared it noisily. "Too late to start now. Come after your tea tomorrow."

Over the next afternoons Spud was down at Whirling Wood as soon as he'd swallowed his last mouthful of tea. Joseph Forrester heard him long before he came into sight and was surprised how glad he was; and how much he missed the boy on the occasion he had to stay home for a visiting auntie.

He worked methodically, explaining to Spud what he was doing and why. Sometimes he'd ramble off into long stories of how everything in nature was linked in a whole complex structure, and the way plants and insects and animals had learned to work together. Spud didn't understand a lot of it, but he liked the idea of so much unseen order. Sometimes they'd end up doing a short circuit of Whirling Wood, looking at insects and things. Twice they saw woodpeckers, and once the flash of a kingfisher along the stream.

Heather Armitage printed out her latest editorial for the Dorringham News and crossed to the window. She had assumed Spud had reneged on his undertaking until his mother happened to mention that morning his daily eagerness to get down to Whirling Wood. In Heather Armitage's limited experience, small boys did not forego a daily 50 p without reason. She reached a decision.

She saw the two figures from some distance away: Joseph bending to examine a sapling, Spud hunched beside him; both far too absorbed to be aware of anything else.

Joseph Forrester, one time Head Gardener at Langham Grey!

Spud looked up and saw her. "Oh cripes," he said.

Joseph straightened, turned and stared. And said nothing.

"So perhaps you would care to explain Mr Forrester," Heather Armitage said coldly.

"You g-got it all wrong," Spud blurted, stammering in his anxiety to reassure her. "Mr Forrester, he knows all ab-bout looking after t-trees."

"I'm well aware of Mr Forrester's skills, thank you Spud. What I wish to know is why he is exercising them on my ... our wild wood."

"Wild wood!" Joseph said scornfully. "Takes a thousand years or more to make a wild wood. And who heard of a wild wood with a parking place and a path and a couple of seats!"

They glared at each other. Heather Armitage's next thought was that this strange old man had voiced her own deepest reservations about paths and parking places; and then that he actually seemed to think he was repairing some awful neglect. There came a first glimmer of understanding.

She said "We're *trying* to make it a wild wood. Trying to think of the next thousand years. Trying to get back some of the wildflowers and mammals and insects we've lost."

Joseph thought, *she talks real queer, but there's some sense in it.* He said "There were Banded Damselflies near the brook last summer."

"Indeed there were Mr Forrester," Heather Armitage said. "And a few Beautiful Damselflies too. These are just the habitats we must protect while re-creating others that we've destroyed."

Joseph grunted. "Won't be no wood if you don't tackle them rabbits," he said nodding at the oak sapling they had been examining.

Heather crouched down beside him. "Oh dear. What do you suggest?"

Spud looked from one to the other in astonishment. He'd never understand grown-ups.

"It's them plastic guards, a lot of them aren't fixed proper." Joseph's tone implied *what else could you expect from a bunch of amateurs.*

Heather looked round in the fast fading light. He was right. She was not one to hesitate.

"I suppose Mr Forrester you wouldn't consider taking charge of checking them ..."

"Big job," Joseph said.

"I'm afraid as a charity we couldn't offer..."

"It's not money I want Mrs" he interrupted impatiently. "It's more hands - like this young'un."

99

An idea was gaining rapid appeal. "You recruit who you like Mr Forrester. But only on the understanding that they take their orders from you." Heather Armitage considered a moment. "You could, in fact, be our official warden."

Joseph grunted. "I'll think on it."

A small pause. "Only no more pruning. Please."

He looked her straight in the eye. "You don't never prune a wild wood," he said.

THE DON'T CARE GENERATION

Sylvie Nickels

Phillida didn't enjoy being angry. It was just that she couldn't bear the slovenly way things were done. The 'don't care' generation she called them, the youngsters who came within her orbit, whether it was cleaning the house, doing the garden, or working in the typing pool where she was supervisor by the time she reached twenty-five. She knew the girls laughed at her: at her mousy hair and old fashioned appearance, and her precise way of talking. But for as long as she could remember, it had been important to her to take pride in what she did and to do it to the best of her ability. By the age of thirty she was in charge of a department in Better Sales, and by thirty-five its managing director. With time, the slovenliness of the young only seemed to get worse.

"No wonder you never married, Phil," her sister Ros said after overhearing her telephone conversation with a junior. Ros was the only one who dared shorten Phillida's name to Phil.

They mutually respected each other, Ros and Phil: Ros for Phil's drive and efficiency; and Phil for Ros's charm and real niceness. Small wonder that Ros married in her early twenties, had four cherubic children by her early thirties. Less predictable was that she should be a widow by her early forties.

By then Phillida was teaching the Africans the benefits of family planning, having given the Malaysians and Bangladeshis similar benefits of her wisdom. No one bothered about her old fashioned appearance there; they were only interested in the fact that she got things done and that it made their lives just a little easier. No one noticed, least of all Phillida herself that her mousy hair had turned to pepper-and-salt and finally to grey. By the time she returned to

Middle England for good. both sisters were in their sixties and Ros's children had turned into Dave the builder; Rob the DiY merchant; Mags the district nurse; and Pris the wannabe artist. Pris was the youngest, wildest, artiest. The other three were reasonably settled with, between them, sensible careers and five grandchildren for Ros. Pris, unmarried, was shortly to produce the sixth..

Ros herself had had a stroke and needed full time care in a pleasant but pricey institution where she was being rehabilitated. Her mind was as lively as ever, but her right side was frozen affecting her ability to do most things for herself. Pris went to see her every day with her growing bump.

"Don't you worry about her?" Phillida couldn't resist asking.

Ros smiled her crooked smile. "I know you used to call them the 'don't care' generation, but they do, you know, especially for each other."

"Hm," Phillida said.

Phillida resumed her charity work, in due course becoming secretary to a support group for dysfunctional families and fund raiser for adopting third world grannies. There was no time for a social life and in any case she felt no need for it. She visited Ros from time to time and was delightedly amazed by her progress. Eventually Ros was released back into the world, spending several weeks in turn with each of her married children before returning to her home now fully equipped with gadgets to make life easier. Pris had decided to give up whatever bedsit she was in to go home and keep an eye on her.

Phillida visited her there on the eve of her own departure for an international conference in Luxembourg on single-parent families. On her return there was a crisis with third world grannies, and then a series of launches to fund nursery care for the progeny of single parents. Not to mention the talks that took her to schools all around the county and beyond promulgating the value of hygiene and safe sex. It was from one of these institutions no doubt that she picked up a bug that knocked her for six..

It was a virus, the doctor said. Nothing to be done but to stick it out. There was a particularly virulent one going about at the moment. Drink plenty and take paracetamol to keep her temperature down. For a week, Phillida lay in bed, alternately sweating and shivering.. She did not even answer the door or the telephone. Early on she rang the corner shop mini-market and asked them to deliver a consignment of invalid food in different flavours, which she mixed with water or milk. It was disgustingly cloying, but the packets told her she was imbibing the right balance of protein, vitamin and minerals. Periodically she picked up the mail, and eventually opened the front door to find two plastic bags of rubbish. People really were disgusting. She dumped them in her wheelie bin.

She had of course cancelled her commitments, but now began slowly to pick up the threads of normal life. Even working part time she was exhausted by the evening. Then the plastic shopping bags started appearing again. Irritably she plonked them in a box by the wheelie bin and hoped they would not attract foxes. Finally she found the energy to go round and see Ros.

"Welcome stranger," her sister said, looking radiant, her smile now only very slightly crooked. She proceeded to demonstrate to Phillida how adept she now was at a whole range of household jobs, including preparing a meal.

"Why don't you stay?" she suggested. "Pris would love to see you and has been a tower of strength. She told me, by the way, how poorly you've been. I did try and ring…."

Phillida shrugged. "A minor bug. And how did Priscilla know that?"

"Oh that group of hers seem to know everything. Probably some of them have kids at one of those schools you talk to."

"Hm," Phillida said.

"Anyway, my dear, did you enjoy that mousse I made for you? One of my first efforts. It was in Pris's last food parcel."

Mousse? Food parcel? Phillida's mind raced and finally settled on a boxful of plastic shopping bags.

"Mm, I haven't got around to it yet," was all she could think of saying.

"Oh Phil. Well, don't leave it too long – there's real cream in it."

As soon as she got home, Phillida retrieved the plastic shopping bags. A nasty whiff came from one of them and she glimpsed strawberries well passed their 'use by' date. But the lemon mousse in a plastic container looked fine, as did a packet of ginger nuts, some camomile tea (how had Pris known that was her favourite?), a container of dried fruit, three cartons of soup, a jar of peaches in brandy, and an interesting choice of boil-in-the-bag meals.

She felt a tightening of the throat as she took the bags into the kitchen and examined their contents. At the bottom of one was a note:

Hi Auntie Phil – Hope you soon feel better. Only three weeks to go now."

Three weeks? Oh, the baby.

She thought of all the charity she had dispensed in remote corners of the world and blessed Pris for dispensing hers nearer home. Then she made a decision. She would drop the child a note and offer her services as a baby sitter.

She found she was humming to herself as she stored her bag of goodies away.

LIFE AFTER DIVORCE

Penelope Brown

I can honestly say, even though I never thought I'd say it, it was a brave decision for my ex-husband to go. I didn't see his decision coming and I never prepared for that day.

I kept myself busy – the house had never been so clean. I tidied up drawers and garage stuff, removing anything and everything no longer required with a zeal I have never experienced since. Then, once the divorce began in earnest, acrimony took over and depression moved in in his place. I knew I would never laugh again. I knew I would never feel what I used to feel about life itself. My natural optimism morphed into pessimism. My smile a grimace. My crow's feet smoothed out by eye bags and puffiness.

Yet had that day not happened my life today would be very, very different. The difference is such that my former life is not something I would choose for myself ever again. Along the way, life taught me to forget the 'why' and get on with re-building my life. For me that took a long four years. Four years of tears, stress, anxiety and suffering. I don't think a marriage breakdown is something one 'just gets over' or 'moves on from'. The person who torments you hasn't died. They are alive. They are well. They become a barrier to being able to properly grieve for a life lost.

I married in my early twenties. He left after I turned forty. At first, I put it down to a mid-life crisis: his, not mine. I spent a lot of time trying to work out why. Was it something I said? I did? Didn't do? Didn't say? What about him? His actions? His selfishness? Him leaving changed my outlook on life in ways I didn't expect. Things I used to enjoy, I no longer could. Beliefs I used to hold about myself no longer held true. Things I thought mattered, didn't matter a jot.

I'd bought into the fairy-tale of marriage, but I didn't have a clue how to *do* marriage. I don't suppose anyone really does when it's all hearts and flowers. As it was, I bumbled through it the best I thought how. Laughable when I look back: between us, our parents had been married no less than ten times – at the last count. My expectations, and my abilities, fell well short. For a long time, I felt I should have known better. I realise now that is ludicrous. It is what I didn't know that contributed most to the failure of the marriage.

As we navigated our way through divorce, the depression moved in and any remaining sense of self moved out. For me, depression is that level of hell when one sinks below tears, when feelings are just a soup, indistinguishable from one another, and none of the ingredients palatable. And when the depression exited stage right, as depression is wont to do, then anxiety took centre-stage. I'd burn myself out. The war between depression and anxiety remained for a long time. My mind was just territory for them to fight over.

Him leaving made me appreciate the importance of looking after oneself first and being there for others second. Everything had to slow down. I was no longer in a position to just 'bounce back' and 'get on with it', like people demand one does. I had to start looking after myself and being a lot kinder to myself. Easier said than done. During marriage, I'd given up my likes, my wants and my needs. Not totally, but I'd compromised to the point that I lost myself. For me, somehow, marriage stopped me developing my own identity, my own self-esteem and my own sense of mind. It became something to hide in. A safety net: no more, no less. In marriage, I discovered that 'good enough' can be a very low bar to attain.

The divorce, or rather the process of divorce, forces one to grow up and find independence. I don't think that is easy. At least, not when it's not your own decision. I fought hard against growing up and gaining independence. I became the most incalcitrant of teenagers. I swore a lot. I drank too much. I stayed up too late. I didn't eat well. I dressed shockingly badly. I thought the world didn't understand me. I raged against the unfairness of it all.

I'm now through those awful, gangly, painful years and on to the other side. Around me, I meet people heading down the dark tunnel of divorce. All I can say is that 'it gets better', that somehow 'you get through it'. As Winston Churchill once said, 'When you're going through hell, keep going!' No one dies from divorce, but there are days when death seems preferable. Murder even possible. It is, without doubt, an utterly brutal and brutalising experience. Not for everyone, of course, but for me it was.

And yet it ends. The day the divorce certificate landed on my doorstep, the sun shone. It was one of those gloriously wonderful spring days. I couldn't have felt more despairing. It didn't feel like a re-birth. I felt like I was dressed for summer in the winter. That somehow, I'd been planted in a shady-spot in the garden, with no hope of ever getting full sun. That I was, as a friend so perfectly described, like a snail without a shell.

I learnt to hate anyone starting sentences with 'At least…' or 'Just…' because it's not that simple, Good enough is, as I've said, a very low standard sometimes. I didn't want perfection, either. I didn't know what perfect looked like. I didn't have a clue what I wanted, or what I needed. I only knew I didn't want what I had.

I tried as best I could to do the 'right' thing. I got a job. I moved house. I moved countries, in fact. A fresh start, with my old black moods, hurt and pain transported along with the sofa, the bed, the cat and the artefacts of marriage that were now mine, and mine alone. I had counselling. I acquired names in my phone book. I obtained a social life. My driving improved. I learnt how to fix things. I put one foot in front of the other. I stumbled all too often. I crawled. And I bawled.

And then came that sudden moment when I realised the best thing that ever happened to me was my husband buggering off. It was over four years later, when I found myself in yet another house on yet another glorious spring day. Walking around my garden I inspected the work I'd put into it over the last few years. Until this day, the physical labour managing a sizeable garden, the endless weeding, the planting out of spring saplings, the noise of the lawnmower, the harvesting and composting, not a single second of it had truly over-rode the endless thinking about the past.

Of course, a new bed had helped, as had a new duvet cover. New friends had helped. Giving up the booze had helped. New clothes, and a new haircut helped. Getting therapy helped. But the moment when I discovered who I was that was the key. The 'why' no longer matter, the 'how' became my focus. How do other people *do* happiness? How do they cope when things don't go to plan? I made a decision to try anything and everything anyone suggested, no matter what I thought of their idea. I forced willingness into myself. Where the body goes, the mind follows.

It all started with a friend saying, 'Have some fun' and I tearfully explained that I no longer knew what fun was. 'Have a bath' she said. I bought smelling salts. A candle and put on music. I sat in the bath talking to no one but the cat. I couldn't fathom how on earth anyone thought this was fun. I forced myself to have a bath everyday for a month. I discovered it was a great place to meditate – yet another person's idea of 'fun'. I went to the cinema, alone. It gave me something to talk to people about. I ate out, sometimes with friends, sometimes alone. I bought homely stuff. I bought a new car. I took up a writing course. None of it felt like 'fun'. 'Do something that no one else is doing', said another. I bought a quadbike. I took it to Scotland. I had a blast. It broke down. I handled it. None of these things stopped me feeling like a person with a minus one.

If a person wants more self-esteem, like I did, then as the knowledgeable would say: 'you must do self-esteemable things.' For me, that was getting out of my so-called comfort zone, a place that was pretty miserable even on a 'good enough day', into the very uncomfortable zone. I had to hang on in there until it got familiar, and when it got too familiar, I had to move further out again. It is not, in my opinion, time that heals, it's finding enough resources to try new stuff and to hell with what other people think about it. Then to keep trying it over and over, until it works. Switching my brain off helped by far. I don't remember when exactly, I stopped asking 'why', and start doing the 'how'. No matter how ludicrous, ridiculous or cringe-inducing the idea, I try it at least a few times, in spite of my reticence or my scepticism. My natural optimism crept back in without my noticing. My smile returned. Laughter reigned. Nothing now can describe my relief now that I am the thing I feared most: divorced.

Some people might say it is 'faking it until you make it' – I don't think that is helpful. I couldn't fake feelings I didn't hold. I couldn't fake happiness I didn't feel. I couldn't muster up energy I didn't have. Nor money. I hate feeling like a fraud at the best of times, let alone at the worst of times. Yet, I learnt I could mindlessly follow instructions. I could ask 'how' and somehow, just somehow, where the body went, the mind reformed. Until that day I found myself wandering around my garden, I realised that had he not left, I wouldn't have my life as I know it. A life full of plans, ideas, friends and activity. I now feel more like the mid-twenty something I used to be: full of optimism, hope and anticipation. Life is back to being an adventure.

NOT A PLACE TO LOSE A COW!!

Olive Hill

The present contains nothing more than the past, and what is found in the effect was already in the cause   Henri Bergson, L'Evolution créatrice (1907), ch.1

From the forest rim a man and a woman gaze down into the canyon. Two thirty-somethings, slim, assured, they seem at ease with each other in the way that evolves with long association. But not in love. An animal attraction perhaps, certainly on his part; but not love.

She glances at her watch. Seven o'clock. The throb of heat is muted now, and the metallic blue of the sky has mellowed to a kinder shade. The sinking sun is bringing texture to the rock pinnacles, as well as deepening colour, so that the weathering of millennia assumes curves and whorls as of man-made sculptures. Temples, almost. Only no human hand has ever wielded a chisel in this unforgiving place.

Hoodoos they call them, these pinnacles of fantastical shapes that characterise Bryce Canyon, created by an unimaginable time span of erosion in America's West.

Hoodoo – to cast a spell.

The man glances at his companion's profile and comments,. "We've missed the last shuttle back to the hotel." He notes again that she has cut her hair and that the gamine style makes her younger, more vulnerable, inviting. It belies that intrinsic serenity which has long intrigued him.

"It's not that far to walk," the woman says, still looking down into the canyon. "Especially in the cool of the evening. Well, relative

109

cool." She turns, her still features suddenly illuminated by a smile. "Give us an appetite," she adds, and reaches out to take his hand.

----oOo----

They say there is no deeper love than the first. I wouldn't know as that is all there has ever been. Danny said it was a marriage made in heaven, but then Danny was full of clichés which he pulled out like rabbits from a hat, always with delight and surprise as though he had just invented them. When I explained about clichés, he merely said, well, even if they were so overused by so many people, there had to be more truth in them than all the unique one-liners clever people came out with. But like most things about Danny, I even got to like his clichés.

It seemed an unnecessary quibble to point out that we weren't actually married. We'd been together in that squat in Granton since forever. Dad had dragged me away when I was sixteen, but we didn't stop meeting, Danny and I, and as soon as I was eighteen, I was back again.

We'd met in a churchyard. He was into gravestones in a big way and, on a balmy July evening, he found me curled up asleep behind one a couple of days after I left home. Mum and I had been far too close for me ever to live in the same house as her stand-in, though it was a while before I told Danny about any of that. You can learn a lot about a place from its gravestones, he said, and proceeded to show me the several that recorded deaths from a plague: not the Great one but a smaller episode that didn't make the history books. Later he led me to the graves of a whole lot of foreign folk – French prisoners from the Napoleonic wars, Dutch who came to build canals, Italian prisoners-of-war to clear World War Two bomb sites and, of course, hordes of Irish. There was a bit of Irish in him, Danny said.

There was an amazing number of graveyards within walking distance of the squat. If I complained about the distance, Danny said we needed the exercise, so what was my problem. Sometimes, if we were a bit flush, we took the bus. When I got bored watching Danny, I started going into the churches and noticing the stained glass windows and wondering how they were made and why. Well, get some books out of the library, Danny said. That's how he'd learned so much about old gravestones.

You can't actually take books out if you haven't a permanent address, but I got to really like being in the library: that thick silence that's louder than the traffic outside. It was warm, too, in the winter.

With Danny's gravestones and my stained glass windows and the library and the squat, we had a great life. When we needed money, we got casual jobs – there are always jobs if you're not fussy what you do. I wasn't so keen on cleaning loos - well, people can be really *gross*. But the washing up jobs were OK and usually we got some left over grub as well. Then, if the Parks people were short-staffed, they'd take us on: clearing leaves in the autumn, or cleaning up after some public event. During all that time, I let my hair grow until it fell over my shoulders in long dark curtains which Danny would spend ages brushing and shaping. He said I was never to cut it as long as we were together which, as far as he was concerned, would be forever. He had this way of making you feel beautiful even when you knew you weren't.

Others in the squat came and went. A lot ... most ... of them were on drugs or booze, and on the rare occasions they weren't stoned they told us about their lives and why they needed oblivion. We weren't into that stuff, Danny and I. We didn't need oblivion and preferred to know what we were about. So I just knew it wasn't true when they said he was drunk and stepped out on to the street in front of that motorbike. It was late evening and he'd gone out to get a bag of chips. A stupid bag of chips. I was holding his hand when he died a few hours later in the hospital.

The police put out requests for anyone who might have seen the accident; but I knew no one was going to bother much about a dead drop-out who'd brought it on himself. Except I knew he hadn't. One of the druggies told me they saw what happened, knew who the biker was: a toe-rag called Crag Blackmoor who'd been regularly carving up the neighbourhood for weeks. But who was going to believe a drop-out? Anyway, by now I was dead too, except I was still breathing and couldn't figure out how to stop. Then Dad came and took me home, and I didn't care enough not to go.

----oOo----

They call this part of Utah State 'red rock' country, but the colours go all the way from rose to cinnamon, lemon to flame, ash to purple.

111

"If you saw those colours in a painting, you'd say 'yuck'," she observes. She fishes into the sling bag on her shoulder and brings out a camera: one of those tiny digital ones.

"You'll get better sky effects if you leave it a bit longer," he suggests. "And I never say 'yuck'."

She grins at him, and he's charmed by this new, unfamiliar lighter mood. So many sides to this amazing woman. And to think he'd once dismissed her as a saddo. He wonders which of her personae he will be sharing a bed with later for that is firmly on his agenda.

He goes to join her, sitting on a rock looking out over tens … hundreds … thousands … of square miles of rock and desert: a mega construction site as this corner of the earth rearranged itself through ever more awesome upheavals. He finds himself wondering what it must have been like to be the first human to set foot in this extraordinary place?

"Just imagine being the first one to see all this," she says.

So they are telepathic soul-mates too. He doesn't usually allow himself to get emotionally hooked by his bed partners. Emotions are dangerous. Better watch it.

---oOo---

It was hard to remember afterwards how long I stayed dead. My stepmother was surprisingly smarter than I gave her credit for. She just left me lying on my bed for hours, days, may be weeks. Sometimes she'd come in to my room and switch on the TV, and I'd get up and switch it off again. Then one day I didn't, and there was this programme about gravestones. I think I cried for two days.

Dad was teaching in adult education and said why didn't I do a course. So I cut my hair and took up computing. Danny had always said he'd learn about computers one day, so I did it for both of us. Anyway, if you're going to go on living in a world where everything is www.-this and dotcom-that, you need to find out what they're on about.

Amazingly, I was good at it. Even more amazingly I enjoyed it. No need for face-to-face confrontations with people asking stupid questions. It was magic: just me and the universe linked by a few clicks. I looked in on chat rooms and newsgroups and discovered there were some seriously weird people out there. One day I checked Google and found there were 508,000 entries for stained glass windows, and 423,000 for gravestones. Then I checked Amazon.com

112

for books on the subject; there were respectively 56 and 116 listed, a lot of them out of print.

How about a book linking the two: 'In Memoriam' for all those dead people? And especially Danny. I didn't discuss it with anyone. Anyway, I didn't care what anyone thought. Danny had given it the OK in my head.

----oOo---

"Perhaps we should get back to the road," he says, but doesn't move. It's quite addictive sitting on a rock next to this woman looking out over this amazing view. And he has become sharply aware of the silence. It is some time now since they heard distant voices or the hum of a vehicle from the invisible road. Everyone else, it seems, has gone home.

"We can continue along the track and pick the road up from the next access point," she suggests. "Have this view for a bit longer. It's only half … three-quarters of a mile." She leans forward to touch a white flower on a slender stem near his foot. "Did you know that's the state flower of Utah? Sego Lily. You can eat the bulbs, you know."

He didn't know. "You have a storehouse of the most irrelevant facts," he teases. ""It's all that time you spend with Google."

"I don't suppose it seemed irrelevant to Ebenezer Bryce and his family when they were hungry."

"You're making him up," he accuses, and it seems all right to slip an arm round her shoulders, draw her a bit closer.

"You obviously haven't read the brochure. Ebenezer Bryce and his family moved here in 1875 and made the road up to this plateau to harvest the timber. So they named the canyon after him." She slides gently away from his arm and stands up to look out over the canyon. "Apparently he said it would be a hell of a place to lose a cow." The colours are truly vibrant now. Give it another half hour ….

"Another half hour and it should be perfect," he says. "Yes it would be. A hell of a place to lose a cow." He takes her hand loosely and she does not pull it away.

----oOo----

Within six months I'd created a huge database, immaculately cross-referenced so that you could check any common denominator between

113

the burial rites, say, of the Aztecs and the Inuit, at the click of a mouse. I couldn't have done it without Danny's help. He was there all the time, encouraging, urging, suggesting; seemed to have an instinctive affinity with computer technology though in his lifetime he never as much as touched a keyboard, let alone a mouse.

By now I'd moved into my own place, a mews flat behind the market place, near the library. This was perfect as I'd taken a part time job in the library. It was at the time they were putting in a new computerised system, so I learned a lot as well. All this I discussed in the evenings with Danny after we'd finished our stint of surfing the 'Net. His presence became so real that for long periods I truly forgot he was dead, and the shock of remembering each time was like a new bereavement. Sometimes I wondered if I might be going just a little bit crazy, but it didn't feel like that.

It was quite a while later and the book was at the almost-ready stage when a headline in the local paper blared out *Local Man Claims World on Full Throttle,* and the name Crag Blackmoor leaped out of the page. There was a picture of him: smiling, cocky, blonde, good looking. They gave his website - www.fullthrottle.uknet – so I went straight to it. Clearly he had travelled a very long way indeed in every sense since those days of carving up a neighourhood in Granton. I followed a series of links leading to Crag Blackmoor testing ever larger, sleeker and shinier motorbikes in ever more unlikely parts of the globe looking ever more debonair.

And alive.

It was then, as though a switch had been thrown, that old unresolved grief turned into new all-consuming hatred.

Somewhere on www.fullthrottle.uknet Crag Blackmoor announced he was planning a series of books on worldwide biking, so if anyone had any experiences they would like to share ..... there followed his email address.

Hi Crag, I tapped out barely stopping to think. Then explained how I knew my way round the 'Net like no one else, and I guessed he could do with a research assistant; and, as I thought he was the coolest thing since MS-DOS, there wouldn't be any charge. And that, while I had no biking experience, I was a fast and willing learner.

114

As I suspected, the prospect of a research assistant, especially an admiring and free one, appealed to the Crag Blackmoor ego. Within no time we were emailing several times weekly. Two years of sifting through the gold and the garbage of thousands of websites had made me ace at turning up the least likely facts in the fastest time. I soon acquired a working knowledge of the biking world and began to pepper my emails with casual references to the comparative specifications of the latest Yamaha and Suzuki. Then there was the impending Harley-Davidson centenary and all the razzmatazz to be associated with it. It was not hard to impress Crag Blackmoor who clearly knew more about speeding than surfing. After a while, and not very subtly, he began trying to find out more about me – age, partner status, interests. Just about everything except ask for my photograph. Finally he came up with *I guess it's time my own private Brainbox came out of the closet.*

Thank heavens for email anonymity. I had needed to go no further than the local telephone directory to check out that Crag Blackmoor still lived locally: now upgraded to a leafy suburb a couple of miles away. And, yes, my gradually unfolding plan still had a long, long way to go, so perhaps it *was* time to come out of the closet.

Crag suggested the Princes Bar of the King's Head on a Friday lunchtime. This was just across the market place from my mews flat, and couldn't have suited me better. I made it sound as though I was doing him a favour, said I could do the small detour on my way to stay with friends in the next county. He'd find me sitting in the bar reading a computer magazine. But I made quite sure I was late and that he was already at the frowning-at-his-watch stage when I showed up.

I had spent some time deciding on and creating a suitable persona before we met. It wasn't hard. Danny had insisted I grew my hair again, but now I drew it back into a tidy, no-nonsense knot, applied careful make-up to tone down the usual clear-eyed healthy glow; modulated my voice to clipped-efficient. I reckoned the effect was clever, reliable and distinctly un-bedworthy, and it was soon clear that Crag Blackmoor had reached a similar conclusion. He was charming, attentive – and showed no hurry at all to meet me again.

But I'd only just begun with him. Where it was all going to lead I had no idea, but how it was all going to end was beyond any doubt.

I set about making myself indispensable. My research skills had clearly impressed and we were in ever more regular contact. Crag was beginning to get commissions from biking magazines, especially in the U.S. and when he let slip how much he loathed having to meet deadlines, I magnanimously offered to help out. So I started a new career in ghost writing. I also began emailing him during his frequent travels with titbits about the latest 'in' places to eat, drink, sleep, with or without a partner.

Then I suddenly announced I'd been approached to do some new work and regretfully would have to withdraw my services in a couple of months time.

"Risky," Danny said, looking over my shoulder as I composed the email. I'd had to work hard to talk him round into grudging support of the whole enterprise.

"I know my Crag," I said.

He replied with the speed of desperation. "For Chrissake, can't possibly cope without you now, Brainbox," and named a figure by way of a retainer that it would have been insane to turn down, even if I had ever had the intention of doing so.

It was some months before we met again. In the meantime *In Memoriam* was completed and made an unexpected impact. It was never going to make the best seller list, but 'the heavies' wrote flatteringly about the author's impeccable research and it became a 'must have' for reference libraries throughout the English-speaking world.

"Clever Brainbox," Crag said when I showed him some of the reviews at that next meeting. But I could see his mind was elsewhere. For this time I had loosened my hair a bit into a bouncy ponytail, adjusted the make up a little, introduced the hint of a drawl.

"You look different," he said, putting a hand over one of mine.

"Do I?" I said, withdrawing it.

----oOo----

High in the evening sky, a turkey vulture circles and is joined by another. And another. Soon there are five.

She gives a small shudder. "Revolting creatures. But fantastic flight."

He follows her gaze, says to the sky "I think I'm falling for you."

She pats his hand. "I'm not your type," she points out. "And don't forget, after all this time, I'm fairly familiar with what your type is. Or should I say types."

"I've changed."

She looks sceptical.

"Well, what's so odd about that? God, no one could have changed more than you. Right little mouse potato when I first met you."

"Thanks."

"I'm serious." She sees that he is. "I can't imagine life without you now."

She looks thoughtful. "OK, we'll talk about it, when we get back."

----oOo----

The next succession of steps was obvious. I gave up the library job, as I was doing more and more ghost writing and it was to everyone's benefit if I became Crag's fellow traveller in the literal sense. By now he was getting showered with freebies, and no one was going to question a minor celeb's need for a companion/p.a. Nor, I guess, would anyone have credited that said p.a.'s duties firmly stopped outside the bedroom door. Crag needed me too much in all other respects to risk jeopardising our working relationship.

In the following years, the world became our oyster as Danny repeatedly put it. As clichés went, it was pretty appropriate. We travelled all over Europe, a swathe of the Far East and did three big trips to the Antipodes.

And then came America. One of their top travel magazines wanted a series to cover all fifty States, a couple each month. Arizona was third on the alphabetic list, and they'd paired it with neighbouring Utah. As always Danny and I did our research very thoroughly, and so we came upon Bryce Canyon National Park. And I knew the time had come.

"They have fabulous national parks over there," I told Crag.

"I leave all the planning to you, Brainbox," he said.

I worked out a dream of a route, starting in Phoenix, where we'd pick up the bike, and make our way gradually north via Grand Canyon and a series of national parks to Salt Lake City. Though it was still early summer, it was hot, hot, hot. Neither Arizona nor Utah legally enforce the use of helmets for bikers over the age of 18, which needless to say Crag thought was really cool; but this wind-in-your-hair stuff is grossly overrated when the wind is straight off the desert and the thermometer is topping a hundred. By the time we crossed into Utah I was wanting out and when I heard about Bryce Canyon, I was pretty sure I'd found the way.

Our hotel was just outside the national park. We took the shuttle bus and reached Inspiration Point on Bryce Canyon's Rim Trail towards late afternoon. There was a still fair scattering of visitors draped in cameras and binoculars; well, these were views almost anyone would be reluctant to leave. They silenced even Crag for a while and he settled beside me in the shade of a pinyon pine while we waited for the worst of the heat to drain out of the day. But I could feel his eyes were as much on me as the view. And I could feel my pulse beginning to race a bit, too.

Then he said "We've missed the last shuttle back to the hotel." And I said "It's not that far to walk," and held out my hand.

----oOo----

He says "I guess this is the moment," and she peers into the viewfinder as he arranges himself elegantly on the cliff edge. "How's that?" His smile is confident. He knows he looks good, blonde hair ruffling slightly in an updraft from the canyon, head slightly on one side.

Later she runs the sequence of events through her head like a video set endlessly on 'repeat'. She remembers saying 'OK, just one more. Let's go for a close-up', and taking a step towards him; but is convinced she does not touch him, though it is her next intention.

She sees him shift into a more theatrical pose, his arms flung out as though he would embrace the world. He blows her a kiss. Then he seems to lean back. Almost as though someone is tugging from behind – only, of course, there is no one. Only space. Though of course they do say that there are more things in heaven and earth.....

118

The smile changes to a look of surprise, then alarm, as he feels his balance begin to go, and that is the last thing she remembers of him: his flailing arms and the shout rising to a scream that shuts off into silence.

She puts the camera carefully down on a rock and goes to the edge; kneels there, gripping a tree stump so she can lean over as far as possible. The heat is like a warm hand on her shoulders.

Nothing seems remotely out of place down there among the debris of immeasurable time. It is just as she had hoped: Bryce Canyon is a hell of a place to lose anything.

THE LOVE CALL

Smithers

Of course, I had heard about that sort of thing. It was rather like 'meeting the Queen', 'seeing a flying saucer', 'winning the lottery'. Very few people had actually experienced it, not many more even knew somebody who had, but oddly nearly everyone knew somebody who knew somebody who had actually experienced it.

It had been a normal enough day on the road in my job as a rep. selling toilet accessories to chemist shops. There were the usual run of successes and failures, and my last call had produced an unexpectedly large order. It had been quite an arduous job, and I was feeling rather pleased with myself. In fact, I was feeling pleased enough to decide that maybe my doubts about Julie were unjustified after all. It's true she had seemed a bit off for some time now. It's also true that I had glimpsed her a couple of times with this guy - certainly younger than me, and some might judge better looking. On the other hand, most couples go through 'iffy' patches. So here was an idea. We'd have an evening out: a really great evening out and I'd surely be able to read the signs as to whether anything untoward was going on. Pulling off the road for a minute, I rang her up to tell her to get her best 'going out' clothes on.

As soon as I had done this, I felt a headache coming on: something I very rarely suffer from. By the time I got home, I was in real pain, and as I walked up the drive I knew that the planned outing was a 'no-go'. I saw the disappointment on her face before she said that she didn't really mind, but she had obviously taken trouble and looked wonderful, in my eyes just as she had done on our first date all those years ago. And she had arranged for her sister Patsy to child sit.

I don't usually take any form of remedy since a good night's sleep seems to be all I need to cure the worst headache. Desperate situations, however, call for desperate remedies. I asked Julie if she had any pain killers, knowing the answer in advance; she took them like children took Smarties. She produced a couple of her 'monthly specials' as she called them, and I took them both right away.

To give them their due, within a few minutes my headache was completely gone, and giving Julie a big kiss, I went upstairs to have a shower and change.

I started to feel a bit queer as I stood naked in the bathroom before stepping into the shower. Luckily I had not locked the door. Why should I? I had nothing to hide from my wife. Anyway, I felt a sudden urge to lie down on the floor and close my eyes. It felt wonderfully relaxing and when, rather reluctantly, I opened my eyes it could not have been more than a few seconds later. To my total astonishment, I found myself on the ceiling.

From this vantage point I saw myself lying naked on the floor. I did indeed look peaceful with a half smile on my face. For some minutes I watched the scene fascinated, until I was aware of it becoming increasingly hazy. Then I found myself walking along a brightly lit corridor not unlike the London Underground, except that it was spotlessly clean. And although I was surrounded by other people of all ages, each one walking in the same direction, there was complete silence. I remember having a feeling of total contentment, even euphoria. Yet, despite this, there was a deep-down sense of unease as if something terrible was about to be taken from me.

All at once, I heard the most piercing scream from behind me, exaggerated by the absolute quiet surrounding us. No one seemed to take any notice. It was as if no one could hear but me. Somewhat reluctantly I felt compelled to investigate. Turning about I retraced my way back along the corridor though, curiously no one seemed to notice that I was now moving in the opposite direction to everyone else. With each step my sense of peace seemed to evaporate and yet, at the same time, there was new twinge of excitement. Finally I was once more looking down at myself lying on the bathroom floor. Julie was crouching beside my body, screaming at the top of her voice, her face contorted with distress. I closed my eyes tightly to shut out the upsetting sight and, when I opened them again, I was looking up at her tear-stained face. As I smiled weakly at her, the door bell rang and soon afterwards the doctor entered the room. He examined me

121

carefully but could find nothing seriously wrong. He suggested that it was probably something I had eaten or that perhaps I had been overdoing things recently, and advised that I should take things easy for a while.

Naturally we had to go without our evening out, but Julie fussed over me in a way that was very pleasing. Fortunately, I was able to re-book the restaurant for the next night, and we had a marvellous time. Nor, since that evening, have I had any cause to revive any doubts about Julie's feelings for me. However, I often wonder what would have happened if I had locked the bathroom door so that Julie did not find me and scream. We joke about the event now, telling our friends how she called me back from death. It's proved a good story to dine out on.

Of course, I told her about my walk along that brightly lit corridor, though not of the hint of reluctance with which I had retraced my steps or that sense of peace gradually declining as I looked down from the ceiling. On the other hand I regularly tell her how deeply glad I am that I did. Deeply glad.

A HERO FOR 2000

Sylvie Nickels

From the check-out next to Cindy's a stage whisper announced "Here he comes, your weekly boy friend!"

Cindy tossed her head of short dark hair, briefly disturbing the lime green streak. But her expression softened. You could set your watch by him each Thursday evening at 6.15. Glancing across to the nearest aisle, between the breakfast cereals and the biscuits, she saw the tall familiar figure: not quite as straight-backed as when she had first noticed him six months ago, though she still always thought of him as a military gentleman. And there was now a special reason for hoping she was right.

That first time, and ever since, he'd had two basket-loads. She was poised between checking through the streaky bacon and a banana yogurt when her scanner went on the blink.

"It could take a while sir," Cindy had said. "If you'd sooner switch to another check-out..."

He grunted "I'm in no hurry."

She noticed the slightly worn cuffs, the neat darn in his jacket. Never good at silences she commented "I'd have thought you'd be better with a trolley than two baskets."

"Oh would you?"

She went on "In fact Thursday evenings is one of our busiest times. The mornings are best, early in the week."

After the smallest pause he said tartly "Do you always shower your customers with unwanted advice young lady?" and she'd felt herself go scarlet. Not a thing Cindy was prone to do, nor stammer as

123

she did then "S-sorry s-sir. Gran's always on about my b-bossiness. So's my boyfriend Jason."

Unexpectedly he'd burst out laughing and agreed "Men don't take kindly to it," adding "But actually your concern is quite refreshing in today's indifferent world."

After that Robert Sinclair came to her check-out every Thursday, always with two basket-loads and a mischievous twinkle in his eye. He was also shopping for a neighbour, liked to keep it separate, he eventually explained. She had gleaned his name and address - Holly House, Bickling - from the pension book he dropped one evening.

There was rarely much time for a chat but Mr Robert, as Cindy now thought of him, always asked after Gran and sometimes about Jason. She told him how Jason was general dogsbody on the local paper though *she* thought he should be on a college course, adding with a grin "OK, so men don't like bossy women."

Occasionally she wondered about him. She guessed he lived alone and this was confirmed one Sunday when a trip out on Jason's motorbike brought them through Bickling village. "Stop!" she yelled in his ear as they came to a large house with a sign which read "Holly House, residential flats for single gentlefolk." She peered over the hedge and saw it was one of those old country-house conversions and found herself wondering if the neighbour he shopped for lived there too.

In answer to Jason's "So what goes on here?" Cindy explained "It's where one of my regulars, Mr Sinclair, lives. Like clockwork he comes, every Thursday evening, 6.15."

"Picking up old men now, eh?" Jason said. "Come here and give us a kiss."

And then his paper began a special series headed *Where are they now?* The boss, according to Jason, had this fixation on World War Two anniversaries. "Reckon it's his way of drumming up readership," Jason said. "A good dose of nostalgia - the oldies love it."

The idea was to trace all sorts of people who had lived in the area and made their mark one way or another in the last hundred years. They published photographs of them from the archives urging readers to help in finding out if any were still living locally; among them were several who had distinguished themselves in some way in the Second World War.

"Can't see the point myself," Jason said. "I mean it's history, isn't it?"

But Cindy was fascinated by old films and the stories Gran had told her, especially of those war days. Then her pulse quickened one day as, among the published archive pictures, she noticed one of a clean shaven young man with the neat short-back-and-sides of the time; and the name under it: Zapper Sinclair.

The text below described how Flight Lt R.E.Sinclair DFC, known as Zapper to his comrades, had won great distinction during the famous Battle of Britain. Later he'd been grounded after multiple wounds received in combat.

Jason peered over her shoulder. "Hey wasn't Sinclair the name of that old boyfriend of yours?"

"Don't be so daft," Cindy said, only later wondering why she felt the need to protect her Mr Robert from the lovable but not exactly over-sensitive man in her life.

Now as Robert Sinclair methodically arranged his purchases on the moving belt of Cindy's check-out she looked at him with new interest. He didn't look a war hero but then what did a war hero look like over 50 years on? She'd put a copy of the local paper by the till.

"That's the rag my Jason works for."

"I'm afraid we don't get it out where I live."

Cindy slid it into his carrier bag. "Have a read."

But in answer to her "What did you think of it?" the following Thursday he merely said "An excellent training ground I would think."

And that's how things might have stayed, only very soon after Jason said more insistently "I suppose that old boyfriend of yours must have been in the war."

Surprised Cindy said "Why?"

He shrugged. "Our photo call's been running out of steam and the boss has got dead keen on this local hero lark. You know, with all this anniversary stuff about the world wars. I told you - it's all about boosting circulation among the wrinklies. I could do with impressing him. How about I come 'n ask the old boy?"

Cindy said quickly "He's more likely to talk to me."

But it was already the beginning of December and time was running out. In a burst of festive indulgence the supermarket management festooned tinsel along the display shelves and dispensed wall-to-wall seasonal muzak. Cindy noticed Mr Robert had added the odd box of chocolates or jar of bath foam to his weekly shop and tried

125

to guess whom they were for. A home-help perhaps? Or a visiting great niece? Somehow she didn't think of him as married with a family of his own. And then what about the lady he did the shopping for, because by now Cindy was determined there had to be a gentle romance in her Mr Robert's life.

Once she nearly reminded him about getting some Christmas wrapping paper and then thought better of it. Just as well because the following week there it was, balanced across one of his baskets: deep red with green sprigs of holly on it. There was also a packet of frozen turkey breast with stuffing, and two mini Christmas puds.

Cindy said approvingly "I see you're well set up for Christmas."

Uncharacteristically Mr Robert looked quite enthusiastic. "An old friend is coming; we haven't met for more years ..." He stopped and smiled "Certainly more years than you can count birthdays for."

Here was her chance. Cindy took a deep breath as she deftly dealt with the contents of his two baskets. "Yeah, I guess it's a time for looking back, isn't it? - what with new and old Millenniums."

Mr Robert went on looking at her, still smiling. "My dear," he said, "The most remarkable thing about the milllennium is that I lived to see it!" And Cindy knew that, in the gentlest possible way, she had been told to mind her own business.

But it would have been useless telling that to Jason.

That last Thursday before Christmas everything happened so quickly it was only later that Cindy was able to get it in some kind of order. She remembered feeling very tired and thinking she never, ever, wanted to hear *Jingle Bells* again. She noticed Mr Robert and his two baskets at almost exactly the same moment she saw Jason come into the store.

Then she saw Mr Robert stumble and crash to the ground. She hurtled out of her check-out to help him and saw Jason vault over an empty counter to join her. She heard Mr Robert say faintly but firmly "Just give me a moment young lady; nothing hurt except my pride," and immediately after Jason's "Excuse me - Mr Sinclair, isn't it? Flight Lieutenant Zapper Sinclair?"

She heard herself say "It's not him you moron. Push off Jason" even as she knew beyond doubt from Mr Robert's expression and the massive scarring revealed by his pushed-up trouser leg that Zapper Sinclair this certainly was.

126

A store supervisor helped him to a seat by the check-out while Cindy gathered up his scattered belongings. Meeting his eye she knew that he knew that she knew - and that what he wanted more than anything else in the world was to leave the past untouched in the privacy of his memory.

She took his hand briefly. "May be now you'll use a trolley," she said.

He grunted "Bossy woman," then gave a small smile. "Better go and make it up with that young man of yours. Which reminds me my girl friend's waiting for me in the cafeteria."

FRIENDLY FIRE

Sammy Birch

Sometimes you could feel drunk with gratitude at being alive, at having survived, and today was one of them. Ahead of Gerald Braithwaite in the formation was Jeffers' Typhoon and four more ahead of that; behind him Bones' brought up the rear. All around them the blue sky pulsated with the sense of victory, the knowledge that at last this damnable war was approaching its end.

Below lay Germany. From 3000 feet it was like a map, its rivers, railways, roads well defined, all of them teeming with life. Well, of course. Everyone was on the move, most of all the Jerries in retreat from all directions, probably shitting themselves in their desperation to get away from the Commies moving in from the east. The bridges over the Elbe had been blown up, so no joy in that direction. And from the south and west the British Army was pretty well unstoppable now. Soon it would all be over and he would be on his way home to his wife, dearest Lily, and his beloved Astra, nearly five and the prettiest kid in the free world. Soon to be the whole world.

"She won't thank us for christening her that," he had warned Lily. But she wouldn't listen. The kid had been conceived in the middle of an air raid when he was home on leave, and the idea of naming her after part of the RAF's motto had become fixed in Lily's head. They said women got funny ideas when they were pregnant, and this was one on which she refused to shift. So Astra it was, with Margaret thrown in as a second name after Gerald's mother.

A voice crackled in his ear. A target had been spotted below and they were going in. Ahead of him he saw the Typhoons point earthwards, one after the other, and followed suit. His head exulted with the noise and the speed and the promise of the future. The earth was approaching, and the network of roads reduced to one, crowded with men, pale blobs of faces turning skywards. They might well shit themselves some more, the buggers. He fired his rockets, pulled back the stick heading back into the sky, noticed with surprise that Bones had broken formation and had headed up and way before any of them.

Bones was almost in tears when they joined up for the debriefing. "Didn't you *see?* That was no retreating army column. That was a straggle of refugees, may be p.o.ws. May be ours."

It was finally confirmed that he was right.

It was nineteen days before the war ended. Gerald never got rid of the memory of those pale blobs of faces turning up towards him.

----oOo----

Jesse Smith mopped up the last of his gravy with a crust of bread – a habit he had acquired from Knuckles – and leaned back in his chair. He ran his tongue over his teeth, felt in his pocket and got out the small gold-sheathed toothpick his father had given him. Knuckles watched him probing for a moment and then said, "Gawd, you don't half have some Nancy ways."

Jesse removed the tooth pick, wiped it carefully on a paper napkin and looked at him. "You said something?"

Knuckles waved a conciliatory hand. "OK Jed, no offence meant."

Jesse grunted, began probing his teeth again. Knuckles couldn't bring himself to call him by his proper name. They had settled for Jed. Jesse didn't mind.

It was a couple of years since the two had met in a bar near Euston Station. Jesse had just got back from several months as a mercenary in a small African republic fighting for a cause he did not understand or much care about. But he was ace at his job and the money was good. He had noticed Knuckles eyeing him for some time and eyeballed him back. After a while Knuckles came over and said, "You looking for a job?"

"Could be."

"I'm looking for someone with a bit of muscle. You look a useful sort of guy. What's your name?"

"Jesse Smith. What's yours?"

Knuckles had stared, started to grin, saw Jesse's expression, thought better of it. "I'll call you Jed," he said. "Most people call me

Knuckles." Glancing down at his companion's beefy hands, Jesse could see why.

It was a construction job, good money, tough conditions in some remote part of the north. "They're a tough gang," Knuckles added.

"I'm tough," Jesse said. He'd been tough since Pa had taught him to handle bullies at that fancy school. They'd laughed at his name, which was also Pa's after Grandpa's greatest buddy, an American, who died in the First World War's trenches. Then Pa had been shot down, taken prisoner of war and got shot at and killed. Just nineteen days before the effing war ended. Things might have turned out differently if he hadn't.

----oOo----

Beyond the fringes of memory Astra reached back for echoes of the fun and giggles as she hid in the garden and Daddy pretended not to know where she was. She would remain hidden for ages and ages until, when she was least on her guard, he would swoop down and scoop her up from behind some shrub or wheelbarrow and, holding her high, twirl round and round until she nearly wet her knickers and Mummy came out protesting he would make her sick. Then he would go away again and she would ask every day when he was coming back until Mummy said crossly "Darling, there's a war on. Daddy is away fighting." She began to wonder if he was fighting this war thing single handedly. Once she asked him, and he put back his head and laughed and laughed.

Then one day he had come home and, when she went to hide in the garden, he did not come looking for her. In the end she went in to find him in the living room reading a newspaper. When she tried to insinuate herself between him and it, he said, "Daddy doesn't want to play at the moment, sweetheart." He had never wanted to play again.

The war ended and still Daddy hadn't cheered up. Once she started at school, it hadn't mattered so much. She had learned to ride a bike, had made friends, had gone out for long bike rides into the country at week-ends. It was then she had noticed how different things were in other people's homes, other kids' Dads sometimes joining in their games or at least asking that question that seemed to preoccupy every adult: *and what do you want to do when you grow up?* What *did* she want to be? Not a teacher, thank you. Not a housewife, not particularly a mum. The only person who didn't ask her was Dad.

130

And yet, and yet. Somewhere on the edge of memory were those echoes of a fun: a Dad who had laughed and come looking for her in the garden, and twirled her high in the air.

"Was Dad always so …. so…." She had not been able to find the right world and ended up with "boring?"

Her mother flared,. "No he was not. He used to be the life and soul of every occasion."

"What happened?"

"The war happened. It changed him almost from one day to the next. He doesn't like to talk about it."

Astra had tried once. "Tell me about the war, Dad. I was too little to remember much."

He had looked up from his book. He was never without a book. "A lot of people killed each other. Some terrible mistakes were made."

"But we won."

"Yes, we won. But it doesn't mean we did not make some terrible mistakes."

"What sort of mistakes?"

"The sort that should never be made again."

But how could you avoid them if you didn't know what they were?

About that time Astra had met her first boy friend. She had her first kiss and wondered what all the fuss was about, but it distracted her from her interest in the war which was fast becoming history. Later she had gone to secretarial college and after that took a job on a magazine in London. Daddy graduated to Dad, and she thought of him throughout those years as an *eminence grise*, monosyllabic for the most part. She could sense the effort he made to share in her pleasure at good exam results, getting a job, her first rise. Occasionally they celebrated with a meal out and Mum chattered non-stop to cover for his silence. It was one Friday when she was at work that Mummy had rung up to say Daddy had had an accident and was in hospital. She had gone home early and then to the hospital with Mummy to find Daddy in intensive care, all strung up with tubes. He had crashed into a tree and died that weekend. She sat beside him for hours and several times he had squeezed her hand. Once he had smiled and whispered "sorry". Then for a moment he had looked like the Daddy she remembered from all those years ago.

Three years later Lily married again. Bob was large and as loud as Dad had been silent. Astra liked him, rather like a favourite uncle, but she couldn't face sharing the same house, thinking of them in Dad's bed. Anyway, it was time she moved on herself. By now she had a job with a glossy county magazine called *Mid Shires* whose offices were in two rooms in a building next door to the library. She found a flat within walking distance and went to a second hand furniture shop to get most of what she needed. She also went up into the attic to see if there was anything she could salvage there, and it was then that she found Dad's diaries. Lily said no, she did not want them as she had moved on into a new life, so Astra took the battered suitcase in which they were contained to her new flat.

By now she had a new boy friend, Mike, the latest of a series. He helped her move in and do some decorating, and eventually moved in too. Her views on sex were much the same as on her first kiss, but it improved with practice. She liked Mike a lot. He was great fun, in fact reminded her a bit of those distant memories of Dad, but so much jocularity got a bit wearing after a while. When he moved out she decided to stay celibate for a while and it was then that she remembered Dad's diaries.

They were notebooks rather than diaries, scrawled in chronological order in the sort of exercise books they used to have at school. He hadn't written daily but in bursts, starting from the time he joined up just a few days after the outbreak of war. He was already married and Lily was pregnant with her. She read in amazement about the enormous amount of fun they managed to pack in to those early war years. How could they have been so unafraid?

She knew mother had been a teacher during the war. She had left Astra with her own mother who lived nearby on her way to school and collected her on the way back. It was a small school for girls. If there had been an air raid during the night, Lily told Astra how the girls had compared bits of shrapnel from anti aircraft shells collected on their way to school. Sometimes lessons were interrupted by air raid warnings and they would all pile into the cellar. Astra thought it sounded a jolly sight more interesting than her school days.

Of course Dad hadn't mentioned any of that in his diary, but he had written about how he felt every time he got back from an operation. He said he felt like God, all powerful and so elated that all he wanted was to go out and do it again.

Whenever he had leave he and Mum would go off into the countryside. As there was no petrol available, they would hitchhike. They had even taken Astra, strapped in a kind of harness on Dad's back, though she couldn't remember that. They had also gone dancing a lot and to one of the three pictures houses in the town. The diary was quite repetitive so after a while Astra started skipping bits. Until, that is, she got to the entry for nineteen days before the end of the war.

----oOo----

After a while Jesse became used to being Jed. Pa would have objected strongly but Pa had long since died on some foreign field. Ma had become senile and was quietly enclosed in her own little bubble. She would not have noticed if he had called himself Jezabel. He saw her as often as he could, joining her in her bubble in the nursing home he paid for now she had used up all the money she had got for her semi in north London. Sometimes she recognised him, more often she did not, but seemed happy to invite him in to whatever fantasy she happened to be living at the time.

"You're good with your mum," Knuckles said. "I'd never have the patience."

He had his own old woman, buxom and jolly, Maisie, and their daughter who was almost a younger clone called May. May had taken a fancy to Jed and Knuckles let it be known he would be glad to welcome him into the family. Their lives had become closely linked. Knuckles clearly regarded Jed as his right hand man in all business negotiations since he had 'a way with words' not to mention 'the right accent'.

They had an import-export outfit for a while and in due course moved into the loan business. Knuckles had a small coterie of brawny youngish men on whom he could call at a moment's notice. Jed refused to have anything to do with strong arm tactics, but he was very good at sweet talking customers into increasing their loans, especially the single Mums to whom he would promise more leeway in return for a night or two of favours.

And then one day Jed was browsing in a charity shop and his eye was caught by the cover of a book showing a picture of a straggling column of prisoners of war. The summary on the back said it was about the great marches many p.o.ws were subjected to towards the end of the war. He bought it for a quid and read it through the night.

The author had researched it by talking to hundreds of survivors from those marches. Jed knew the camp where his father had been, and the date of his death. He read how weary columns of p.o.ws had inched their way first east, then west, across the dwindling map of Germany. He read how one day the p.o.ws were in two parallel columns and one of these had been mistakenly shot up by Typhoons, and fifty killed.

It was nineteen days before the end of the war. The day Pa died.

----oOo----

The entry for April 19th 1945 in the diary of Astra's father was almost illegible, as if he had written it when he was very drunk. In the end she decided this must have been the case. There were few words, many repeated over and over again. *Poor bastards. Just as it's nearly over. Poor bastards. How come only Bones twigged. Poor bastards.* At first she thought some friend of Dad had been shot down and he was appalled it should have happened so close to the end of the war. But it didn't really make sense. And who was Bones, and what had he twigged? Finally, she understood that Bones had twigged they were mowing down some of their own.

The next entries of the diary were even more terse. Sometimes just a word: *haunted.* Occasionally there was a scrawled reference to nightmares of pale faces. A longer more coherent entry described how Bones had been hospitalised with a nervous breakdown.

Astra rang her mother. "Did Dad know someone called Bones? Someone in his squadron?"

Lily said straight away, a laugh in her voice, "Yes, a lad called John Bowman. Everyone called him Bones because he was so skinny. Very serious." She paused. "I think he was invalided out with a nervous breakdown. Not sure your father wasn't on the verge of one himself. He was really very odd after the war. I often wondered... " She broke off.. Why do you ask?"

"Something in Dad's diary. Nothing serious."

There followed a gap of several weeks in the diary. Then Gerald Braithwaite wrote a long and obviously carefully considered entry. From it Astra understood that the nightmares from which he had suffered were connected with pale blobs representing the faces looking up as the Typhoons hurtled town towards them and let loose their rockets. Each blob seemed to trigger a fresh nightmare peopled by strangers connected with a blob. Gerald, clearly convinced he was

134

going mad, had consulted a doctor who diagnosed him as suffering from post-war trauma. He had prescribed some pills, the equivalent of modern tranquillisers, which blotted out the nightmares but made him feel like a zombie. The doctor suggested a psychiatrist but Dad was of the stiff-upper-lip generation which sorted out its own problems.

Lily tried to draw him out but was of the same generation so that when he spoke of being stricken by guilt for the deaths he had caused, she reassured him that death was what happened in war and he must put it behind him and move on. Finally, in desperation, he tracked down Bones.

"He's just beginning to get a modicum of peace of mind," Bones' wife warned. "Please don't stir it all up again."

But Gerald's diary recorded that Bones had seemed remarkably together and quite obdurate in his refusal to discuss that morning nineteen days before the end of the war. He'd been to hell, he said, and was now on his way back. He could only recommend that Gerald did what he had done. It meant psychiatrists. For whatever reason, Gerald couldn't.

The diary ended about a year before her father's accident. Astra consulted her memory focussing on key events in her life when Dad had been around: exam results, job promotions, broken relationships. All she could remember was her mother's chatter to cover her father's silence. Until the accident. Accident? Or had he just given up the struggle with the pale blobs of his nightmares? Had that quiet "sorry" been for something other than just being a silent Dad?

----oOo----

It took a while for it to sink in: that Pa's death and the friendly fire were on the same day and that one could have resulted from the other. As the idea took shape, glowing embers of resentment grew to flaming anger. He had looked up to his father, adored him. It was Pa who had taught him how to stand up for himself. With the abrupt removal of his role model he had concentrated on consolidating his ability to be self sufficient. Then came the army. He did well. Some of his peers recognised in him the potential that would make for a good career as a mercenary. They hadn't sussed out that softer side that Pa had stressed was so important to make you a really strong person, but he had developed cunning as well as strength and it wasn't too difficult to find a way of opting out of the messier aspects of some assignments. And when it became too difficult, he simply opted out of the mercenaries. It was soon after that he met Knuckles.

And now he learned that the loss of Pa was probably down to some trigger happy moron within days of the end of the war.

The thought began to dominate his days.

"What's up Jed?" Knuckles asked on several occasions.

"Something on my mind."

"Then for Gawd's sake get it off. You're a right Jeremiah. Take May out and give her a good time."

He had done what he was told. May could take your mind off anything and after a night in her bed he wondered what the fuss had been about, though by lunch time the thought was back, and he knew it would stay there until he did something.

The next time he went to see his mother, he probed gently: how had Pa died in the war. It was one of her more lucid days. "Telegram," she said. "I got a telegram saying he was reported killed. April, 1945." No more than that, he'd asked? "Later," she said. "Later they said it was some place in Germany. Funny name like something in the kitchen. I never found it on the map."

He started on some research. There was amazing stuff of the internet and he followed leads in the wildest directions. Through the War Graves Commission web site he found that Pa had been re-interred in a big war cemetery in Berlin. The web site for that said that many of those buried had been prisoners of war marched out of the camps as the Russians approached from the east. He wondered why Ma hadn't had Pa brought home, but by then Ma was starting to be odd. He reckoned she had never got over Pa's death either. Further enquiry yielded the information that the original internment had been a mass grave in a place called Gresse. Gresse … grease…. something in the kitchen?

OK, so he had confirmed the time and place of the friendly fire and Pa's death were identical, and even where it had happened. He went to the library and went through several atlases until he found the place: in tiny print about 20 miles east of the Elbe, near a place called Lauenburg. Now all he need was to know who. He emailed the RAF Museum and had a sympathetic response, but all they could tell him was that seventeen squadrons of Typhoons had been operating over Germany at the time. Seventeen! It was suggested that he approach the National Archives who would have the records of each squadron. And would such records admit to friendly fire?

And then Knuckles had a crisis and it went out of his mind. Several years later Jed had married May and had first a daughter and, two years later, a boy. They called him Jesse despite Knuckles' protests. And then one day, aged eleven, the child demanded to know what had happened to Grandpa.

"He died in the war," Jed told him. But he didn't add it was only nineteen days before it ended.

----oOo----

At 28, Astra moved in with Roy soon after he was appointed advertising manager of *Mid Shires*. She had told Roy about Dad and the friendly fire, but after initial interest he expressed the view it was an obsession she had to rein in or she risked becoming a war bore. Only Astra found she couldn't and by the time she was 30 Roy had moved out. She was making him feel claustrophobic, he said, and anyway he wanted to try his luck in London. It was true that Astra's obsession only increased with time. Though she did not have her father's nightmares, she inherited the pale blobs which intruded as soon as her mind was not especially occupied and even sometimes when it was. She did not visualise the strangers connected with each of them, but she tried to imagine them and in what way they had been affected. It seemed you could inherit the sins of your father.

The intrusion of the pale blobs continued to affect her relationships. Roy had left her with the flat and in it she was successively joined by Eric, Bill and Nathan. In between Eric and Bill, she took a posting overseas with V.S.O. for several years working in different schools in a number of locations in Africa. On her return, during Bill's tenure, she wrote a book about her African experiences. It didn't make much money but established her reputation as a practising liberal. It was about then that she glimpsed herself in a shop mirror and noted with a small shock that she had slipped, unawares, into middle age. Following Bill, Nathan lasted the longest – nearly five years, in fact, - as he had a penchant for 20th century military history and initially an interest in the fate of Astra's Dad. But her pale blobs were not part of history and in due course indulgence gave way to irritation and eventually to his departure. Her mother gave up exhorting that it was high time she settled down.

In due course Astra followed many of the same leads as Jed and acquired the same information with the same gaps. Trawling through the list of those buried in the Berlin cemetery she made a list of all those who had died on the relevant date. Some of them came from Canada, Australia or New Zealand, but most were listed as Royal Air Force Reserve. Usually the name of the parents and wife of each were given, and the town where they lived. Astra made a list of all the wives and then checked the electoral list of the towns concerned. One of them was named Smith which inevitably produced a large number of links. Some had remarried, some moved away, some simply disappeared but she eventually had a list of half a dozen wives and a couple of elderly parents.

It was surprisingly easy to dispose of the wives. Astra's standard opening was "I'm really sorry to trouble you, but I'm trying to trace relatives of a friend of mine who died in World War Two. Name of Jesse Smith."

The usual response was "Sorry I've not heard of her."

"Not her, him. Jesse was a man."

There was inevitably a pause then a faintest hint of amusement in the concluding "No, I'd certainly remember a man called Jesse. Sorry I can't help."

Which left a couple of elderly parents: a man in his nineties living alone in Oxfordshire and an old woman in a home in Norfolk. The man's home was a cottage near the village of Deddington in north Oxfordshire, just a few miles away. Astra checked in at one of the local pubs. A cheery barmaid knew quite a lot about Jimmie Smith. "Comes in like clockwork, two minutes passed six every evening, has a couple of halves, then goes home again."

Astra was waiting for him, watched him for a while exchanging witticisms with a youngster in his seventies. When the other man had gone, she approached him. "Jimmie Smith?"

He'd looked up, studied her for a moment, then said "It's a while since a handsome wench was asking after Jimmie Smith."

Astra smiled dutifully. "I just wondered if you were related in any way to Jesse Smith who died in 1945?"

The old man put his glass down. "Who wants to know?"

"I'm the daughter of a friend of his."

Jimmie Smith grunted. "Jesse was my brother. We never saw eye to eye, but no one deserves to die like that. Amy, his missus never got over it."

Amy Smith, the last name on her list, the old girl in a nursing home.

Jimmie picked up his glass, had a sip, put it down again. "In a nursing home she is." He tapped his head. "A bit doo-lally poor old

138

girl. I reckon it started with Jess' death. Just nineteen days before the end of the war, it was."

----oOo----

That day Jed approached his mother's room from the garden entrance. He was in time to see a strange woman come out of the room and disappear down the corridor. A member of staff was seeing to his mother, settling her into her chair with a cup of tea on the table beside her.

"Who was that?" he asked. "That woman who just left?"

"I don't know, dear. She said she'd come to see Mrs. Amy Smith, but I told her that Amy wasn't well enough to see anyone at the moment and she said she would come back another day."

Jed strode back along the hall, down the stairs to reception and demanded to know who the woman was who had visited his mother. The girl scrabbled among the papers on her desk and produced a visiting card: Astra Braithwaite, researcher, he read, and underneath an address in Banbury, Oxfordshire. Astra – what kind of name was that? Wasn't it something to do with the stars? *Per ardua ad astra* Pa's voice suddenly boomed in his head. Of course, the R.A.F. motto. Somehow that seemed to clinch things.

He rushed to the door, saw the tail end of a plum-coloured Audi receding down the drive.

He went back to the receptionist. "So what did she want>?"

"Something to do with your father, Mr. Smith. She said she thought she knew someone who was connected with him."

Yeah, too much of a coincidence.

That Spring, Jed suggested they start going for country drives.

"Do we have to go so far?" protested May, as they regularly headed for the M40.

Jed pointed out that the Cotswolds was a beautiful area and the children would love it. Sadly the children were soon bored by picturesque villages, venerable churches and old pubs where they weren't allowed to run about. They weren't even very impressed by the splendours of Blenheim Palace or the fact that Winston Churchill had been born there. But Jesse became very excited by the lake and the flotillas of ducks on it. So Jed did some more research and found the wildlife park at Burford, and some farms open to the public.

Gradually he widened their range until Banbury s started appearing on the signposts.

"There's someone around here I want to look up," he told May.

Astra Braithwaite's cottage was on the outskirts of the town in a suburb that had no doubt once been a separate village. They parked across a patch of green. After a while Jesse asked impatiently why they were just sitting there?

"Daddy know someone who lives in that cottage," May explained.

"That lady coming out?" asked Jesse. And as the woman walked briskly away from them, Jed recognised her as the woman who had visited Ma's room. She looked older than he remembered, perhaps ten years his junior.

"So why are we just sitting here?" Jesse asked again.

"I want an ice cream," said Jesse's sister.

"Let's go and find one then," Jed said.

After that, the family outings dwindled. Maisie said she was too busy, the children expressed no opinion and Jed preferred to go on his own, sometimes parking for long periods outside Astra Braithwaite's house. He still hadn't worked out what he intended to do. How do you approach somebody whose father may have killed yours nineteen days before the end of a war?

It was Astra's neighbour who noticed Jed's car first. She was a noticing sort of person when it came to local happenings. "Perhaps you are being stalked," the neighbour suggested. But Astra knew she was not the sort of person that anyone would stalk. All the same, now she had had her attention drawn to it, she noted the make and number of the car, and its occupant. The latter was a well built, rather good looking man, probably well into his sixties. Once or twice he brought a rather buxom lady and a couple of young children with him. She thought they were his grandchildren until the little boy called him Dad. Usually, though, he was alone.

One day she saw the same vehicle leaving the pub car park as she was going in.

"Hi Astra," the landlord greeted her. "There was a fellow in just now asking after you. Left his card."

She read 'Jed Smith, import/export', and an address in Swindon. So why hadn't he come knocking on her door?

But there was nothing now to stop her knocking on his. And she knew what she wanted to say. She wanted to say Jed's Dad should never have died; that his death in a way had killed hers. She wanted to get the pale blobs out of her head.

May, taking a breather from her weeding in the front garden, noticed the Audi parked across the road. At the same time she noticed Jesse surreptitiously letting himself out through the front gate, pushing his bike. He knew damned well he was not allowed to cycle on the main road yet.

"Jesse!" she called, and then more urgently, "**Jesse!**"

The boy was clamped to the i-Pod they had given him for his twelfth birthday. Of course he couldn't hear her, any more than he would hear the traffic coming up behind.

"*Jesse! Jesse!!*" screamed May, bringing Jed hurtling out of the house.

Jesse had his bike on the edge of the kerb, had swung one leg over, one foot resting on the offside pedal.

A woman had come out of the Audi, was crossing the road towards them. She started yelling "*Jesse*", too. Then, as the boy began to move off, oblivious of the white van fast approaching from behind, she hurled herself in front of it, knocking Jesse to the pavement.

In a moment the boy was sobbing in his mother's arms. Assured that he was all right, Jed went to kneel down on the kerb where the woman's head was just visible. There was a lot of blood and the van driver saying over and over again "Came from nowhere….didn't stand a chance…."

Her voice was so quiet that he only just distinguished "So sorry about your Dad."

Jed reached down and held her head gently. "You saved my boy. Oh God. It wasn't supposed to happen like this."

She gave a little smile and said something that it was even more difficult to understand. It sounded like "pale blobs" and then, with a gasp of relief, "gone". She was probably hallucinating, poor woman. He stayed there, holding her head, until the ambulance came.

REACHING OUT

Olive Hill

She was in the kitchen cutting up peppers for a *ratatouille* when the doorbell rang. Culinary work was proving one of the better therapies for being dumped.

"Sugar," Alison said, followed by a silent monologue. *If only they would leave me alone. It's got to the point where I hardly dare leave the cottage for fear of bumping into Jill ('how about a coffee and a chinwag?') or Georgina (' have you thought some more about joining our reading group?')*

The associated '*it will help take your mind off things*' was never stated but patently implied. Damn Darrell.

From the end of the hall she could see the frosted glass over the top of the front door. Well, it was a male-shaped head, so that was a blessing. The head disappeared as the letterbox was pushed open and a voice said, "You there, Alison? This won't take long."

It was Sim Johnson who did the computer courses at the library. "Hang on, just washing my hands," she called and went to turn the taps on in the kitchen.

Sim had been looking after a terminally ill partner before she died a few weeks ago. Alison had noticed them soon after they moved into the village a year or so earlier. Well, it was difficult to miss them. Amanda was already in a wheelchair and Sim was always at her side. Otherwise they kept themselves pretty much to themselves. Sim was a big, broad man, and Alison had been struck by his gentleness; Amanda did water colours and was good at them.

In those days Alison had been very much part of the social scene herself, and they had all speculated about Sim's job.

"Builder?" Jill suggested.

"Handyman," offered Georgina. "I could do with someone to put up a shed." Georgina could always do with someone to put up or pull down something

It turned out he was a computer wizard, mostly working from home, designing websites. Then he began Computing-for-the-Terrified classes in the library. Alison, though not terrified, had gone to a few to polish up on desktop publishing. Darrell had fancied himself as a computer nerd but was too impatient as a teacher. Sim, on the other hand, was very patient and Alison looked forward to the lessons. She missed them when Amanda's condition deteriorated and Sim stopped the classes.

By then she and Darrell were an item, the sort that she had truly thought would remain an item forever. Yes, she knew he was married, but he had totally convinced her that it had gone wrong for both of them ages before. Shelagh, his wife, ran a small art gallery in a desirable little market town in the Home Counties. She had a partner whom Darrell suspected did not limit his affairs to the business variety. Though they had never put it into so many words, Alison took it for granted that she and Darrell would formalise their lives together sooner rather than later. In the meantime they had opened an arty shop in the village and moved in together in the small flat above it. Alison had kept on the cottage, as much because it had been left to her by her parents and it was stuffed with memories. But her commitment to Darrell had been total. So total that, encouraged by him, she had retired from a string of community involvements which he said took her away from him.

"Can't you see this place is gobbling you up!" he'd said more than once, and Alison had begun to notice how claustrophobic it could seem. And he'd been marvellous at finding new things to do as they rushed off round the countryside visiting art exhibitions and artists and 'finding out what life's all about'.

Then he had started going up to London to see this or that person, initially for the day, then overnight and gradually staying away longer. There was always a good reason to do with building up their reputation, networking, checking out this or that new name. Then she had found a photograph of him and Shelagh in his wallet, raising glasses to each other in a bar. There was a clock giving the date hanging on the wall It was a very recent photograph indeed.

When she had challenged him he had not attempted to make excuses. He and Shelagh had coincided at some art exhibition, had a drink together, she had asked him for advice on some show she was promoting, and it had gone on from there. And finally it came out. They were going to try and make a go of it again together.

"But we can stay friends, can't we?" Darrell said. Was he really that thick?

At the time of Amanda's death and funeral, Alison had been floundering at the bottom of a black hole. It was the week after Darrell had left. Alison had moved back into the cottage and lost herself in a frenzy of redecoration and gardening.

Now, as she let him in, Sim said "It may well not be your sort of thing. It's just that a mate of mine is organising a willow sculpture workshop on Saturday."

"Willow sculpture?" she repeated blankly.

"Yes, making shapes from willow whips, that sort of thing. The general idea is that we should learn enough to run our own workshop at next summer's festival. The guy who's running it is offering a special rate of seven people for the price of six."

"Like loo rolls."

"Mm, something like that. We did have seven. People, not loo rolls; but someone's had to drop out and it's short notice to fill the gap."

"OK." Well, it was something different and she had to rejoin the world some time. "Do you want a coffee?"

Sim shook his head. "Things to do, I'm afraid." Sim always had things to do, usually rescuing people with ailing computers. Perhaps it was his way of coping with loss.

It was arranged that they should travel in two cars. Georgina was going with three from the PTA, Sim said he would take Jill and Alison.

As it turned out, Jill was a good person to make up the third in the carload as she did not stop talking. Mostly it was about the forthcoming village festival on whose committee she was a prominent member. It was agreed that there was real talent in the village, mostly of the musical kind. At least two people were professionals – an oboist and a violinist - retired from major orchestras in other parts of the country. They had an excellent choir, an up-and-coming composer. Then there was the art group, one of whom had been hung in the Royal Academy. And there was Jill herself who was no mean cook and was featured on a local television programme entertaining a group of celebrities in her own home.

"What about you, Sim?" Alison managed when Jill at last paused for breath.

But before he could answer, Jill was already informing her that the festival would collapse if it were not for Sim's skills in ensuring the sound systems were working in the church, setting for most of the concerts, and the lighting system in the village hall, venue for the art exhibition not to mention sundry craft displays. By the time she had finished, they had reached the venue for the workshop. Several other groups had already arrived and settled in various parts of a large shed. Their mentor led them to an empty area, showed them the various bundles of willow whips, explained briefly what to do, demonstrated some knots and then left them to it.

The whips seemed to have a life of their own as Alison tried to exercise control over them. Around her murmurs of protests faded into silence of concentration. Glancing round after a while she saw recognisable shapes emerging before hunched figures.

She looked up to find Sim watching her. "You're good at this," he said, a statement, not a question. "But of course you ran that arty place for a while, didn't you?"

Dangerous ground. Alison concentrated on weaving the end of a whip into the circle which formed the right ear of the bear she was creating.

"What happened to that fellow – can't remember his name. The one that used to work for you?" *Not an assessment that would have pleased Darrell.*

"Oh he and his wife moved away from the area."

"Ah. So what's happening to the shop? Sometimes when we were passing, I'd peer in and Amanda would remind me that I'd once been rather keen on water colours and stuff."

"Really?"

"No I wasn't any good, though Amanda was really clever at water colours. I just liked the idea of capturing moments, so you could make 'em last forever, bring 'em out and dust your memories. Amanda expanded from painting into arts and crafts, especially after she fell ill. She was ace at making things: rag dolls, puppets. And tapestry. She said they were what kept her sane. I remember us on country outings: me with my art block, Amanda with a bagful of bits and pieces. I guess that's what I wanted to capture, some of those good moments. Silly really."

It was the longest speech she had ever heard him make. "Not silly at all. It's how a lot of artists feel." Well, Darrell hadn't. He was into post-post-Modernism and you needed to be a mental Houdini to try and grasp what he was getting at. But fair enough. She returned her attention to her work in progress, deftly twisting a frond of willow to anchor her bear's right ear.

"I used to have bear," Sim said unexpectedly. Alison found herself pressing her lips together to suppress a grin. He looked at her severely. "Now you're laughing at me. It's because I look large and tough."

"Not 'at you, but with you'. I have a bear too. Mother gave him away once - thought I was too grown up for such a thing. And then had to rescue him because I was so upset. He only has one eye and one ear is almost, off despite her best efforts.."

"A bear after my own heart." Sim touched her shoulder briefly and then moved off. She noted he spent a lot of time talking to each member of the group, but an especially long time with Georgina who always managed to seem the odd one out. He was that sort of nice person who would want everyone to feel included.

They had a break for lunch, and admired each other's handiwork. The most popular choice of subject proved to be a bird, and handsome many of them were too, if sometimes a bit wobbly-legged. Jill had gone for a kind of cage rising out of a basket from which you could train a trailing plant.

It was Jill who demanded "And how about you, Sim?"

"I'm just the chauffeur." But they would not let him get away with that and finally, sheepishly, he produced from behind a partition something tall and gangling.

"It's another bird," Jill pronounced.

"An ostrich someone suggested.

"An emu," said someone else.

But no bird had a head and neck like these.

"It's a giraffe," Alison said, and Sim's grin confirmed she was right.

Everyone agreed it had been a great day out. Alison could not remember a time when she had gone so many hours without fuming about Darrell.

It had been decided that the Festival willow workshop would be held in the gardens of the old people's home. On the following day there would be an organised walk down to the local Millennium wood, with optional picnic, and the results of the willow workshop would be scattered about the wood with a prize for the one voted the best. Alison planned to place her bear in a tree.

Sim had made himself responsible for ordering the bundles of willow whips needed for the workshop, and when she offered to collect them from their source in the next county he said it was okay, Georgie had already said she would do it. Georgie?

During the run up to the festival, life suddenly became busy. Whether Sim had put the idea into her head, or whether it had been there all the time, Alison decided to reopen the shop but broaden the focus to arts and crafts generally. Jill's Mum who headed the county arts and crafts association was almost overwhelming in her enthusiasm and advice, not to mention her contacts who filled Alison's answering machine and email box with recommendations of what she should stock and where she should obtain it. Alison planned to reopen the shop during the Festival.

The willow workshop was planned for the first week-end of the festival. Sim set it up on a fortuitously fine day and by lunchtime the gardens of the old people's home were buzzing. The kids from the primary school were the most enthusiastic, producing a preponderance of fish and caterpillars. Some of the fish acquired a mast and scrap of material and turned into yachts. Birds were popular and of amazing variety and proportions. Sim wandered from creator to creator looking increasingly satisfied.

"How about a willow craft section in the shop," he said to Alison as she helped a 12-year-old with a particularly recalcitrant peacock's tail.

Why not? She could establish a supply with the growers. She could even start a class in basic willow sculpting. She began filing away in the back of her mind various ideas for further thought. For the moment the appeals of "Please Miss, what do I do now?" or "Allie, give us a hand with this," had her scuttling all afternoon. There was hardly time to notice anything else, except that Georgie was doing a lot of scuttling too: a new Georgie, brisk, confident as she kept an ever-growing record of everyone's creations and provided labels by which to identify them when they were set up in the Millennium Wood later. Once she saw Georgie and Sim absorbed in discussion and felt a twinge of envy. Georgie was gesticulating and animated in a way Alison had never seen before. It reminded her of her early days with Darrell. Darrell. She hadn't thought of him for days.

Next day the walk to the Millennium Wood gathered momentum as it proceeded through the village. Many people came as families, some with dogs, most with picnics. Sim and Georgie had made a great job of displaying the willow sculptures, and the wood rang with excited cries as youngsters found their creations and showed them off. Alison found her bear jauntily perched in the fork of an ash tree. She settled beneath it with her picnic, feeling a surge of contentment at the success of the event and a sense of belonging she had not had for a long time.

"It's great news about Georgie, isn't it?" Sim's voice said from above her.

"What about Georgie?"

"She's been offered a place on some posh estate in the Midlands. Overseeing a new garden centre."

"Good Lord."

"No, not surprising. She has really good ideas when you can excavate your way through the layers of diffidence."

Alison thought for a while. "And you're good at that, aren't you? Getting under people's skin." She stopped, laughed as she realised what she had said, added, "In the nicest possible way, of course."

Sim grinned back. "Yeah, you could put it that way. Mandy used to call me an interfering so-and-so."

"Mandy? Oh, Amanda. I've never heard you call her that before."

He looked wry. "It was strictly forbidden when we were kids. She could shorten my name to Sim, but then Mandy was an angel and could always get away with anything as far as Ma and Pa were concerned."

Alison found she was staring at him, open-mouthed, got herself under control. Ma and Pa? Sim and Mandy were brother and sister?

But Sim was still talking. "I came to agree with them when our parents were wiped out in an accident. Mandy just took over. She was only a couple of hours older than me, but she always did get the hang of things quicker than I did. Well, girls do grow up more quickly, don't they?"

148

Alison murmured something noncommittal, then managed "How old were you?"

"Twelve, rising thirteen. I don't think I'd have survived those years on the farm without her."

"On the farm?"

"We were sent to an aunt and uncle in the north. The farm was OK, spectacular hill setting. But aunt and uncle were dire. They'd a hard life and didn't see why it should be different for us."

"So what happened?"

"After school, Mandy did a business studies course, I went in for computer technology, so we started a desktop publishing service: fliers, cards, posters, booklets." He paused. "Then she started dropping things, losing her balance." He paused again. "It was payback time."

Alison found there was a lump in her throat. "What a wonderful relationship."

"Mm. Mandy had a man in a her life for a bit, but he soon disappeared when she fell ill." He stopped. "Sorry, I have been rabbiting on. And it looks as though people are clearing up."

He was right. Picnickers were folding blankets, stowing away remains of food. A couple of the team were touring the site with plastic bags, picking up rubbish.

Sim pushed fingers through his brown thatch of hair. "We'd better give a hand." He began to stride away, paused, turned. "I've got some ideas for the shop opening next week: things you might think of stocking, and courses you might run. I have a few contacts that might be useful. That's if you don't think I'm interfering. Fancy a drink and a bite when we've finished?"

"Yeah," Alison said. "I rather think I would."

AVALANCHE IN NEPAL

George Spenceley

The 1950s have been described as the Golden Age of Himalayan
Mountaineering when, after many attempts, Everest had at last been
climbed in 1953, followed two years later by Kangchenjunga. Other
countries were also active in the Himalayan ascents by men of much
experience who had already proved themselves at high altitude. But
the Himalayas is a vast range with a wealth of lesser unclimbed peaks,
lower in altitude if not less in difficulty. It was at the Y.R.C. Annual
Dinner of 1955 that the idea of a Club expedition took root when
Charles Evans, recently returned as leader of the successful
Kangchenjunga expedition, was in conversation with Crosby Fox.
With Crosby's enthusiasm and with the full encouragement of the then
President Harry Stembridge, the plan for a Y.R.C. Himalayan
Expedition was formed. It was not appreciated at the time this was to
be the first Himalayan Expedition to be sponsored by a club.

The team finally selected was Crosby Fox as leader, a position
fully merited. I was appointed deputy, less for my mountaineering
ability, more for my recent expedition experience and glacier travel.
The team was completed by Wilfred Anderson as secretary, Dan
Jones, the medical officer, and finally Arthur Tallon and Maurice
Wilson. For the objective of the expedition, Charles Evans was
consulted and Jugal Himal in Nepal, a little to the east of the Langtang,
was his suggestion. It was a little known area, unclimbed and visited
only once by an earlier expedition. More interesting, among some
mountains of considerable difficulty, the highest of the group, a peak
of 23,240 ft. in altitude, situated on the Nepalese-Tibetan border,
seemed an attainable objective. At the time of the expedition,

150

although its height had been calculated it lacked a name, but the Sherpas called it the 'Big White Peak'. It has subsequently been called Lanpo Gang and has now been climbed by a Japanese expedition.

The financing of the expedition was a major hurdle for the cost far exceeded the modest donations of the participants, but by the generosity of the club and some of its members, together with a substantial donation from the Mount Everest Foundation, a sufficient sum was raised. Further assistance was received from a national newspaper and various industries. Much of the food and equipment was donated free or at cost price.

On 16th March 1957, the expedition members together with club well wishers gathered in London for an early flight the next morning from a diminutive Heathrow. We walked out across the tarmac to our twin-engine piston B.O.A.C. aircraft for our flight to Calcutta. To compare it with my recent jet age flights, it is well worth recording the six refuelling stops. They were Frankfurt, Rome, Istanbul, Baghdad, Bahrain and finally Karachi where there was a change of crew. We were an exhausted party when we disembarked thirty-six hours later in the heat and dirt of Calcutta where we were welcomed by members of the Yorkshire Society who were to be our hosts.

From our Base Camp there stretched ahead a long line of steep and unstable moraine which would lead to the foot of the Phurbe Chyachumbu Glacier which would become the highway to our peak. A tedious but safe route was established along it, leading to Camp I, a noisy place with much creaking of the glacier. It was at two points along the moraine that the terminals of the base line were established for survey was much in our mind. It was this responsibility that occupied the time and efforts of Anderson and myself in those early days, by establishing two survey spots on the rocky ridge to the west of Base Camp overlooking the Dorje Lhakpa Glacier. It was desperately hard work for we were far from being acclimatised to the altitude.

Meanwhile Crosby Fox, good leader that he was, had drawn up a plan of operation for the following two weeks, allowing us to move up the glacier in three parties with our Sherpas, stocking and restocking each camp up to Camp IV. The plan of operation allowed the maximum lift to the greatest height without imposing undue strain and allowing time for acclimatisation.

151

Camp III, lying under the shadow of Phurbi Chyachu, was established at about 19,000 ft. by 26th April, and through much gruelling work in the next few days was adequately provisioned. After an earlier reconnaissance, Crosby Fox and I, with our two Sherpas Mingma Tensing and Lakpa Noorbu, set out to establish Camp IV from where we hoped to climb to the site which we hoped would be our final camp. Dan Jones and Arthur Tallon came up in support.

It was cold as well as the altitude that in the morning numbed our senses. It took us an hour with well gloved hands to scrape the tents free of the ice that had formed during the night and to make up the loads for the new camp. We were away at 7.15 a.m. on two ropes of four, Jones and Tallon with their Sherpas on one rope, Lakpa Noorbu, Mingma Tensing with Fox and myself on the other. The tracks of yesterday were almost obliterated and for the man in front it was desperately hard work. At 8 a.m. we were out of the shadow of the frontier ridge where we removed sweaters and gloves and briefly basked in the sun. We had gained perhaps a thousand feet of height.

The route was straight-forward but not without interest for we were now threading a way through a mass of intricate crevasses and the slope was steeper than any before encountered. It was satisfying to look back at the two tiny specks of Camp III on the level glacier.

At last we reached 'the Corridor', a level and uncrevassed highway. Now we could see the problem ahead. Beyond the point where we would pitch Camp IV the glacier abruptly narrowed and flowed between walls of fantastic steepness – it could be described as the jaws of the glacier. They might not be the jaws only but the fangs too, for here the glacier became steeper and more broken up, the whole area split by crevasses. We knew then that we should be lucky to find between these walls a route free from objective danger. But that was tomorrow's problem; now we had thought only for the soft snow and our overburdened backs and the release soon to come at the end of 'the corridor'.

Another hour or so, punctuated by many halts, brought us the release. 'the corridor' which had safely conducted us above the lower difficulties of the icefall had petered out and here the glacier mounted to its height. Close by, where there was little else but seracs and great chasms, was a level bed of snow adequate for our camp. We might have preferred a site a little further removed from the bounding wall, but we were on a slight rise and were additionally protected by a series of open and wide crevasses. We had little cause for fear. Wishing us

152

luck, our support party left us alone hurried down to Camp III. Soon the tents were up and the Primus roaring to give us hot lemonade for which we most longed. Already the weather was deteriorating.

The next day, April 30th, dawned clear, gone were the troubled skies and the wind. We were out of tents just as soon as it was light. It did not take us long to gather the survey equipment; on this reconnaissance we needed to take little else. From the tents we moved round a serac more centrally into the glacier. We could see the jaws, but standing below them, all was too foreshortened to see the problem. We could not plan our route, we could but progress upwards hopefully, taking the least tortuous route, avoiding the bounding walls. We were still in shadow and it was extremely cold. For several hundred feet we mounted keeping safely in the centre of the glacier. There were crevasses in plenty but so far they were bridged in some part of their length, although but thinly.

We were slow too for another reason; we were higher than we had been before, there was soft snow and Fox for the first time was troubled by altitude. It was this last that caused me to take over the lead somewhere through the icefall, a position I was to keep for the remainder of the day. Fox now came second, to give me security over the fragile bridges. For a little way more we climbed, moving in a zig-zag pattern, but safely in the centre of the glacier. But this was too good to last; suddenly we came to a series of large crevasses, unbridged and unbridgeable, spanning the greater width of the glacier.

There was one way round them, easy and short on the true left bank of the glacier. But here where we proposed to turn them, we were for perhaps ten minutes in the ascent exposed to the possibility of an ice avalanche from a series of ice cliffs high above. We turned the crevasses and in ten minutes we were once more central in the glacier. We did it quite casually, time was not wasted nor did we desperately hurry; we may have cast the occasional glance up at the seat of danger but we suffered no strain or great anxiety of mind. The odds were too heavily in our favour. Soon we were close to the summit of the icefall, only a few crevasses remained, and for a while it seemed that things were going our way.

What faced us now was a weary plod which was to continue for four hours. Distance had again deceived us. It always appeared that a few yards more and the angle would level out; it never did. Our pace was slow; we were all conscious of the altitude and the soft snow did not help. Fox remarked that never before had he suffered such a

153

hard mountain day. We seemed to be immensely high; Phurbi Chyachu, which soared so majestically above the Base Camp, appeared from here quite insignificant. Over the col to the north of it we could now look, and beyond it in Tibet, were noble unknown peaks. In front, obscured partly by its eastern ridge was the 'Big White Peak'. There was nothing in its appearance to suggest defeat and no longer did it fill us with awe as when first we saw it, as an aloof, utterly remote triangle of snow.

Still we plodded on but at last the angle did relent. If we were to survey, then we must do so while we could. It was 11 a.m. and for half an hour we worked in this cwm of great peaks until deteriorating weather put an end to our task. We lingered there no longer, the wind was rising and we were glad of an excuse to leave.

A few crevasses warned us when we reached the head of the icefall but we had not now the visibility to know exactly our position. When we heard an avalanche for half a minute we stood and listened. We were not alarmed; it was close but not dangerously so. It was the usual small snow avalanche of the kind that every day we heard and saw; behind it there was no great force. This had not the roar of the great ice avalanche that we had seen come down the face of Phubi Chyachu, there was no boom to it, just a gentle swish of slowly sliding snow. When silence had returned we continued in our tracks.

A minute later we recognised our position. The crevasse on our right was the one by which to turn, hazarded by ice-cliffs as we had noted that morning. Now on the descent, our moments of peril, if so they could be described, would be even briefer. We certainly gave them little thought. Soon we were at the furthest point, the point nearest to the cliffs. We turned the crevasse and were now walking back towards the centre of the glacier and safety, walking between two great crevasses. Thirty seconds more and we should be free from danger, but our thoughts were of other things and nothing ominous clouded them.

Then, just as the last man on the rope had turned the crevasse we heard it: a might roar from high above. There was no mistaking what it was or where it was coming. It was a great ice avalanche. We ran as fast as we could, every second the thunder swelling, but we could only make a few paces before it was on us. We knelt down, crouched pathetically braced for the impact, as if with our muscles we could beat off its force. In the last second I looked round. On the upward slope was the gaping crevasse which gave a feeble hope, behind a great cloud of snow advancing and outlined against it, bent and braced as myself, three figures, Crosby Fox, Mingma Tensing and Lakpa Noorbu. That was the last I ever saw of them.

I was in motion, pushed by an irresistible force, then almost immediately I felt myself falling. I knew I was going into a crevasse, but my fall was not far. A great force of snow followed me which I tried desperately to ward off with my arms. Buried, or partly buried I must have been, for all was dark yet I could fight still with my arms.

How long I lay there I cannot say, but abruptly vision returned. All was strangely still and quiet. I was 25 feet down at the extreme end of the crevasse. Where I lay it was narrow, my body almost spanned the walls. Although still alive and apparently uninjured my position would have given me little comfort, but I could now see that in the centre of the crevasse where it was widest, the avalanche debris had formed a cone, mounting up to within a few feet of the lip of the crevasse. At least I knew I could get out.

I was still suffering from shock and it was some time before the full horror of the situation entered my dazed mind. I could not yet believe that Fox and the Sherpas were not just outside, unharmed as was I; the awful alternative I refused to grasp. When I had struggled free from the snow I tried to shout to them, but no sound could I make. I was gasping for breath as I had never done before and for some minutes I had to lean against the wall before I could make a second attempt. But my voice was lost, absorbed by the ice around me. I had strength now to move and I made a few steps up the slope towards the centre of the crevasse to be halted shortly by the rope. Before I had not thought to look for it; the rope that tied me to my companions 20 feet apart. It was not broken. I followed it back to the little pit from which I had emerged. It descended vertically into the floor. Only a few feet could I pull free; no portent could be more ominous. I had now no axe and I could dig only with my hands. At first the snow was soft and a little of the rope I cleared, but soon I came to hard compacted snow and ice in which I could make no impression. I knew then there was no hope, below that solid floor no man could live.

I untied from the rope and climbed out. For some time I walked around trying to orientate myself. I peered into another crevasse, likewise filled with debris, one of the dark pits round which we had walked that morning, but I could see that no victims could be there. The crevasse into which I had fallen was immediately below the position the whole party must have occupied at the time the avalanche

155

struck. All must have the same grave, yet with a fragment of hope I looked around and called out once more. It was an awful deathlike silence into which my voice feebly penetrated. Nothing relieved the whiteness around me. I don't think I have ever felt so alone and it was some time before I could motivate myself into any action.

I need not describe my descent nor the thoughts with which I was accompanied. Soon, a little below, I picked out our morning's tracks which I hastily followed, now crawling over the more dangerous of the snow bridges. I stopped at the pathetically empty tents of Camp IV and found a message from Anderson and Wilson. They were having trouble with the Primus stove at the lower camp and had decided to return that day to Camp I. This was a blow indeed. I packed a rucksack with a sleeping bag and a duvet jacket; I felt strong enough then but some sort of reaction might follow before I could go so far. Again I set out.

Fortunately there was no difficulty and little danger. I was in a sorry state of mind but as I came down the last slopes leading to Camp III, imagine my joy to see, standing beside the tents, a figure in red windproofs: Anderson. The camp after all was occupied. Soon kindly hands were looking after me while I told my tragic tale.

Only I had seen the crevasse and knew with certainty that there was no hope, but it was necessary that this should be confirmed. After a rest and time for reorganisation, I returned with Anderson and Tallon and Sherpas Ang Tembu and Pemba Gyalgen to the scene of the accident, but any hope of digging in the ice floor of the crevasse was shattered.

Perhaps the full force of the tragedy had not made its impact upon the Sherpas until that moment. Our return and the sight of the empty tents brought it forcibly home. It was natural that it should be as great a blow for them as it was for us. They came all from the same village; all had lost friends, some relatives. They are simple child-like people whose faces portray their emotions and now they were as quick to tears as before they had been to laughter. But it was not only for their own race they wept.

Fox was loved as leader and man not only by ourselves and his loss took some share of their grief. Lhakpa Tsering, the least sophisticated and most lovable of our men, emerged weeping from the tent holding in his hands, plaintively, Fox's few personal possessions, his face reflecting the desolation that filled all our hearts. In these solemn moments of mutual anguish the gulf between us of race, religion, language and culture was firmly spanned and we felt a close affinity with our Sherpa friends.

I returned to Base Camp and, while others in the party continued to work on the survey, I made preparations for what was now my responsibility: a return to Katmandu to report the accident, the saddest of all missions.

Well after Istanbul

- a kind of love story

Sylvie Nickels

'Drive carefully' it's what everyone says, isn't it, when you set off in a car? Whether it's a few miles to the supermarket or overland to India. It's what our neighbour said when we dropped in the house keys (she waters our plants) before heading for Turkey.

It was to be our last big trip, so Rex said. He says it every time we plan another big trip so I don't take too much notice.

"Best go back before the EU ruins it," he said this time, as we began to make inroads into the 21st century. Both of us were aware that time was passing.

It looked a very long way on the map. I imagined our ageing camper van inching across the map, and thought it was a bit like life: setting out from A and creeping – though in the case of life with ever gathering momentum – towards Z. Of course, who's to know precisely when, or where, Z will be? Judging by statistical averages, we're both, as it were, well after Istanbul already.

Rex has always been the route planner; loves doing it, is good at it. He spread maps all over the dining table for days, working out the best if not the quickest routes. Once he looked up from manoeuvring a way through the industrial Ruhr and grunted "Trouble with getting old is that so many place names resonate. I passed over most of these on those 1000-plane raids of Bomber Harris."

"Perhaps not mention that if we're camping in the area."

"Hmmm." He gave me one of those grins which takes 70 or so years off his four-score and three: the grin of a small boy caught in some mildly wicked act, or of a deeply familiar friend complicit in some shared experience.

He is also ace at packing the camper van so I left him to that, too. It involves elaborate lists, much muttering under breath and innumerable to-ings and fro-ings between house and car port. Plastic containers of all sizes and shapes crowd every surface of the kitchen for some days as dry goods are stored in each, labels applied, and boxes acquired from the local co-op, the measurements of each appropriate to the space it will occupy. My task is to keep track of what is in each container, box and space, but given the number of changes that occur in the packing process, this aim is quite unrealistic.

I'm also the one who does the paperwork, relentlessly pursuing every scrap – tickets, insurance certificates, lists of camp sites, road tunnels, toll charges, traffic regulations for a dozen countries – that is briefly borrowed as 'just want to check something; do stop fussing, woman'. I do the note for the milkman, for the plant-watering neighbour, the post office for holding our mail, the gardener, and notify all persons likely to contact us while we're away. It takes at least the 3-4 hour drive to the Channel port to stop agonising about what we might have forgotten.

So we set off from A, in this case Harwich, for a millpond crossing to Hook of Holland. Our European Sites guide listed one near Arnhem, so we mused over the bridge whose taking cost such a spectacular and largely avoidable sacrifice in 1945. I was at school at the time, but Rex – by then a prisoner-of-war for nearly three years – was being marched back and forth across a dwindling chunk of Germany. A column parallel to the one he was in got shot up by some of our own Typhoons. Fifty dead. Some of them had been prisoners almost since the beginning of the war and they were then within a month of the end of it. Rex weeps when he speaks of it.

Next day we crossed into Germany. I always think that *ausfahrt,* the German word for a motorway exit, sounds rather rude and tends to distract me from the destinations to which it is *ausfahr*ting. I was, however, jolted by memory into noticing the *ausfahrt* to Ingolstadt, north of Munich. Then I was straight back to that steamy July day on the river Danube, me in a kayak on the second day of a course, Rex on the river bank, except I hadn't known he was Rex then. Fast forward to me *in* the Danube under the kayak, and something grabbing and pulling at me as I fought for breath, desperate not to die. On the bank I found myself surveyed by very blue eyes. He was a bit breathless himself, and said "You look like a drowned rat."

I vomited up water. "A nearly drowned rat" I choked. And he grinned that memorable grin at me for the first time. Sixty-plus years ago.

Autobahn- motorway-autostrade-autoput-driving by whatever name is unspeakably tedious, but in Austria it at least has the compensation of the kind of scenery on which you can refresh your soul. And so into Slovenia, the first of the six republics that had made up the former Yugoslavia before that terrible civil war of the early 1990s, and may be E on our life's journey to Istanbul.

We'd stayed at the camp site at Bohinjska Bistrica before and the young receptionist, Lisa, remembered. But then Rex is rather unforgettable. She had been a student that last time when Rex re-climbed Triglav, Slovenia's highest mountain, on his 80th birthday. Happily another ascent did not appear to be on his agenda, so we went instead to admire Lisa's chubby new baby and meet her bus driver husband. The house was a traditional Slovene chalet, with wood stacked under the eaves, and tubs overflowing with geraniums and petunias. The garden was a strip of meadow scattered with apple trees and a tethered dun cow grazing. It was one of those multitudinous moments in our travels which affirmed why we continue insatiably to do them, and why we do them together.

The Dalmatian coast had not changed for the better with an ever-lengthening ribbon of *sobe-zimmer*-rooms, *apartmenti*, motels, pensions, and half-built houses to replace those destroyed in the war. I thought back nostalgically to our earliest visits when the Dalmatian *magistrale* was slowly inching its way along that magnificent coastline, turning stony dusty lanes into a sinuous ribbon of tarmac. A Croat friend, who was something in tourism, pointed out the tiny terraced fields, cleared with painstaking dedication, stone by stone removed to create the walls separating one few square metres of field from another: here an olive tree, there a handful of vines.

"The next generation won't bother with this," our friend said. And now it was patently obvious that the next generation hadn't.

"It's called progress," Rex said when I voiced the thought.

"Is it?"

"Well, would you want to break your nails and your back on that soil?" he asked, reasonably enough. "Those sort of life styles are mainly romantic to those who don't have to live them."

Below our ribbon of tarmac, crystal clear water shaded from turquoise to purple. We found a camp site in a meadow atop a steep

160

descent to that sea at Mlini, a few miles south of Dubrovnik. May be 'M' on our alphabetic journey. We liked it so much we stayed several days, caught up with the laundry, dipped in and out of the sea and, in the family-run restaurant on the shore, nibbled at juicy *raznjići*, the Croatian version of the shish-kebabs that would form our staple diet when we got to Turkey.

Rex was looking younger by the day. A semi-insomniac at home, he sleeps like a babe in the camper van. His ability to relax seems to be in ascending ratio to our increasing distance from the mail and telephone. Especially the telephone. He argues that it is an instrument of the devil and will go to extremes to avoid picking it up.

While we were at Mlini, Rex collected a Swedish couple and a lone birdwatching Dutchman, demonstrating another unfathomability of my unfathomable man. At home he is affectionately known as O.C., acronym for old curmudgeon from his self-professed antipathy to the social round. Yet pop him into a camp site with a load of strangers and in no time he has ferreted out the most interesting.

We usually end up with a small party, and I love it as much as he does. In fact, each trip provides an opportunity to renew acquaintance with a Rex who, between times, burrows under protective layers. "Cultivated old-fogeyism," one of our closer friends said and was probably right. I wished it were not so. Our sons rarely saw the real Rex, and it was the discerning youngest, now approaching middle age himself, who glimpsed through the layers and kept in closest touch, his concern expressed in a kind of bantering resignation over what eccentric caper would be the next on his father's expanding repertoire.

"Where have all the donkeys gone?" I mused a few days later.

We had crossed into Bosnia-Hercegovina, which I've always thought to be one of the more accessible of Europe's few remaining areas of wild magnificence. Rushing green torrents, precipitous gorges, soft uplands studded with wild flowers beneath rocky crags; women, faces lined with an eon of wisdom, spinning wool as they watched their flocks; and wide rackety carts drawn by horse, mule or donkey. Now replaced entirely by tractors and clapped-out cars.

The theme for one of those freedom songs had been haunting me for hours. I found myself putting words to it:
"Where have all the donkeys gone?
No more trotting.
The tractors in their place

161

Will never have their grace. "

Rather pleased with that I started:

"Where are all the roadside geese? "
"No more honking," suggested Rex.

"Now only plastic bags
Flap in a world of tattered rags. " I finished

"Hmmmm. Doesn't quite scan. But not bad, not bad."

It was late afternoon when we reached Mostar, spilling down steep slopes to the Neretva river. There was no camp site so we booked into a pension next to a mosque from whose minaret, at sunrise, the recorded call to prayer gently nudged us into the new day.

The old town was pitted with destruction – burnt-out shells of homes, rubble and rubbish everywhere. Framed by the gaping walls on one building we got our first glimpse of the reconstructed single span bridge built in 1566, destroyed by the Croats in a matter of minutes of mortar fire. The new bridge was a clone of the original, but it looked what it was: spanking shiny new. It had taken its predecessor over four centuries to acquire its patina.

A couple of days later we found that we had the Oaza Camp site at Ilidža, a few km from Sarajevo, to ourselves: a fine grassy meadow with well laid-out trees and a superb shower block that didn't work. I guessed we must be at 'R or 'S' by now.

Ilidža is a spa where the Archduke Franz Ferdinand spent his last night before reviewing his troops in June 1914 in the capital of the then Austro-Hungarian protectorate of Bosnia. An 18-year-old terrorist/freedom fighter called Gavrilo Princip shot and fatally wounded him, providing one of the triggers for the First World War. Indeed, that 'war to end all wars'. Sarajevo, it seems, has an unfortunate talent for making the world's darker headlines. We took the tram into the city the next morning. There were regiments of highrise blocks of flats, pitted with black window sockets where yet another mortar had hit and destroyed yet another home during the siege of the 1990s; there were new mosques, their multiple minarets pronouncing the Saudi origins of the aid which had rebuilt them; there was the rebuilt Holiday Inn almost obscene in its shiny gaudiness, long-robed figures sweeping in and out of it. But the older parts of the city were visually pleasingly, as long as you didn't notice the gravestones hurriedly erected, usually in the middle of a mortar raid, wherever there was a space.

Yes, well, the 21st century has produced other terrorists, other freedom fighters.

We were beginning to feel we were in the Balkans now, and the feeling increased as we headed into Serbia. The inconvenience of having to cross borders every hundred miles or two where earlier there had been none triggered unanswerable question as to who had gained, and what, by so much destruction and bloodshed. We asked one or two people if things had changed much and were usually replied with a shrug and 'not really'. So what had that all been about then? The border crossings which were relatively straight forward along the coast and across the plains became less obvious among the labyrinth of winding mountain roads. And these Serb-Bosnian borderlands, deeply ravined, thickly wooded, were the same as those which provided shelter and a bloody setting for guerilla warfare in World War Two.

"It must have been around here that I was dropping supplies during the war," Rex observed. "For that Tito fellow. Don't imagine he would have thought much of this new mania for borders."

And the next moment we had crossed yet another one as we drove passed an onslaught of acronyms representing the international presence in Kosovo.

The main highway through Kosovo serves what must service Europe's biggest building site, slightly reminiscent of the approaches to any major US city with its gas stations, shopping malls, and barrage of advertising signs. It all seemed a far cry from the smoke-darkened ancient monasteries we had visited years ago peppering the valleys and mountains within a 50 miles radius: relics of Serbia's medieval empire, wrested from them by the Ottoman Turks following the seminal battle on those very fields of Kosovo in 1389.

Before long we were into the three-day crossing of northern Greece. I was beginning to feel twitchy and Rex noticed, but I knew better than to share the A-Z superstition which had seized me, imagining the snort of derision that would greet it.

This late in the season, there was not much delay at the border beyond Alexandropoulos. The landscapes of European Turkey did not differ to any marked degree from those of northern Greece. The main difference was in the gas stations where we were offered small glasses of tea while they filled us up and where I spied a small mosque at the end of the forecourt for those whose visit coincided with one of the

163

times of prayer or a desire to meditate; or maybe it was a reflection of the standard of driving.

When I drew his attention to it, Rex agreed that it was a mightily appropriate facility. The Turks are, in the main, a delightful people in any circumstance other than behind the wheel of a vehicle. They do not seem to have grasped the purpose of a rearview mirror, of indicators, or really any feature of the car except its horn which is in constant use.

"Not many women drivers," I thought aloud.

"Hmmmm," Rex said.

We had agreed that under no circumstance would we drive in Istanbul, had selected a camp site on 'our' side of the city and put our trust in Allah. At least I did on behalf of both of us for Rex's relationship with his Maker is tenuous to the point of non-existence. When we eventually found it, it was one of the worst camp sites we had come across. A disconsolate Frenchman was standing guard outside the Gents' showers while his wife splashed away behind an unlockable door. "The water it is salt, of the sea, and only for the *Messieurs* is it heated," he explained.

So had we reached 'Z', I wondered? Was this it? But it didn't really feel like the end of everything or, indeed, anything.

Istanbul was hectic in a loud, colourful, human way; culturally dazzling; and tiring. "Let's go clockwise," Rex said, meaning directionally round the country, and I felt absurdly safer once we'd crossed the Bosphorus and left the outskirts of the city well behind us.

We barely heard a European language along the north coast which, in all honesty, we didn't find terribly attractive. Having made the grave error in some inland village of succumbing to home-made ice cream, it didn't help that we were both afflicted by violent diarrhoea and holed up for some days in a Black Sea-side camp site.

Once he started feeling better, Rex began plunging down memory lane, something that he was doing more and more. At one time he never mentioned the war and only referred to the scenes of his more colourful escapades when they were mentioned in the news or some documentary, usually to pronounce they did not know what they were talking about. The sole survivor of an avalanche in Nepal, scooped off the Greenland ice cap in the nick of time, precipitated into an Antarctic crevasse, he had had a worrying number of near misses and I couldn't help feeling he was not due for many more. Now, though, his reminiscences were geographically more immediate. Forty years ago he had climbed a Turkish mountain, befriended a family who lived in a mud-brick hut whose son had been their donkey boy, helping them to carry their equipment to establish a base camp.

"I'd like to go and see what's happened to Ali," he said.

Ali and the relevant mountain were still some distance away in south central Anatolia. I thought this heartland of some of our earliest cultures was one of the dustiest places I'd ever seen. Then we reached the little road, blessedly wooded, that led into the Aladaglar mountain range. Rex had a photograph of the donkey boy, his family, and their mud-brick hut, with the hulk of Demirkazik soaring up behind it. In one of those coincidences that makes life so much stranger than fiction, we showed the photograph to a young man in a small village at the end of a road. He became very excited. "That is my father, and there is my grandfather," he shouted. "Follow me!"

The grandfather had died. But the father Ali, one-time donkey boy, duly arrived and burst into tears when he saw Rex, remembering everything about his earlier visit, even the colour of the car in which they travelled. He had progressed from the one-room hut to an attractive pension he now ran for the trekkers who came here to walk and birdwatch. His son helped when he was on holiday from university and now cooked us an excellent meal of local river fish.

It was difficult to get away. Ali wanted us to go with him to the coast to see his kid sister Fatima, now mother of three, whom Rex had last seen posing on his car bonnet aged four. But we'd lost too much time with our sick stomachs and had to get on. We hit the south coast near the Mediterranean port of Silifka and spent a couple of nights in a pension. Rex said we were going 'soft' but the fact was that camp sites are extremely thin on the ground in 'off-beat' Turkey, and in the more well trodden areas most of them have been covered by high rise hotels or self catering flats. We liked Silifka. It had some very good restaurants where we spent the evening watching the evening ferry load up for its regular connection to Turkish Cyprus, a reminder of one long-running European sore that needed healing before Turkey's acceptance in the EU family.

As we progressed westwards, Rex became increasingly depressed. Upon his long cherished memories of deserted beaches on which he had spread his sleeping bag to sleep in the open forty years ago was now superimposed the reality of miles of highrise 'tourist nonsense'. We scuttled through Alanya and Antalya as fast as possible.

Worse was to come at Altinkum, with its wall to wall hotels, pensions, restaurants, souvenir shops, tattoo parlours. Altinkum (justifiably meaning 'golden sands') is one of a scattering of popular south-west Turkey resorts, each dedicated to the every need of a particular visiting nationality. In this case, the Brits were the chosen people. All signs were in English, all prices in Sterling. Menus blared out *Full English Breakfast, Roast Beef and Yorkshire Pudding, Bacon Butties.*

We went for a stroll. The fine sandy beach was crowded with our compatriots of all ages, shapes and sizes wearing the minimum. Mountains of reddening flesh bulged from bikini tops and bottoms, paunchy overhangs wobbled over swimming trunks. Not a pretty sight. In a cyber café where I went to check our email, the youngish owner showed me to a computer, put his hands on my shoulders. "You like massage?" he asked. "In your dreams," I said and he seemed to get the message. Rex roared with laughter when I reported this.

We escaped to some of the world's greatest archaeological sites, which were numerous and extensive enough to dilute our fellow tourists into acceptable proportions. Ephesus, Pergamon, Troy – you could become dizzy with the resonance of such quantities of history and human experience. Suddenly Rex had had enough. "Let's miss out Istanbul on the way back and side-track through Gallipoli."

I thought of my A-Z. We'd seemingly sailed through the alphabet unscathed. Superstitiously it seemed a good idea not to tempt fate. "Fine by me," I said.

Our visit coincided with howling gales, plummeting temperatures and coachloads of schoolchildren being taught the importance of this seminal battle to the birth of modern Turkey. At the museum they were more interested in us than in the exhibits.

"They think you're a Gallipoli veteran," I whispered.

Rex was delighted and posed happily with them as they took each other's photographs. Such quantities and freshness of youth made a poignant contrast as we looked down on Anzac and other coves where boys not much older than these had made the ultimate sacrifice.

By the time we reached Edirne near the Bulgarian border, I reckoned we were going through the alphabet for the second time. Edirne's Selimye Camii Mosque was designed by the same architect as that of Aya Sofya in Istanbul, and I thought it was the most beautiful in Turkey. And a good place to hear the call to prayer for the last time. "I shall quite miss that," Rex said. "Especially the dawn one. It kind of makes a reassuring start to the day."

It was out of earshot that last morning. We were only a few miles from the Bulgarian border when Rex said "Well, we made it." Had he been harbouring his own superstitions? I opened my mouth to say "Don't tempt Providence," when an oncoming car came out of nowhere round a bend and on the wrong side of the road. Our side. I didn't hear the crash and the blackness which followed gave way only gradually to flickers of greyness peopled by white shadowy figures talking in an incomprehensible language.

"Speak English," I tried to say crossly, but my tongue was too thick to form the words.

"Ah, you're awake," said a voice sounding like Stephen Fry, though its owner looked the archetypical man from the Embassy. His expression was sad and gentle, and I think I knew, as it were, before I knew.

"Rex," I said.

'Stephen Fry' consulted someone behind him, and there was some shuffling about while a wheelchair was found and I was transferred into it. Painful.

Rex was in a little room by himself. He looked like a monstrous mummy punctured by an intricate network of tubes, but his face was unmarked and uncovered and his blue eyes open. He looked quite peaceful and smiled that smile that had captured me well over 60-70 years earlier.

"The boys are on their way. They will look after you," he said.

It was too early for grief, but I thanked God he had thought of summoning the boys.

He went on, "I have always loved you."

"I know," I said. "And I've always loved you."

"Hmmmmm," Rex said, before he closed his blue eyes and moved gently towards wherever there is beyond the dark.

"Drive carefully," I said in my head.

Did he respond or was it my imagination that he squeezed my hand?

167

THE TIME OF THE STORKS

Olive Hill

It was soon after the stork returned that the foreigners came, almost as though one heralded the coming of the other. The male stork was always first and for Pia it was a special moment when she first saw him, wheeling over the village before landing with such certainty on the shaggy remains of last season's nest. Father had fixed a platform for it on the angle of the shingle roof all those years ago, before he died. Odd to think it could even be the same stork since her teacher said it could live 25 years. Twice her own age!

In fact the stork was late that second spring after the revolution. Though there was still snow on the tops, the plum trees were well in bud in the orchard behind the farm, and Baba's cows already tethered out all day in the meadow. Pia was bringing the first two in for evening milking when she saw the strangers.

First she saw Baba standing in the yard, hands clasped over the back of her heavy dark skirt, which was the way she always stood when faced with some alien circumstance. Beyond her was a silver grey car and behind that a quite amazing white caravan: as big - no, surely even bigger than the truck that brought them all back from the fields after haymaking.

But there was barely time to wonder at it before she saw Mother and the strangers. The lady was tall with short dark hair, and brilliant blue eyes, and a full red mouth, and skin so clear; not at all like Mother's or Baba's that was weathered like leather from years of all seasons in the fields. Pia thought she had never seen anyone so magnificent. Not even in the city where she spent all last winter with her aunt Lisa.

Strangers were rare, very rare, in Gorena, which was as far as the road went in this remote valley in the Carpathians. Pia had taken its remoteness for granted until her winter in the city. And, of course, since the white satellite dish brought the world bursting noisily into their living room. The satellite dish had been Aunt Lisa's idea.

"It's rude to stare," Baba said sharply now: Baba who spent hours sitting by the village track staring at anything that moved! But when you were old you could get away with many outrageous things; that much Pia had learned in her 12 years.

She asked "What do they want? Where do they come from?"

Baba jerked her head towards the satellite dish. *Out there, a long way off* the gesture meant.

Then the magnificent lady said "What a very pretty child," and when Pia blushed the man said "Why, I do believe she understood that."

To Pia's great relief everyone's attention was abruptly distracted by a loud disturbance above their heads. A female stork had arrived on the nest and the two were greeting each other in a frenzy of clacking bills and twisting necks.

Enchanted, the magnificent lady exclaimed. "Our very own storks," quite as though they belonged to her. "How very lucky!"

They hadn't stopped Father being dead, Pia thought. And then to her amazement the strangers got into the car and began to tow the caravan into the field behind the farm.

Later while Pia and her mother Rakela were getting supper ready, Baba took her needlework out on to the verandah. The English woman would probably buy some of the embroidery. Perhaps a lot. The craft market stallholder down in the valley where Baba sent her embroidered cushion covers said the foreigners couldn't seem to get enough. It confirmed the impression Baba had from the white saucer programmes that no one out there had time any more for using their hands.

She looked down at her own, so crooked now, so slow; but in spite of that, and the pain that varied but was always there, the needlework still brought her the greatest sense of quiet and fulfilment. It was as if she were stitching her very life into the intricate patterns passed on from generations beyond the ashes of the big war.

Baba glanced up across the yard. She could see the top of the caravan well down the field. Perhaps these were all right, but in the past foreigners had meant at best trouble, at worst anguish. She had taught herself not to dwell on this; but a year back there had been shooting and death in the city again and though everything seemed all right now, you could never be sure. And now these foreigners. Bringing aid, Rakela said.

And then she was where she didn't want to be: back half a century in 1942, 23 years old with a small child. It was Spring. The first of the stork eggs had hatched and little Jokim was laughing as the ungainly youngster plaintively mewed its hunger. Everyone said terrible things were happening but here life still seemed impregnable. Until the noises began to reach them from further down the valley. When he looked anxious she told little Jokim it was a distant storm; and wished big Jokim would come.

The rumbling grew loud and close and great clouds of dust were curling up the track towards them. Suddenly the yard was full of soldiers with guns, shouting in a strange language, and little Jokim ran to cling to her legs. What happened next, in spite of the noise, was like a silent film: seeing big Jokim running down the hillside, a lamb draped round his neck; the soldier lifting his rifle; the spreading red patch over Jokim's chest. In the fraction of a second before he fell, he stopped in his tracks looking so astonished.

The Germans had shot the lamb too and ransacked the house for food before they left. Baba sat holding the head of her dead husband in her lap, feeling the last warmth drain away. There was more shooting in the distance. She didn't know how long she sat there, with little Jokim clinging to her. Then neighbours came and they had helped each other bury their dead.

"But what are they *doing* here?" Pia asked again as she sat on the back porch slicing potatoes.

"Be sure to take out the blemishes," Mother said. She went on chopping peppers and cucumber for infuriating moments before saying "It's something to do with that new clinic they're building down in the valley" She meant the main valley 30 kilometres away carrying the main road and railway from the city to distant frontiers and the world of the satellite dish. She grunted. "And you're not to pester them mind."

As soon as possible Pia retreated to the little cubby hole of a room she had inherited from her brother Miru when he left to work in Germany. From the window she could just see a small corner of the caravan over the yard fence. Think of it. Foreigners in their field. A magnificent English lady who had said she was pretty; and whose language she understood.

They had insisted on her going to her cousin's school while she was in the city. Her aunt was a doctor in the main hospital and Pia had been sent to stay with her while they treated her for leukaemia. At first she'd felt terribly ill and very homesick for the farm and all the country sights and sounds. And smells. Until she got used to them the city smells were quite awful.

At her cousin's school they taught English. This was something new and to do with the shouting crowds they'd watched on televison the previous year. There'd been shooting too but then the army decided to go with the people and the crowds became wildly happy.

After that there were a lot more changes, like being able to buy a lot of foreign things and teaching English in the schools. Pia found she learnt surprisingly quickly. It was fun rolling strange words round her tongue and being able to understand some of those foreign programmes on TV. And now, even better, she would be able to practise with the foreigners in their field.

From the open door of the caravan the woman saw her swinging on the gate and called her over. Pia didn't need asking twice.

Everything inside the caravan looked bright and clean and smooth. At the far end the man was chopping up onions and emptying

171

a tin into a saucepan. Pia was astonished. Reading her expression the woman said "He's a very good cook." She smiled "I'm Emma Lambert, and that's James."

Pia said "My name is Pia and I am nearly thirteen years old. And I have a brother Miru who is in Germany."

"Hello Pia who's nearly thirteen years old." The woman patted her arm. "And your father, where is he?"

Pia could not take her eyes off the man. "He is dead before my birthday."

To her surprise this James stopped what he was doing and looked up, quite upset. "You poor kid," he said.

"I think," Emma said, "Pia means her father died before she was born."

Wasn't that what she had said?   James went back to his onion-chopping saying "Ah, that's bad luck. Terrible for your poor mother. And grandmother."

Before Pia could examine this curious idea of death and luck she heard her mother calling and hurried guiltily to the door of the caravan.

"*What* did I tell you about not pestering those foreigners? If you annoy them they'll go away," she went on scolding even more insistently as she approached.

Reading her tone Emma put a hand on Pia's shoulder and said "Tell her we hope you will visit us a lot. Tell her it will be good for your English."

Mother grumbled "She probably doesn't know what it's like to have a disobedient child. And you forgot to get the water."

"Sorry Mother," Pia said meekly, her heart singing because the magnificent lady wanted her to visit them and *a lot.*

Emma watched mother and daughter walk back across the field. Had she been able to understand Rakela she would have agreed that she did indeed not know what it was like to have a disobedient, or any other kind of, child. May be that had been much of the problem.

She would be a heart-breaker that Pia in a few years. Far too skinny at the moment, breasts only just forming under that awful pink

T-shirt, hips still tomboy-narrow. But with a natural grace and impending beauty already clear in those dark eyes, pointed chin, full mouth.

James joined her. "Bright kid," he said looking towards the house. "Given half a chance she'd go a long way."

At least this one's too young even for you James, Emma thought, but aloud said "Smells good back there." He wrapped his arms round her from behind, buried his nose in her hair. "I adore you Emma Lambert," he said softly.

And I you, Emma said in her head, leaning back against him. *Warts and all*

Theirs had been the match of the year in their corner of middle England: Emma, fashion writer turned modestly successful romantic novelist; James a construction engineer with an architectural flair who'd crashed his way up the social scale from inner city roots he was at pains to forget, in the process changing from Jimmie to James. Once his house conversions had made the pages of the glossies there was no looking back.

He'd put on a bit of weight but twelve years ago he'd been outrageously good looking. They couldn't take their eyes off each other at that book launch; or, later, their hands. If she'd read such stuff in a romance, Emma thought wryly, she would have cringed. But it had been out of this world; still could be. In bed and out of it.

She'd moved in to the barn James had just finished converting on the edge of the village within easy commuting distance of London. It wasn't long before she found there were other women he couldn't keep his hands off - usually the wife of whatever house he happened to be converting at the time. When hurt turned to rage, Emma understood that their unavailability was one of their chief attractions. And finally he'd admit it, pleading over and over that he could not survive without her, that she was the only one for him. And she knew she wasn't ready to let him go.

Their reconciliations were memorable. It was soon after the last one they had seen the documentary programme on the dire conditions in parts of newly 'democratised' eastern Europe. An initiative was under way to build a series of clinics in the most

173

deprived rural areas and they were looking for technicians and designers who could be available for a minimum of six months.

Between books, Emma said "May be it's what we both need," And still deep in his latest slough of remorse James agreed.

"Dinner is about to be served," James said now "Lamb ragout *a la Gorena* for Madame, in a bed of quick-boil rice!" He could do quite remarkable things with a couple of tins, a few vegetables from the market, a herb or two.

"It smells like heaven," Emma said, feeling ravenous.

"And later, Madame, I have further heavenly proposals,"

Emma put up a hand to touch his cheek. "I can hardly wait," she said.

On the day the first young stork fledged Pia knew that she had never known such happiness. She could pinpoint the precise moment because Emma had just looked up from reading her essay and said "Pia dear, this is really very, very good." Then "Look!" she exclaimed, and Pia turned to see the young stork teetering on the edge of the nest while a parent circled anxiously overhead.

At the same moment James arrived back calling "And how are my favourite women?" Laughing Emma held up Pia's essay saying "Just see what this clever lass has written." and, smiling, James said "I think we'll have to take her back to England with us." It was then Pia thought that if she could die of happiness this would be the moment she would choose.

Several weeks had passed and life had settled into a magic routine. Early each morning James set off down to the main valley. Sometimes Emma went too, but usually she stayed in Gorena working on her new novel. Pia knew the caravan was out of bounds to her until four o'clock each afternoon.

At first Emma had come over to the house then and sat at the scrubbed table on the back verandah while Mother prepared vegetables or baked bread or sewed. It was quite surprising how Emma and Mother managed to communicate, each learning a few words of the other's language and roaring with laughter at the results. At least Emma roared; Mother just gave her quiet smile. It was one of the things Pia noticed about the English people: how loudly and confidently they talked or laughed. Another difference was how they answered, or sometimes didn't answer, questions. Where Baba or Mother would give a categoric "yes" or "no", Emma, and especially James, would temporise with "Well, it rather depends" or "Well, let's see shall we..."

Later Emma started giving her English lessons and Pia went to the caravan instead, usually taking some of the embroidery that Baba had set her to do. Emma had got very excited when she first saw the handwoven and embroidered wall hangings and cushions they had all over the house. Not many English girls, she said, learned embroidery nowadays. Pia hadn't thought of embroidery as something you learned. You just did it, unless you got really crooked hands like Baba.

Once the school holidays began and Pia started working in the fields it was agreed she could still go back to the caravan at four o'clock. "Don't forget the water," Mother would call automatically after her. But she wasn't likely to forget again, especially after James started coming with her most evenings. They had their own well in the yard, of course, but it had become brackish long ago and they drew all their drinking water from the communal well several hundred metres away.

Pia loved these times with James. She wondered if this was what it was like to have a father. He started calling her Princess and talked to her as if she were another grown up. There was a lot about "unbelievable red tape" and delays which she didn't understand, but she tried to look wise and hugged to herself her gratitude for the delays.

James also started coming with her to collect brushwood, initially with the handcart but later they took Shana, the mare, to go further afield. He learned to put on her harness including the red pompom that warded off evil. He became quite good at stacking the brushwood neatly, and later the logs which they went to collect ready for the next winter. By then there would be no Emma and James. Pia snapped her mind shut on the thought.

One day early in July James took her to see the clinic. She was dismayed to see the building almost complete.

James said "We're waiting for the final official inspection before we can begin installing equipment. These damned bureaucrats take forever..." Pia's spirits rose at this further welcome delay. Then James said "They're holding a meeting down on the coast to discuss progress. Next week. We'll probably stay on a while. Explain to your Mother we'll be away for a bit, Princess"

Pia's heart was a stone falling, falling. She stared at James. "You're going away?"

"And coming back." Seeing her expression James touched her cheek. "Of course we're coming back Princess."

Pia stood on the track watching the caravan's swirl of dust progress down the valley. Then she went to sit in the field, now so much bigger in its emptiness. A clacking of bills caught her attention and she looked up to see the two young storks circling over the fields. They had been flying for some time, rapidly improving their skills but not venturing far. Now they headed steadily, purposefully away. Perched on the nest the parents appeared unconcerned.

From a window Rakela watched Pia thinking *there's nothing I can do to stop the hurt, and it will be much worse when they leave for good* And she was not thinking of the storks.

Now, though, there was an alternative. She went back to her spinning, drawing and twisting the rough wool through her fingers. These were often the best times for unravelling her own thoughts. *They do not think like we do,* she told herself now. *They come from their world with their good intentions and their gifts. And then, like the storks, they go away.*

She knew she was being unfair for the Lamberts had brought something far more permanent than gifts and good intentions. And she liked them. Especially Emma, and especially after finding that she, Rakela, was in many ways much more experienced in living, for all her lack of travel and knowledge of books. Alas there was no time for books.

"You're just as clever as Lisa. You should have been a teacher," Jokim had said many times. And then it was 1969 again.

Daily the protest marches on the streets grew bigger, louder, in the city. He had to go Jokim said, to add his voice to the revolution, to be part of the dawn of that new era.

Such fine words, but they came thirteen years too soon. After he'd gone she could hardly bear to leave the television set with its blurry black and white pictures. The crowds looked so happy that sometimes she wanted to rush to the city herself. But Baba, already arthritic, could not run the farm alone. And, anyway, she had to protect the new life just beginning to stir inside her.

The invasion from their eastern neighbours - liberation so *they* called it - came without warning. Rakela watched the TV screen stiff with horror as the tanks moved on to the streets, and heard the appeals going out to the West from the TV station still in revolutionary hands.

Then there were pictures of wounded people being carried away and the cameras zoomed in on a student, a middle-aged woman, a man. And the man was Jokim. It was several days before she finally learned he was dead. It was months before her thoughts were not dominated by the memory of his body sagging, his head lolling in the arms of his bearers. She was haunted by the thought of such a public dying.

"So what shall I do Jokim, about Pia and the English people?" Rakela was surprised to hear herself ask aloud.

On the day Pia had told her they were leaving for the coast, her face as long as a wet week, Emma and James had come to see Rakela with a colleague who could speak both their languages. They explained how fond they had become of Pia, what a bright girl she was. They said they would like her to come and stay with them next winter, go to a special school. It would be a wonderful opportunity for Pia and it would not cost Rakela anything.

"It will cost me months without Pia who is all I have left of you Jokim," Rakela said in her head, but she knew she would not stand in Pia's way.

As she emerged from the rim of the forest with a panier full of bilberries, Pia saw the bright blob glinting in the field behind the farm. They were back! She rushed down, spirits soaring, arriving breathless at the open door of the caravan. Emma was sitting at the table, James pouring wine into a glass. She sensed hostility; something was not right.

As soon as he saw her James' expression changed. "Princess! What a sight for sore eyes. And I'll swear you've grown."

It took some moments longer for Emma to smile and say "You've got bilberry juice all round your mouth."

Pia looked from one to the other. "You are all right?"

"Just a bit tired after the journey," James said. We'll tell you all about it later."

"*All* about?" Emma queried in a strange voice.

James watched Pia walk back across the field. Despite his own discomfiture he noticed that she really was changing: a little girl suddenly become half woman. She would be a stunner all right. He looked beyond her to the farm crouching under its shingle roof, and the meadows sloping behind it to the dark line of the forest, and high above that to the bare tops. There had still been a lot of snow up there when they first arrived.

Those weeks had been an idyll. They'd found a harmony, he and Emma, of a kind they'd never known before.

On the coast he'd blown it. At the time it had seemed harmless enough to buy that pretty Swedish woman a few drinks and that had somehow led to a moonlight clinch on the hotel terrace. Well, not so much harmless as inevitable. Good lord, she was crying out for it, and in all truth he hadn't planned at stopping there. He felt desire stir at the memory. But it hadn't meant a thing, any more than it ever had before.

Emma had walked in on it. She had screamed at him like a fishwife, so out of character that it was shocking. "You can't get enough can you?" she shouted. "You're sodding sick." The Swedish woman had wisely disappeared and Emma sagged suddenly and said hopelessly "It was so *good* what we had."

He had known then at gut level that this time would be different. This time there was no possibility of denial; there would be no earth-moving reconcilations.

"One more chance," he'd pleaded over and over, as her anger gave way to bitterness and finally sadness, far into the night. "Just

178

one. It'll be as good as ever. Better. I promise. You *know* you're the only one. Dear God, you must know."

Emma said flatly "I don't believe you James. I don't think I ever have. Just cared enough to hope..."

He had sensed a chink in the defences, homed in on it with the fervour of desperation. "And Pia? What about Pia? We owe her that one chance."

They had both grown so fond of her: her youth, her freshness, her trust in and obvious affection for them both.

Emma said wearily "Let's see how we feel when we get back to Gorena."

It was only much later that she thought: *perhaps in the end Pia would be their salvation.*

"Live in England? With Emma and James?" Pia repeated astounded that first evening of the Lamberts' return.

It was the most incredible, fantastic thing that could ever happen. And yet... and yet...

In the coming days Pia was astonished to find she had even the smallest reservations. Of course there were the obvious ones of the unknown being scary, and missing Mother and Baba and the farm. But more persistent was something far less definable, to do with that alien feeling she had walked in on when Emma and James returned from the coast.

Yet on the face of it everything was as it had been before. Or almost. Emma had lost some of her jolliness but was every bit as insistent as James that Pia should come to England. Perhaps even more so. She even made it seem as if she, Pia, would be doing them a favour! At times these foreign ways were very strange.

"It'll be a time you'll remember for the rest of your life," James said. "I promise you."

They were in the forest picking the first wild mushrooms of the season. Now he called her over "What about these Princess?" He still got hopelessly muddled between edible and poisonous fungi and,

179

crouching down to survey his latest find, Pia giggled and said "You could kill all Gorena people with those."

Still giggling she looked up and, surprised, saw James' face only a few inches from her own, his expression quite odd so that for a moment he was like a stranger. There was just time for a flicker of unease before he shook his head and said with a slight shake in his voice "We can't go around committing mass murder now, can we?"

The incident stayed in Pia's mind. It had never happened to her before that someone so familiar could, in a moment, become so unknown.

For the first time she found herself looking at her friends in a new way, comparing rather than simply noticing the differences. She tried to imagine what it would be like to be with lots and lots of people like Emma and James; to have no escape to the familiarity of the farm, the comfort of Mother's quiet, Baba's gruffness, the sense of presence of a father and a grandfather she had never known, the everyday familiarity of a score of people.

And then she thought of what it might be like if she met that stranger in the forest again. The idea would not go away.

She thought about it a long time, and then she made her decision. Emma put both her hands on Pia's shoulders. "If you change your mind ...."

Pia nodded. She knew she wouldn't.

James was very quiet. "We'll miss you Princess."

And she them. She watched the silver grey car and the white caravan bump away down the track, finally disappearing in a gathering cloud of dust.

"I could do with some water Pia," Mother said, resting a hand briefly on her shoulder. She had sensed something had happened the moment she saw Emma after their return from the coast, been aware of Pia's growing uncertainty. It had been a relief when she had reached her decision and Rakela had not questioned it.

Overhead the parent storks were circling. The slow steady beat of their wings seemed to imbue them with infinite wisdom. Soon they would be leaving too; autumn would come - some of the leaves on the sweet chestnut were already turning. And things would get back to normal.

Except that Pia knew they would never quite be the same ever again.

'Then' and 'Now'

a chat between Henna and Shameem Ramzan; and Sylvie

How often do we actually find ourselves taking the time to sit down with those of different generations and beliefs to discuss where we used to be with relationships, and where we are now?
This question came up recently when I was talking to some very good Muslim friends, a mother and daughter, originally from Pakistan. Henna in particular had been pondering over the fact that looking back might not always be recommended though by ignoring the past you could be left feeling short-changed. And, coming from a much older generation, I had some questions concerning Muslim marriage customs. So we decided to explore this question of relationships in general and marriage in particular, beginning with a conversation between Henna and her Mum.

Henna: I feel strangely nervous because how often to mothers and daughters sit down and talk about the past in this way?
Mum: Well, I think it's really important. We tend to talk about what we're going through in the present but not our views on things that have been.
Henna: Mum, the other day whilst you where cooking you said "I know that I'm only 49 years old and in the grand scheme of things that isn't particularly old, but you have to understand that I come from a time that doesn't exist anymore". So, what elements of life from when you were younger do you wish were still practised today?
Mum: Well, I wish people cared more about each other and were kinder and more giving. When I was younger, we had hand-me-downs and you may not have had a lot yourself but if someone was struggling you would give anything that you could to help them out, and vice versa. Growing up in the '70s in Sheffield felt very community driven. There was a connection which I don't think we have anymore.
Henna: That's quite sad. Do you feel as though nurturing relationships was prioritised when you were younger?

Mum: Yes, they definitely were. I think it has changed because there isn't as much "togetherness" now. I feel as though we have to live up to so much, do so much and compete with so much that everyone ends up just feeling a little bit lost. And for example, we'd knock on our neighbours doors when the electricity used to go down. Or if it was snowing we'd check they were ok. Perhaps let them know we were just off to the shops and see if they needed anything. That was the normal thing to do. When I used to take you out on the bus when you were small so many people would speak to you or buy you a lolly. It seems that these days' people are too scared to do things like that.

Henna: Well, I think it might be frowned upon.

Mum: It's partly because we lived in Sheffield and it's slightly different there than down south, but even in Sheffield it seems to have changed. Of course there was always racism and things but people took things at face value, weren't influenced by things that they'd seen or read. And it's still friendlier than the south but people are definitely more wary of speaking to people they don't know.

Henna: I feel that because everyone has smartphones and iPads these days, people don't look up as much. Also because of that the media is more in touch with us than ever. So it has the ability to manipulate how we think. And do you find it as sad as I do that we forget certain birthdays unless we get a reminder from certain social media apps? Because I hate to say this and I hope none of them read this (she pauses to laugh) but I might forget certain friends' birthdays unless I get a notification reminding me of them.

Mum: Yes, but if you think about it, it isn't because you're not a good friend. I genuinely think we have so much on our minds. And though we might seem more connected because we can ring someone in a different country straight away or send them a message there and then, by fostering those distant relationships we're actually distancing ourselves from the relationships that are close to us. The relationships with the people that we live close to are being destroyed because everyone is in their own rooms or looking at their own screens. Even when we sit as a family we are on our phones. Now you and I have stopped we are having this conversation without other distractions.

Henna: Well it feels really mindful doesn't it?

Mum: Yes it does. I think technology occupies our minds to the point where it doesn't allow us to have thoughts such as "oh. That person looked really upset. I'm just going to check up on them". A lot of the time our minds don't have the space to think about those things.

Opportunities for care and compassion get missed even towards ourselves. I think social media and such things take away a bit of our humanity. When I was younger, we had to go to my grandparents' house if we wanted to watch TV. So we made our own entertainment. We made toys and we explored. Today it may be a bit of a "health and safety" worry but we explored derelict houses. We would make jam sandwiches, take them in the morning, and not come home till teatime. Nobody would question where we were. We made go-karts or kites or just our own entertainment. My uncles would make bonfires and we would put potatoes in them. We played with animals and my granddad used to have a sheep that he would take for a walk. We were exposed to nature and we explored it so much. We would pick blackberries and gooseberries. We made friends in the community. Neighbours spoke to each other.

Henna: Well I was asked recently how often I interacted with the neighbours and I realised that actually, I didn't at all. This is a bit of a change of topic, but one thing that always interests me is how the dating game has changed. I always have this idea that people are less willing to work at things nowadays.

Mum: Again for me, it comes back to technology and social media. When you met people years ago you would take the time to get to know them and that is how you would base your opinion. These days people seem to have a list of everything they are looking for. You know, hair colour, eye colour, shape, ethnicity, economic status. People will have a rigid list of what they want and as soon as something isn't their ideal, that's it. They're not willing to compromise. We as women are not perfect so why do we expect men to be and vice versa? Communication is key. I'm going to be 100% honest with you, sometimes when you don't find someone 100% attractive at first glance, you would still open up an opportunity to get to know them more.

Sylvie interrupts: Sorry to break in, but I've been absolutely fascinated by your conversation, and it sounds so much like others I've heard or read about - perhaps not nowadays but say from an earlier generation or even read in earlier books. Carry on Henna, and let's see where this leads us.

Henna: Well, I think if we all explored our relationships a bit more we'd discover some amazing people - even if it didn't work out romantically.

184

Mum: For me, I love people's stories. So the more people I get to know the more stories I hear. It's interesting. Whether things work out or not, I believe whatever will be, will be. It's not a loss to me if I meet someone, speak to them and then it doesn't work out. Do you know what I also think? It seems that society isn't as accepting of us if we are single or we are not doing what society expects us to do as a whole. Being single on the whole, isn't very accepted in society. People think "ooh why aren't you married yet? Why haven't you got kids yet?"

Henna: Do you think that's social pressure or do you think that is pressure we put upon ourselves?

Mum: I think it's social. We are socialised to expect certain things in life. You go to school, you go to college, you go to university, you meet your life partner, you buy a house, and you have kids. That's the social norm and that's the expectation of how your life should go. We are socialised to think like that. So when we are not doing what everyone else is doing we think that it is a failure but it isn't. We are all on our own journeys.

Sylvie: That's just as well since I didn't marry until quite late and it was too late for children. I considered my books as my children.

Henna: And surely that is reason enough. That is one thing I have to say that is particularly great about social media. There are people out there breaking these boundaries. People who I don't think I would have known about if I didn't have certain accounts and platforms. On the other hand, that comes with its own pressures and so far the pressure to be someone you're not is still greater than the pressure to be your true self. Hands down.

Mum: But I do think social media increases the pressure to be perfect.

Henna: And how crazy is that? Logically we know as human beings that perfection doesn't exist. It never has. Yet we still seek to be perfect - just think of this massive issue we have with fast fashion. Do you feel proud of the time that you grew up in? I always feel really proud that I grew up in a time where things like social media didn't exist. I cherish that so much.

Mum: Yes I am proud of the time I grew up Though life was difficult there were more things that made us human. Life was difficult but people were compassionate, caring and kind, and they would look after each other. If my mum and dad weren't in, our neighbour Carol would have us round for something to eat after school.

Henna laughs: Now it would be like "I'm going to be out when you come home so do not speak to a single person and as soon as you get in, lock the door". But I wanted to touch upon the fact that you said life was difficult.

Mum: It was particularly difficult because of my family. The boundaries just weren't in my favour. For example how was I allowed at the age of fourteen to have a fiancé? At that time however, it wasn't even questioned. Why was it acceptable for someone of that age to get married with the consent of her parents?

Henna: You were fourteen? How didn't I know that? That's why it is important for these conversations to take place.

Mum: I was yes.

Sylvie comes in again: I would really be grateful if you could explain how such an arranged marriage would work. It's so alien to us.

Mum: In fact it isn't if you go back far enough. And you must understand the difference between arranged and forced marriages. The latter were really bad and, of course, are now illegal in some countries like Britain. In these cases the participants didn't have a choice, whereas in the case of many arranged marriages they did and do. Usually such a marriage takes place between two families who know each other very well. In the old days the couple might not meet until their wedding day, but nowadays they have an opportunity to meet and get to know each other, though usually with a chaperone. It's like they are going through a period of courting each other. So they get to know each other without any pressure.

Sylvie: But when you divorced, then whose decision was it?

Mum: In my case it was my decision but at that time, that was unusual. For Muslims there are two parts to the divorce: the civil and the religious one. I got the first one quite quickly, but the religious one took much longer as my husband had to agree. And you have to understand that many of the customs you might regard as the rules of Islam are not at all. They are part of our culture not our religion. Perhaps the same as in the case of your rules, for example in the 19th century, when women were expected to act in a certain way and this probably varied quite a lot depending on the kind of family into which they were born. If you think about it, in Christianity too many women covered their heads as a mark of modesty and can you imagine some of your ancestors dressing as the young do today!

Sylvie: And I've noticed that the way women dress, for example, in Pakistan and other parts of the Far East, seems much less strict, for example, than in the Middle East. And recently I was in a partly Muslim country in the Balkans and many of the young women wore very elegant scarves to cover their hair, so it was like a fashion item. In fact. I've noticed that in some countries - especially in the Far East. women don't seem to follow the so-called 'rules' as rigidly.

Mum: You're right and there are other differences. For example women in Pakistan are much more likely to be driving than in, for example, Saudi Arabia; and also taking a wider variety of jobs. And there are also differences in attitudes towards the opposite sex. It's true that in the past, sex was not very widely discussed, which is possibly true in quite a few societies even today. But the arranged marriage did give couples the opportunity to get to know each other before undertaking the other responsibilities that go with marriage. Whereas nowadays if you saw an older man with very young women or teenage girls, you would automatically suspect that there was grooming going on.

Henna: What was it like growing up as a Pakistani girl in the 70s?

Mum: To begin with, I didn't feel like I was British. I lived in a house where my every movement was controlled.

Henna: Was that due to culture?

Mum: Yes. From puberty onwards. From the age of 11, all of the playing outside was monitored. I was expected to do all of the housework, the cleaning, washing and ironing. We were lucky if we got to sit in our bedrooms and listen to music. When we did that it felt really special. It was special if I got a chance to record a song off the radio. Books were my connection to the outside world. School and books. One thing that I will be eternally grateful for is that on a Saturday we were always allowed to walk to the library and get books. That was my connection with being British. We weren't even allowed to speak English at home really.

Sylvie: And at what age were you expected to cover your hair?

Mum: Pretty well at any age if you went out. And that applied to the way you dressed generally. For example Henna's father does not approve of the way she dresses.

Sylvie: As far as I can see she dresses like other young people in their twenties.

Mum: Exactly, and that's why he doesn't approve!

Henna: Would you say that when you were young Pakistanis were less willing to integrate with the wider community?

Mum: We had lots of English friends, but we weren't allowed to socialise with them a lot. Our lives were controlled. For example our neighbours had small boys and we'd play with them, as long as our father wasn't around. But we were lucky because we could go to our grandparents' house. That was a special treat.

Sylvie: And what about getting a job after you left school?

Mum: No way. Girls were brought up to understand that once they had left school, then they would get married.

Henna: You must have felt a big divide between Pakistanis and other cultures at the time.

Mum: I'm afraid we did, partly because there was one. But also, though it seems terrible to remember now, people would set their dogs on you. Those were very different times. People would threaten you. My mum used to be scared to walk us to primary school because she couldn't speak English and people would swear at her. People would go out of their way to make sure that you knew that you were not the same as them. A lot of the times we would walk ourselves. That was partly because she stopped getting up in the mornings for us though. Even in primary school we would get the younger ones dressed, give them breakfast and walk them to school with us.

Henna: That's crazy to me because you're saying "the older ones would get the younger ones ready" but you were young yourself! Do you think that was to do with culture?

Mum: No, it wasn't to do with culture. It was my mum and dad.

Henna: So you don't think that there were a lot of Pakistanis that operated in such a way?

Mum: Not to that degree no. I had cousins and their lives were not like that. So I think it was my mum and dad. We would get back from school and make our own tea. When my little brother was born, I was thirteen years old and we would make him his milk during the night. My mum wouldn't get up.

Henna: Do you think she had depression?

Mum: She suffered from domestic abuse herself. But I think she may have also had postnatal depression.

Henna: Well with your midwifery background I imagine you'd be able to make that connection. It seems like at 13 you were an adult in the eyes of your parents. And only a year later you are already organised to become married.

Mum: Henna, I was regarded as an adult at aged 11. At 11 your role as a Pakistani girl was to serve. You served your family, your parents, your husband, you served. And, of course, you didn't know anything else. But in one respect, I think we were a lot better than many British people: that was in the way we looked after older relatives. We would never dream of putting them in a home for old people. It would be the extended family's responsibility to take care of them unless, of course, they were really ill and needed to go to hospital.

There is quite a long silence while Henna and Sylvie take this in.

Henna: How long has it taken you to undo all of those behaviours you took for granted?
Mum: I don't think I have yet. A big part of it is still there. I still feel like I have to give to people.
Henna laughs: You definitely do. You'd give away the house if we didn't stop you.
Mum: Well, I've been programmed to believe that my role in life is to serve other people and make them happy. So my whole life I've tried to make people happy.
Henna: It isn't your responsibility though mum. It never was.
Mum: But I was made to feel like it was.
Henna: I stupidly had a question written down which asked "do you think you'd be a different person now if you hadn't had experienced those things?" but I already know the answer…
There is a small silence.
Mum: Don't get upset about it Henna. I don't like to see you getting upset. I'm not that person anymore. I've cried over it and got the tee-shirt. That was another me, so I have the experience of knowing both ways. And there were a lot of things about my childhood that were good. Having family close and being allowed to stay at my grandparents. Up until a certain age we were allowed to explore and play.
Henna: But there shouldn't have been a stopping point. You should be allowed to play and explore at 49 if you want to because it is your life. So not just taking into account Pakistani traditions or northern traditions, are there any that you feel are dying out? Any traditions that you wish would stick around?
Mum: As I said, looking after older people. And I think it's sad that shops open on Sundays these days because back then, people had time to spend time with their families. You know, it was like "at least we all have Sundays off". How has the world brought us to the point where

spending time with your family, going out in nature and doing all of these things aren't as normal? Now we get told "studies show going out in nature helps your mental health". We knew that all along. That was the norm. What changed? Consumerism and materialism caused that. Let's be honest, the more we want, the more we have to go out and work, and it's a cycle. We used to be environmentally friendly, we didn't waste, we reused, we recycled, and we fixed things. All the things we get told to do these days, we were already doing at one stage. That wasn't long ago.

Henna: Well somewhere along the lines something went wrong. In that space of time from when you were young up until now, I'm ashamed at the damage we have done.

Mum: Well we have devastated the earth.

Henna: How bleak. I do have to say, a lot of these things seem obvious to me because you raised me. So I have grown up around the importance of these values. You always used to talk about trees and we would wind you up and say "oh bore off". Then the other day I said something about trees and thought "I am becoming my mother."
She laughs again.

Mum: For me, looking back has helped me try and give you a better life. I know I've failed along the way…

Henna: There isn't a guide book mum.

Mum: I wanted to give you everything that I didn't have. I wanted you to be yourselves because I was never allowed to do that. I had to be what someone else decided. But then one major thing I've learned from this conversation as well as others we've had - when we've stopped looking at our screens! - is that things are not so very different from one culture to another. Well, of course they *are* different in the sense they are affected by climate and the conditions under which we live; but social morals aren't that different except in one part of the world they may have started earlier than another.

Sylvie laughs: Yes, well I remember when the Americans first started coming over in any numbers, they thought we were 'real quaint'- sort of about fifty years behind them in almost everything. I felt quite offended in fact! Then I suppose if Islam started six or seven hundred years after Christianity they might have some catching up to do…

Mum: Yes, if that's what you choose to call it.

Henna smiles: And I suppose that could be a subject for a whole new discussion!

Sylvie, wryly: So, how about we do another book in a few years time... ?

And that seems to be a subject on which they can all agree.

IS ANYBODY THERE ?

Sammy Birch

No one could say I'm of a nervous disposition. Indeed I have been accused of lacking imagination, not least by my daughter Eleanor. But then she was only nine when John died: hardly of an age to reason that, as her father was the ultimate day-dreamer, *someone* had to have feet planted firmly on the ground.

Anyway it was such a gentle voice there was no cause for disquiet. There it was on my answering machine on Wednesday evening, the second week of Lent.. "Could you, er, telephone me please on 013701-8092". Someone not used to modern technology, I thought amused, but when I rang the number I got an unobtainable noise.

It didn't seem worth mentioning when Eleanor rang later.

"Thought I'd pay you a visit next week-end," she said. "If you're free?"

"Lovely darling," I said surprised, but didn't mean to add "That will be a real Easter bonus."

"Yeah," she said.

With even odds she'd take after John I shouldn't have been so unprepared when a few years back she'd thrown up a steady job and set off in pursuit of some pipedream. I'd never stressed of course the sacrifices made to provide extras like the special art classes. It had even all seemed worth while when she found that nice job with the architects. It was a dreadful shock therefore when at 30-something she announced she was joining Larry, one of her arty friends, in some crafts centre in Wales. I had met this Larry once and was not impressed.

Soon after came my retirement, and I'd taken on the Parish Council, the W.I. and some charity involvements. Somehow I was always tied up when Eleanor suggested a visit and it was some months since I had seen her.

Twice in the next week the answering machine produced odd splutterings. Then came another message, now more urgent. *"Please ring me on 013701-8092."*

The number was still unobtainable. I called the operator who said sorry there was no such exchange. My attempts to vary the figures only yielded a couple of irate 'wrong numbers'. Exasperated I left a new message on the answering machine: "Would the caller on the 013701 exchange please ring me at 9 p.m."

As nine o'clock approached I became quite edgy, and when the phone rang at 9.30 I actually jumped. It was Eleanor.

She sounded amused. "Who's the caller on 013701?"

"Probably a wrong number," I said shortly. "I can't think why you ring me in the evening when you know I'm rarely here."

"Yes, well I never was the organised type, as you've pointed out so often. Anyway I could leave a message on your answering machine. It's just to say I'll arrive around seven on Friday."

The mystery caller finally made contact at 9 a.m. that day.

"Oh what a relief," the very little voice said. "I assume I am addressing Eleanor's mother? These technical things are really very difficult and we are still trying to perfect our emergency connections."

I was in too much of a hurry to try and make sense of gibberish and interrupted "Well what is it you want? I was expecting your call at 9 p.m. and haven't much time now."

"Oh dear, did I get the p.m. thing wrong too?"

I couldn't believe this conversation. "Look, is this a hoax?"

The voice became agitated. "Indeed no. It is of profoundest importance to Eleanor's happiness. Let me introduce myself. My name is Lucy and I am her space guardian ..."

"Her *what*?"

The voice suddenly sounded strong and determined. "I appreciate it is difficult for you, but you must accept that I am Eleanor's space guardian concerned entirely with her happiness." Now speechless I could only listen. "She is very fearful of your reactions this week-end.."

I said weakly "Reactions to what?"

"That I cannot tell you. I have already broken some ... some codes by preparing you." There was another pause. "Remember the name Robbie. Now I must go."

Suddenly, at all costs, I had to know more. "No, stay. Please. Preparing me for what? All right, all right, you can't tell me. But Lucy ..." I *am* going mad I thought "... tell me does - does Eleanor know about you?"

"She knows without knowing." The voice was beginning to fade. "That is the way it must be. She is one of the lucky ones. Many are not even so intuitive ..." She had gone.

As Eleanor's battered little estate car drew up that Friday, I hurried out to meet her. She came towards me with a defiant small smile, looking extremely attractive - and very pregnant. As I put my arms round her and, aware of a tightness in my throat, said "Well, well. Seems there's news to be caught up on," I could actually *feel* her relief.

Over supper it all spilled out: how happy she was, how marvellous Larry was, what plans they had . Then looking suddenly uncertain, "We got married last January. Should have told you I know, but I couldn't face the disapproval."

"You could have tried me," I said, smiling so the hurt didn't show. "But I'm glad you're trying me now."

Amongst many spinning thoughts one persisted. At last over coffee I asked "By the way who's Robbie?"

She looked at me startled. "Are you getting psychic in your old age Mum? Robbie's the baby. Robin if it's a boy, Robina if it's a girl. We wanted it to be a surprise."

"Must be telepathy," I said carefully.

We had an amazing week-end, not yet with all the barriers down but a lot of them crumbling.

"Bring Larry next time," I said on Sunday afternoon as Eleanor eased her bump behind the driving wheel.

"May be next month? Better not leave it any later." She patted the bump and started the engine. "And Mum - thanks, really thanks."

I walked thoughtfully back into the house and dialled Lucy. But they still hadn't got their technology sorted out.

Acknowledgments

The three contributions by the late George Spenceley - *The March,*
p.12; *Through the Iron Curtain,* p.76; and *Avalanche in Nepal,* p.150,
formed part of his series of illustrated lectures which he gave from the
1950s until his death early inthe 21st century. More about his life and
adventures can be seen at https://georgespenceley4.wordpress.com

Immigration Control, p. 23, and *A Man of Passage,* p.49 by the late
Ian Mathie are reproduced from his book *A Man of Passage,* Live
Wire Books, 2006. Ian's website updating his published works is at
www.ianmathie.co.uk

Lightning Source UK Ltd.
Milton Keynes UK
UKHW010636261119
354261UK00002B/89/P